MURDER
AT THE
ROYAL
ALBERT

MURDER
AT THE
ROYAL
ALBERT

A DANIEL JACOBUS MYSTERY

GERALD ELIAS

LEVEL
BEST BOOKS

To my fellow musicians and authors, for all of our adventures and for all of your encouragement and support.

Praise for Murder at the Royal Albert

"A cleverly-constructed mystery, a delicious peek behind the scenes of a world-class orchestra, delightful settings that capture the vibrancy of London and the quaintness of small English villages—an irresistibly entertaining trio!"—Cynthia Baxter, author of the Reigning Cats & Dogs Mysteries and the Lickety Splits Ice Cream Shoppe Mysteries

"*Murder at the Royal Albert* is a clever and serpentine mystery and, like the famous snake that eats its own tail, it twists and turns on itself in the most unexpected of ways. Readers who enjoy classical music—especially Mahler's Sixth Symphony—will appreciate how, despite the triad of Means, Motive, and Opportunity, famous in solving crimes, there's no accounting for Fate's darker note. Gerald Elias is a maestro of mystery."—Gabriel Valjan, author of the Shane Cleary Mystery series

"*Murder at the Royal Albert* is a near perfect mystery. Suspenseful throughout, and always smart and elegant. Most importantly, this story has heart. Gerald Elias has created a community of friends and family with the endlessly cranky, brilliant, and noble Daniel Jacobus at the head. He makes us care, and care deeply for characters old and new, and genuinely grieve the lives lost. The Daniel Jacobus series simply never misses."—Victoria Dougherty, author of *Welcome to the Hotel Yalta*

Autumn

Allegro
   The peasant celebrates with song and dance,
   the harvest safely gathered in.
   The cup of Bacchus flows freely,
   and many find their relief in deep slumber.

Adagio molto
   The singing and the dancing die away
   as cooling breezes fan the pleasant air,
   inviting all to sleep
   without a care.

Allegro
   The hunters emerge at dawn,
   ready for the chase,
   with horns and dogs and cries.
   Their quarry flees while they give chase.
   Terrified and wounded, the prey struggles on,
   but, harried, dies.

Sonnet written by Antonio Vivaldi for his
Violin Concerto in F Major,
Autumn from *The Four Seasons*

Chapter One

It had been a week of firsts for young violinist Natasha Conrad. Her first concert with the world-renowned symphony orchestra, Harmonium. Her first travel outside the United States. Her first time in London's legendary Royal Albert Hall. Her first pint in an English pub.

It had all happened so quickly. All those years of practice and study that were concentrated like sunlight through a magnifying glass into a single, intense half hour. That's when, last spring, her life turned on the head of a pin and she won the Harmonium audition even before receiving her degree from Juilliard. Yumi Shinagawa, her teacher, mentor, and idol, and the concertmaster of Harmonium, was so proud of her student—now former student—that she organized a party to celebrate the event and did all the cooking herself—no alcohol, of course, as Natasha was not yet of age—inviting Natasha's parents, all the way from Lawrence, Kansas.

At the party, Yumi had even convinced John and Helen Conrad to buy their daughter a gorgeous-sounding new violin. Well, not truly new. New for the young lady. It was an old violin, and Italian, and it had cost $125,000, which everyone in the know considered a steal. Yumi had haggled over the price with the New York violin dealer, Boris Dedubian. If it had been possible to categorically identify the maker, the instrument would have been worth four times as much, but all that could be determined with certainty was that it was probably made in Turin in the 1730s in the style of the great G.B. Guadagnini. As it was, Dedubian had been asking a quarter-million dollars for it, a reasonable price, given its quality. But as Yumi had bought instruments from him in the past—much more expensive ones—and with the promise of a long-term business relationship with this new young violinist, Dedubian was swayed. As good a deal as it was, Natasha's parents still had to get a second mortgage on their house to pay for it. But this they were glad to do because they were so proud of their daughter.

And now, with the downbeat just moments away, here she was in Royal Albert Hall, sitting just three desks behind her former teacher, who, at their first rehearsal, insisted that Natasha no longer call her Ms. Shinagawa, but Yumi. That might have been the hardest transition of all for Natasha to make.

Sitting to Natasha's immediate left was her kindly stand partner, Frederic "Fritz" Wohlfart, an older gentleman who had been in the orchestra for forty-one years and who, from time to time, still displayed the skills of the virtuoso violinist he once was. Fritz, who always wore a jacket and tie to every rehearsal, decades after everyone else had transitioned to the informality and comfort of jeans and T-shirts, had taken Natasha under his doting, avuncular wing. He had helped ease her into the new, intimidating world of the professional symphony orchestra, where everyone's playing was examined under a microscope by the audience, by their colleagues, and by the conductors, every time they mounted the stage for each of the hundred-odd concerts they performed every year. Fritz had taken it upon himself to introduce Natasha to musicians in the orchestra who had been her heroes since childhood and guided her through the myriad ins and outs of her new job. Job? It had been such an alien thought for Natasha: Playing in an orchestra—a job? It wasn't a job. It was a dream!

The orchestra had arrived in London from New York a day and a half earlier, allowing the musicians time to rest and become acclimated to the time change. They were staying at the Park Tower Knightsbridge, the fanciest hotel Natasha had ever been in, with her window overlooking expansive Hyde Park. It was like being in the city and the country at the same time. That morning, buoyed by the invigorating chill of early autumn, she had floated like a Hyde Park swan to Royal Albert Hall for her new orchestra's rehearsal.

There was something so...so English about the park: the gardens, the open grassy areas, and those regal swans, posing like royalty as they floated motionlessly over the pond. Even the golden retrievers looked English. As much as she enjoyed Central Park in New York, somehow this seemed so much more civilized. So tranquil. She had stopped for a moment at the Princess Diana Memorial Fountain and reflected on her good fortune and how easily life could turn.

The concert hall itself was breathtaking. It was like being on the inside of the Roman Coliseum turned into an enormous wedding cake. Looking upwards from the stage, the ornately decorated cylindrical auditorium could have been a mile high. It made her dizzy just seeing those tiny people on the top tier. Mr. Wohlfart told her that there was room for over five thousand two hundred people, more than twice the capacity of most American concert halls. "And you're lucky," he said. "Until a few years ago, Royal Albert had neither heating nor air conditioning. Sometimes we almost had to wear gloves, other times, we almost passed out from the heat."

Natasha couldn't believe the orchestra would be able to be heard in such an enormous space, but as soon as they had begun rehearsing, she felt the sound expand to fill the entire hall. There were risers built for the orchestra, more than at Harmonium's hall in New York or anywhere else she had played or attended concerts for that matter. Usually, most orchestral string players sat on the level stage. Here, everyone sat on risers, which were also banked so steeply that the brass players in the back seemed to be in the stratosphere. As large as the Harmonium orchestra was, it inhabited but a small wedge in the perimeter of the auditorium, as if a pie slice of seats had been removed. The result left the audience on either side, which would also take getting used to. The lowest riser, on which Natasha and the other first violinists sat, was elevated above the floor of the hall, called the Arena. That enabled Natasha to observe the biggest difference from American concert halls. There were no seats! Everyone in the Arena stood! Up to fourteen hundred music lovers, Fritz had told her, who, when the concert started, would be squished together like sardines. For an entire concert! They must really love music, and have a lot of stamina! It was like the Globe Theatre on the other side of the city, where, the night before, she had fought her jet lag to attend a performance of *Much Ado About Nothing*. She had been one of the groundlings, just like in Shakespeare's day. And afterwards, she went to her first pub. A real English pub, where she drank her first room-temperature beer, and they didn't ask her age.

But what was perhaps the most important first for Natasha Conrad on this occasion was that this would be her first performance of the monumental Symphony No. 6 by Gustav Mahler. Just the sound of the orchestra! It had been unbelievable in the rehearsals. She had thought the Juilliard orchestra was good, but everyone in Harmonium was a superstar. It was like being on an all-star team. One of the amazing things about the orchestra was the age range of almost sixty years. And they were all her colleagues, and she was being treated like an equal. *I guess I'm one of them, now!* Natasha thought, as she warmed up onstage. A little swagger there, but just a little.

They had all been so nice. A group of the younger ones invited her to go to another pub after the performance. She was starting to get the feeling it would be standard practice to celebrate into the night after concerts. For the first time in her life, she was on her own. She felt like an adult!

The hall was jam-packed for the concert, the groundlings in the Arena bobbing up and down with anticipation. The energy was intense, in a positive and contagious way. Natasha couldn't wait to start. She had never been nervous about an orchestra concert before. At school, playing in the orchestra had become pretty boring, in fact. She had been a little nervous when she had given her graduation recital and when she had performed the Saint-Saëns B Minor as the winner of the concerto competition. But now she had so much adrenaline she could barely sit in her seat.

Everyone had said this sold-out concert was undoubtedly going to be the highlight of the Proms season. It had garnered even more buzz than the wildly popular Last Night of the Proms, the finale of the eight-week summer festival. Held on the second Saturday of September, the Last Night featured British music of a lighter, patriotic variety. Harmonium's concert, scheduled for the night before, had been dubbed "The Second to Last Night," and was anticipated with more excitement than any "serious" Proms concert since Leonard Bernstein conducted Mahler's Fifth with the Vienna Philharmonic.

There was a unique buzz with this particular performance. Mahler Sixth was famous—or infamous, more like it—for its three thunderous hammer strokes, each several minutes apart, that supported the finale of the eighty-minute symphony like three gigantic pillars. But Mahler crossed the third hammer stroke out of his score. Why? No one is sure, but credible historical speculation suggested that Mahler, who was intensely superstitious, deleted the third hammer blow in order to steer clear of a three-fold jinx of fate. His efforts turned out to be as futile as they were prophetic: In the years after he composed the symphony, Mahler was indeed assailed by three tragedies: the death of his eldest daughter, Maria Anna; his expulsion from the Vienna State Opera; and the diagnosis of what would eventually become a fatal heart condition. Some conductors respected Mahler's erasure of the third hammer stroke because, in the end, it had been Mahler's decision. Other conductors retained it for musical reasons.

Mahler, a master orchestrator, stipulated the sound of the hammer strokes should be "brief and mighty, but dull in resonance and with a non-metallic character, like the fall of an axe." Other than that, he never defined exactly what the instrument should look or sound like. Every orchestra had its own version. The Harmonium carpentry crew had constructed a hollow wooden box, a three-foot cube. It had to be heavily reinforced because they also built a monstrous wooden sledgehammer. The handle was two feet long, and its head was massive. When the percussionist struck the box with all his might, it made a gut-wrenching impact that cut right through the densest orchestral fabric.

Harmonium's guest conductor, Klaus Kruger, was acclaimed as one of the world's greatest Mahler exponents. For the past week, he had toyed with the concert-going public and the media about whether or not he would signal the percussionist to play the third hammer stroke. He would decide on the spur of the moment, he said. It didn't matter how many times people asked, he couldn't say what he would do because he wouldn't know himself until that very moment. He would let fate itself dictate his decision.

The overflowing and swirling audience—especially the Mahler fanatics standing in the Arena—went wild when Kruger appeared from backstage at the orchestra's top riser, and descended, king-like, to the podium. Natasha couldn't believe the electricity surrounding her. Would this, her very first performance, be the performance of a lifetime? What would be left to look forward to?

The audience listened in rapt attention for an hour, through the monumental *Allegro, Scherzo,* and *Andante* movements of the symphony. Then, the half-hour finale, which had been described as a hallucinogenic nightmare as it jaggedly caromed back and forth between abject despair and ecstatic euphoria. The first triumphant climax approached, only to be shattered by the hammer stroke. The audience audibly gasped when the hammer came down. With the second stroke, the excitement increased, though Natasha had not thought that could have been possible. As they neared the moment for the third and final hammer stroke of death, Natasha glanced into the audience. People were jumping up and down! Several of the more fervent Mahlerians literally seemed to be pulling their hair out. Natasha had never experienced anything like this. She couldn't wait to call home after the end of the concert, now only a few minutes away, to tell her parents how much she loved her new job.

It was the moment! Maestro Kruger raised his arm high above his head. Would it come down, signaling the percussionist to bring down the mighty hammer? Or would he leave his arm suspended in the air and let the moment pass?

Everyone—the musicians, the thousands in the audience, and especially the percussionist—stared at Kruger's left arm. Will he? Won't he? A Roman Caesar signaling thumbs up or down to an expectant gladiator. To kill or not to kill?

His arm came down. The third stroke! The percussionist's effort was shattering. A sonic boom. Cataclysmic.

There was a shout. Rising above all else, a shout!

"Stop!"

It was Fritz Wohlfart, Natasha Conrad's stand partner.

The orchestra came to a ragged stop. What could it mean? At first the audience was agitated. Rebellious. Who would do such a thing? Who would bring the performance to a halt? But then, understanding why, five thousand passionate music lovers fell silent.

Natasha Conrad slumped awkwardly, her head finding a resting place on Wohlfart's trusty shoulder, as if the symphony had exhausted her and she had to pause. She held her violin out to hand to Wohlfart, who instinctively caught it as her grasp on it loosened, saving it from breaking when it most certainly would have fallen to the ground. When he looked at Natasha's face, he understood what had happened and began to cry. She opened her eyes wide to him, seemingly bewildered. Then they closed. A single bullet had pierced Natasha's right temple. Her first concert was her last concert. Mahler's third hammer stroke had claimed its victim.

Chapter Two

Who can predict how thousands of people will spontaneously react in such a situation? The only safe assumption is that there will be any number of responses. Hundreds of people, mainly those closest to the stage who had the best view of the carnage, immediately swarmed for the exits, creating a wave of panic as they fled. Ushers and security personnel attempted, with little success, to maintain an orderly exodus. The unruly mass pushed and pulled to get through doors that were suddenly too narrow. Some were trampled, others had clothing ripped off. Miraculously, no one was killed.

Others remained frozen in their seats or, if they were standing in the Arena, were as immobile as Prince Albert's statue, unable to take their eyes off the gruesome scene on stage, so unlikely and so horribly out of place.

Yet others shouted, calling for help. Or screamed, or cried. Some of the musicians, fearing a mass murderer, dropped their instruments and fled the stage. Others, either more courageous or less astute, congregated around Wohlfart and his young, mortally wounded colleague. Through all the mayhem, Wohlfart, as if posing for a portrait, sat motionless, his violin in one hand, her violin in the other, her head on his shoulder. A surreal, macabre *Pietà*. Tears streamed down Wohlfart's face, the only evidence he was alive. Blood down Natasha's, showing the opposite.

Within a two-minute eternity, security personnel had called the police, who began to secure the building. The hall's EMTs rushed to Natasha Conrad's assistance. They were too late. She had died almost immediately, and so their primary concern became Fritz Wohlfart, who appeared he was about to go into shock. With soothing words, the two violins were gently pried from his hands. With gentle care, he was slowly and quietly escorted from the stage on uncooperative legs. The massive building, which, until a few short moments before, had literally been shaking with sound, was now eerily silent.

When Wohlfart had raised his voice in alarm for the music to stop, Yumi, being a disciplined musician, had not turned around. Instead, she had looked up at the conductor, Klaus Kruger, asking with her eyes, *What is going on?* Looking over Yumi's head, Kruger's own eyes had widened, and he had suddenly turned pale. His legs seemed to lose their ability to support him, and he had to clutch his music stand to prevent himself from falling. Only then did Yumi turn around to find out what had prompted one of her colleagues to ruin what had been, until that moment, a spectacular performance. Such an outburst was simply not to be tolerated. There would be hell to pay.

That was when she saw Natasha, her protégée. Yumi rushed back to her, hoping that what she immediately knew was true was not true. Hoping that as her teacher, she could bring this intelligent, talented, dedicated, enthusiastic, beautiful young lady back to life. She took Natasha in her arms and cried along with Fritz Wohlfart, until the EMTs arrived and separated her from the dead girl. "She is so innocent," Yumi cried. "Why?"

The police arrived on the scene en masse, led by Detective Chief Inspector Christopher Mattheson. Though stout and short and florid-faced, he had one of those personalities that somehow exude an air of quiet, natural command. He was dressed in a trim, well-tailored business suit with a neatly folded handkerchief in his jacket pocket and a silk tie fastened with a large pearl tie pin. His hair, parted with a line as straight as the Prime Meridian and meticulously combed, with razor-edged, short sideburns, advertised he was all business and not to be toyed with. The meerschaum pipe, with a long, curved briarwood stem, did nothing to diminish the overall effect of Mattheson being the man in charge.

DCI Mattheson requested—it was actually an order, politely disguised—that all the musicians retire immediately downstairs to the visiting orchestra dressing room area. They would be interviewed, one at a time, in the musicians' café. He answered questions that had not yet been asked, but he knew they would be: No, at this time, we do not suspect anyone in the orchestra. Of course not. The shot came from somewhere in the audience. But perhaps someone saw something. Perhaps someone is aware of someone who might have wanted to harm the young lady. We must be organized, and we must be methodical if we're to find out who did this horrific thing. And we shall.

Yumi, unwilling and unable to make the final disconnect with Natasha Conrad, was one of the last escorted from the stage. Forensic and ballistic teams were already at work. Two officers knelt on either side of Natasha, still seated in her chair as if she were waiting to be excused, inspecting her as if she were a contemporary art installation at a trendy gallery exhibition. It infuriated Yumi, though she knew it was necessary.

Oh, my God! she thought. Someone has to notify her mother and father. She would offer to do it, she decided, when it was her turn to talk to this Mattheson. Better her than a faceless policeman.

A cordon of uniformed police lined the curving stairway as the musicians, still in their black formal dress, now as appropriate for a funeral as for a concert, slowly descended to the hall's lower level below the stage. The somber formality of the procession was almost ludicrous, in a way. At the same time, the musicians descended into the bowels of the hall, another phalanx of police, supervised by DCI Mattheson's assistant, DS Damien Littlebank, established control of the hall's myriad exits. They were charged with patting down every member of the audience who had not yet fled, inspecting their bags, asking them pertinent questions, and taking their contact information.

As Mattheson made his way along the basement corridor to the café, he passed dozens of what he surmised to be the musicians' travel wardrobe trunks. On wheels and approximately waist high, each trunk had a latched door at either end and a pair of large stenciled numbers on its side. All of that suggested each trunk supported the concert wardrobe needs of two musicians. Most of the trunks were black; a lesser number, red. That approximate ratio led him to suppose the black ones must be for the men, the red for the women, so that when the stage crew arrived at a new hall, the trunks could be accurately segregated into the appropriate dressing rooms. Apparently, there weren't enough of those in the Royal Albert basement, but then again, it hadn't originally been built for that purpose.

Mattheson gave the orchestra's personnel manager, Wendell Barton, permission to sit in on the interviews. Actually, he welcomed Barton's presence. With the musicians still stunned at the turn of events, having Barton there would provide them with a bit of emotional security, which would aid Mattheson with the investigation. Barton was a roly-poly, middle-aged gentleman with an easy smile who always seemed a fish out of water in concert dress, which, even though he was not one of the musicians, he was required to wear at concerts. Barton was also useful to Mattheson in that he had the personnel list of the entire orchestra, ensuring that everyone who needed to be questioned would be accounted for.

Though it would have been ideal to sequester each musician in order to prevent the cross-contamination of speculation and rumor, there was simply not enough room or enough rooms in the warren of the hall's basement. Aside from Mattheson's cautions not to discuss the events, the musicians were otherwise left free to communicate with each other, expressing their sentiments as much by tearful embraces and handkerchiefs as with words of shock and consolation.

"You're exactly right," Wendell Barton said when Mattheson asked him if his conjectures about the wardrobe trunks were accurate.

"Good. We'll have to examine Ms. Conrad's. Ah, here you are, Littlebank," Mattheson said, momentarily diverted. Then, back to Barton. "Which is hers?"

"Number 56."

"And what should we expect to find in it?"

"Each musician's trunk has a pull-out hanging rack and four drawers. They're instructed to pack only those items that they need for concerts: clothing, accessories, shoes. Those sorts of things. Customs agents have gotten very fussy in recent years. They have the authority to examine any trunk, and if they find anything that they deem inappropriate for the purpose, they won't hesitate to open every one of them."

"Thereby creating an unpleasant delay."

"Absolutely. And they can confiscate what they don't think should be in there. Also, the stage crew has as many tons to schlep as they can handle. They don't want to see musicians stuffing their trunks with souvenirs, either."

"You used the phrase 'are instructed.' "

"I did?"

"Yes. You said, 'They're instructed to pack only those items...' et cetera, et cetera. Do I detect a note of qualification in that?"

"Well, we treat the musicians respectfully, so we don't inspect the trunks. We don't want to be the Gestapo about it. We just give them the guidelines and tell them just to make sure whatever they pack in the trunk on the way out is the same as on the return."

"Did you get all of that?" Mattheson said to Littlebank.

"Yes, sir."

"Good. Then please do the honors and let me know what you find. And her hotel room too."

"Of course, sir."

Little by little, Mattheson worked his way through the orchestra's roster, first come, first served, in no particular order. Sympathetic and patient by nature, he understood that if he were to demonstrate exasperation or irritability from having to answer the same questions over and over again, it would serve no good purpose, either to the musicians' pain or his own investigation. So, when asked for the twentieth or thirtieth time, "Who could have done this?" "How long will this take?" "Are we allowed to go?" and other assorted questions, few of which had real answers, he responded with the same thoughtfulness as when he had been asked the first time. It was a form of professional hand-holding. Empathy 101, perhaps, but it worked, and it always surprised him how many of his colleagues in the field were incapable of using it as a basic tool of the trade.

Barton crossed off names as the musicians came and went, answering Mattheson's standard barrage of questions: "Where exactly were you?"

"What did you see?" "How well did you know Miss Conrad?" "Do you know of anyone who might have had a reason to harm her?" Mattheson, filling his pipe after each interview, quickly ran out of tobacco. He took one ten-minute break for tea, which he brewed himself, finding the necessary components behind the café counter.

Mattheson looked at his watch. "Is that it, then?" he asked Barton when the last of the hundred and two musicians, the librarian, and the stagehands had been questioned. Several hours had passed, and the musicians were exhausted, both physically and emotionally, and he wasn't far behind them.

"That's everyone who's here," Barton said.

"Meaning?"

"We had one musician absent today. He called in sick. He was ill."

Mattheson took down the musician's name and phone number. Donald Stroud, violinist.

"Isn't that a problem for the performance if a musician is absent?" Mattheson asked.

"If it's a wind or brass or percussion player, yes," Barton said. "We'd have to scramble to cover that part, because there's only one player per part. But because Donald is a violinist, and we've got thirty-plus of them, we can get by if we're missing one or two."

"Are you saying the triangle player is more indispensable than, say, a cellist?" Mattheson, for the first time that day, was truly surprised.

"It depends on the program. But conceivably, yes."

"But surely, the cellist is paid more. Is he not?"

"The orchestra's collective bargaining agreement sets a minimum salary for all the musicians. Most of the string players are paid just that, plus seniority, of course. The percussion players generally are paid above scale. So, it's the triangle player who gets a higher salary than the cellist. But you should also know that the triangle player has to be able to play dozens of assorted percussion instruments."

Mattheson was doing his best to understand the inner workings of a symphony orchestra. Such insight could conceivably become critical to his investigation. But it seemed so contrary to his own intuitive sense of value that he hoped not.

"But let's say the triangle player only had ten notes to play compared to the cellist's ten thousand?"

"Makes no difference," Barton replied with a smile. Like Mattheson, it was apparent he had been asked that question a million times and was answering with the same indulgent patience with which Mattheson had responded to the musicians. "When a composer writes ten notes for the triangle, you can be sure they're highly intentional and will be clearly heard. If a cellist makes a mistake, chances are no one will hear it, but if a triangle player came in at the wrong moment, it could throw the whole performance off. That puts a lot of extra stress on him. Besides, each musician in the orchestra plays a different number of notes. Do you suggest the musicians should be paid by the note?"

"No, I suppose not," Mattheson said, but he was not quite ready to run up the white flag. "Many of the concerts I've attended have had no percussion at all. Certainly, they don't get paid the same amount as those who are onstage, playing their hearts out."

"All of the musicians had to go through a grueling audition gauntlet in order to win their position with Harmonium," Barton said. "Some say we're the greatest orchestra in the world. We expect each musician, regardless of their instrument, to always be prepared to perform at the highest level. Though the number of notes each one plays might differ, the standard is consistent. So, to answer your question, whether a musician plays in fifty concerts a year or a hundred and fifty, the base salary is the same."

Barton smiled. So did Mattheson. Barton's soliloquy had been so smoothly delivered, it had undoubtedly been repeated often, if not verbatim.

"Thank you for the education," Mattheson said. "We'll contact this gentleman, Stroud. You can release the musicians. Please instruct them to return to their hotel and stay there until further notice."

Almost wordlessly, the orchestra slowly climbed back up the staircase to ground level, their footsteps a hollow echo on the marble steps, like a funeral cortege. Typically, one of orchestra musicians' favored pastimes is to spice up their quotidian labors with juicy rumor and idle gossip. But with

Natasha, there was nothing negative to be said. Nothing that wanted to be said. She had been with them for such a short time, they had hardly known her, and what they knew of her was only to her credit. Why had the police questioned them? It was unimaginable that anyone in the orchestra would want to do her harm. And even if they did, how would it have been possible? They had all been sitting there onstage, playing music. Great music. Could any of them ever perform Mahler Sixth again?

Mattheson stationed himself at the top of the stairs, just inside the artists' exit, as Yumi passed him. She slowed her pace, preparing to offer to contact Natasha Conrad's parents, but, before she could, Littlebank approached with a loping gait. He was the carnival mirror image of his superior officer. Tall and lanky, Littlebank wore a suit no less appropriate than Mattheson's, but Littlebank's was too snug in some places and too slack in others, not even mentioning that his trousers, an inch too short, displayed white socks. Littlebank was the younger of the two by a few years, but only a few, and though both men were clean-shaven, one got the impression that Littlebank needed to spend twice as much time and effort in front of the bathroom mirror to be able to make that claim. From all appearances, he was a dutiful second-in-command—if anything, overly dutiful—and with emphasis on *second*. He began to speak to his superior in a low voice, with some urgency.

"Sir," Littlebank said. "The bullet was a small caliber, probably a .22, and struck the young lady directly in the temple."

"Maximum effective range of about a hundred yards," Mattheson said. "Odd, wouldn't you say?"

"Yes, sir. Even at half that, you'd already have to compensate a few inches. From where the young lady was sitting and gauging the trajectory, that's what we're estimating, about fifty yards."

"You're suggesting the shooter was at approximately the same level as the victim? In the Arena?"

"Yes, that's what we believe."

"With a .22, he would have to have been an accurate shot, if not an expert marksman. Somehow, he managed—"

"Or she, sir."

Mattheson recalled an episode when he was a zealous young constable and made the unpardonable error of correcting his superior, Sergeant Rohan Baker. Baker had believed a cigarette found at the scene of a break-in proved that the man they had arrested, a smoker, had been there. Mattheson made the blunder of pointing out that the cigarette was a filtered brand and that the accused smoked a non-filtered variety. Though Mattheson was right, and though Baker would have otherwise appreciated the revelation, Mattheson had made the mistake of correcting Baker in the presence of a roomful of policemen. The suspect was freed, as he was innocent, but Mattheson spent the next month on the graveyard shift for his indiscretion, for which he was undoubtedly guilty.

"Pardon my grammatical lapse, Littlebank," Mattheson said. "I shall endeavor to be more precise. He...or she...somehow managed to hit his...or her...target whilst standing in the Arena among the crowd. *They*, emphasis mine, would had to have aimed and fired extremely quickly to avoid being observed."

That should be sufficient chastisement, he thought, being a much more humane boss than Sgt. Baker.

"Yes, sir. We're guessing a Smith & Wesson 43C or a Ruger LCR 22. I would lean toward the Ruger."

"Why?"

"Because it's so lightweight. Fits your description of the events."

"And lightweight enough for a woman to use, perhaps?"

Littlebank hesitated. "If you say so, sir." Ah, he had understood the message.

"Has the floor of the Arena been inspected?"

"We're doing that right now," Littlebank said.

"Good."

"But it's a bit of a mess. A lot of people dropped everything when they saw what happened and raced for the doors."

"I'm confident you're capable of handling the mess, Littlebank," Mattheson said.

"Yes, sir."

16

Yumi felt that it was not an inappropriate time to interrupt. She re-introduced herself and offered to call Mr. and Mrs. Conrad. She knew them well and, as Natasha's colleague and former teacher, she thought she should be the one to break the news rather than the police.

"Very kind of you, Ms. Shinagawa," Mattheson said, "if you are up to it."

"And would you mind, Detective, if I kept Natasha's violin for safekeeping? I'd like to have it to return to her parents."

"When will that be, do you suppose?"

"I assume they will need to come to London to…."

"Yes, if it's at all possible. I know it will be difficult for them. And expensive. But we can help them out once they're here. The sooner, the better for all involved."

"Whenever that is, then. When they get here. That's when I'd want to give them her violin."

Mattheson considered whether the violin might be needed for the investigation.

"See Littlebank, Ms. Shinagawa. Tell him that I've decided to hold the violin until such time as the young lady's parents arrive. Once they are here, they may have it back unless, in the meantime, we discover it has some bearing on the investigation."

"Thank you."

Musicians continued to file by Mattheson. If anything, they looked away from him, perhaps hoping to avoid the practiced gaze of someone who might misconstrue their facial expression and subject them to further interrogation.

"But let me ask you," he said, "in the little privacy we have here, since you were her teacher. Can you think of any reason anyone would have to kill the young lady?"

"No. None at all."

"You mention the parents. What do they do?"

"Her father, John, is an insurance agent, and Helen, her mother, has an office job at the University of Kansas School of Music. In Lawrence. That's where Natasha first started getting into music. But both of them are the most honest, hardworking people. You can't think they were involved, could you?"

"We have to obtain all the information we can and work from there. We're starting from nothing, and if we're to find who did this, and why, *nothing* will get us nowhere. So, please tell me a little about the young lady. Of anyone in the orchestra, you knew her the best."

"I don't know where to start."

"How long were you her teacher? Let's start from there."

"She auditioned for me four years ago."

"A prodigy, was she?"

"Far from it. She had had good previous training. And she was smart. But in terms of natural talent—whatever that is—she was somewhere in the middle."

"To what, then, do you attribute her success?"

"Hard work. Determination. A positive attitude. Even when she struggled with a concerto or Paganini caprice, she was always doing her best. No excuses."

The young lady reminded Mattheson of himself. Never the star pupil. Yet, somehow, with enough late-night hours, he had managed. Others hadn't. Where were they now? "The ideal student," he said.

"Yes. In every way."

"Enough to make other students jealous?"

"Meaning?"

"Some with more talent, perhaps, but not as motivated? Who might not have appreciated a less gifted student going to the head of the class?"

"I can see where you're going with this, Detective, but let me disabuse you of your suspicions. First of all, all my students get all the attention they need. That means not only do they receive weekly lessons, I help them prepare for auditions and competitions, and summer music programs. I help them search for and buy better instruments. I try to make sure they maintain good health. I counsel them when they've got troubles, whether it's with other classes or with girlfriends and boyfriends—"

"But certainly there must be—"

"Yes, sometimes there are petty jealousies. Little grudges. There's nothing new about that. But almost all of my students make it."

"How do you define 'make it'?"

"They get into orchestras, or college teaching positions, or string quartets. You name it. So, they'd have no reason to have harbored any hard feelings against Natasha. But the truth of it is, everyone loved her. She was special."

"How many students do you have?"

"A dozen a year, more or less, with usually three or four graduating every year."

"Could you provide me with a list, please?"

Yumi bristled at the thought that Mattheson would investigate her students. It was absurd.

"If you insist."

Mattheson bristled at the thought that Shinagawa would think he was doing anything other than a thorough job.

"I prefer not to insist. Consider it a request. It would be very helpful. I would want to find out if any of them are currently in the UK and if so, whether they might have been in attendance at the concert. It is an easy way of eliminating them from our inquiries, and it would quickly put your mind at ease if what you say is accurate."

"All right. Is that all?"

"One more thing." Mattheson removed the handkerchief from his coat pocket and handed it to Yumi.

"What's this for?" she asked.

"You still have some of her blood on your cheek. You might want to remove it before going outside. You may keep the handkerchief."

Yumi joined her colleagues as they trickled out of the artists' exit into the night. Barton, the personnel manager, stood at the door to inform each musician who had a room at the hotel to return there directly and remain in place. Management had made unusual arrangements, requested by Mattheson, for the orchestra to be fed at the hotel restaurant, so there would be no need to go out. Any musicians not staying at the Park Tower should be available at all times if there were any change in plans. Finally, there would be an orchestra meeting the next morning at nine o'clock to determine whether the tour would continue or be canceled. Everyone must attend. Until then, management would be consulting with law enforcement to see what the options were.

Surprisingly, after all the chaos, after all the interviews, a substantial number of well-wishers was still congregated outside the exit. A somber crowd, perhaps, but a supportive one. In a display of goodwill, many of them had purchased bouquets that they handed to the musicians of this orchestra from America as they emerged from the hall, accompanied by hugs and tears and words of condolence. It was a touching gesture for total strangers to take the trouble to wait for hours simply to express their grief and solidarity with the musicians.

One such stranger was a tall, elderly woman who approached Yumi. Though the late summer night would have recommended no more than a light sweater, she was buried in a long, gray wool coat. Her face was pale and drawn with deep lines of age and sorrow.

"You must be Miss Shinagawa," the woman said. "I read your name in the program. You're the orchestra leader. That's what we call the concertmaster here. The leader."

"Yes," Yumi said, who didn't need the lesson in vocabulary but appreciated the woman's effort to reach out.

The woman handed Yumi a single red poppy.

"I had been so looking forward to the performance," she said, attempting a smile. "I am desolated beyond words. I simply don't know what to say."

She began to cry quietly.

"Oh, dear. Oh, dear," she said.

Yumi put her arms around her. The dam broke, and they cried together.

The woman pulled a handkerchief from her pocket and dabbed at her eyes, and wiped her nose.

"I'm being an old fool," she said.

"Not at all," Yumi replied. "You've made me feel better."

"Oh, thank you for saying so," the woman said. She took a deep breath. "The young lady seemed such a wonderful child. Could you tell me a little about her? You see," and the tears welled up and overflowed, "I lost a daughter. Many years ago."

Out of the corner of her eye, Yumi saw Fritz Wohlfart approaching. Not wanting to be discourteous, she quickly told the old woman a few details about Natasha and, in response to the woman's concerned observations, of the tumult backstage after the concert was so tragically and abruptly interrupted.

"Well, I mustn't keep you any longer," the woman said. "You've had an exhausting slog. I will pray for the young lady." The woman took Yumi's hand in both of hers. With reddened eyes, she looked deeply into Yumi's.

Wohlfart, with his own reddened eyes, burst in between them, seemingly oblivious to the old woman's presence. He embraced Yumi more tightly than she thought he had the strength to and began to shake.

In Yumi's estimation, Fritz had a heart of gold and the courage to match. When she had won the audition to become concertmaster of Harmonium, there were some veterans of the orchestra who expressed concerns that she might be "unqualified." It was their buzzword for "She's too young," "She's Japanese," "She's a she," or any combination of the above. At the end of her one-year mandatory probationary period, as per Harmonium's collective bargaining agreement, the audition reconvened to determine whether Yumi would be given tenure, have her probation extended, or have her employment terminated. Fritz had defended her. He stood up in her tenure meeting, pointed at each of the naysayers, and asserted that Yumi was the finest musician on the Harmonium stage, that he had full confidence in her ability to lead the orchestra, and if they didn't believe that, they should get another job, because it meant they were deaf. After that, the daggers were returned to their sheaths, and she received an overwhelming vote of confidence.

Now it was Yumi's turn to be Wohlfart's pillar of strength.

"I know, Fritz," Yumi said, consoling her senior colleague, trying to smile. "I know. It will be all right. We all loved her. Didn't we?"

"Mahler's ghost has taken his prize," he sobbed. "Mahler's ghost has taken his prize."

Over Wohlfart's shoulder, Yumi looked apologetically at the woman, still standing there. She mouthed the words, "Thank you," and waved the red poppy in her hand, in response to which the woman mouthed back, "Farewell." She waved and lost herself among the crowd.

Kate Padgett, Yumi's maternal grandmother, was the first of the group to spot Yumi in the thinning crowd.

"There you are!" Kate said, waving. Curmudgeonly Daniel Jacobus, Yumi's revered mentor, and Nathaniel Williams, long-time Yang to Jacobus's Yin, were with Kate, but hung back to allow her to be the first to embrace Yumi.

"Blood is thicker than water," Nathaniel said.

"Age before beauty," Jacobus replied.

Wohlfart, sensing that the time of sharing his anguish with her had expired, patted Yumi on the cheek and joined waiting colleagues on the orchestra bus to return to the hotel.

Yumi had paid £105 each for Grand Tier seats for her grandmother, Jacobus, and Nathaniel. They had demurred, but she insisted on treating them. This was important for her, she said, for everyone to be together again after so many years, and to hear her play such a special concert. And she certainly wasn't going to let them stand for two hours in the Arena! Yumi invited Auntie Leonia, too, but she had opted to stay home. She was not a big classical music fan, she boasted—"too highbrow for my taste"—though she did admit to liking *some* Andrew Lloyd Webber, but not his later things.

It had been such a happy reunion only two days earlier. Yumi had flown to London separately from her Harmonium colleagues in order to escort Nathaniel and Jacobus. She had never seen Jacobus, her former teacher and long-time counselor and father figure, so nervous. His anxiety was not the result of having to leave the friendly, familiar confines of his cottage in the Berkshires Hills of Massachusetts, or of flying, or of traveling to a foreign country. It was none of those. Rather, it was because Jacobus, after many years, would be reuniting with his partner-in-spirit, Kate Padgett. Jacobus and Kate had communicated infrequently and irregularly, mainly with Yumi as the go-between, and had not seen each other—"seen" was a bit of a misnomer, as Jacobus was blind—since Jacobus's frenzied journey to Japan more than a decade earlier, when he uncovered her family's plot to steal the ill-fated—some had called it "cursed"—"Piccolino" Stradivarius from Carnegie Hall. In that unlikely episode, Kate and Jacobus had earned each other's mutual respect and admiration, and though Jacobus was loath to admit it, their mutual affection.

Soon after arriving in London, his anxiety quickly dissolved into what, for him, was an unfamiliar sense of being: contentment. Settling comfortably into Leonia's spacious and posh Belgravia home with the rest of his friends, Jacobus couldn't remember when he had felt so at peace. It would have gone too far for him to admit he was actually happy or blissful, because those emotions were reserved for listening to the Schubert String Quintet in C Major or Mozart's Piano Concerto in G Major. But his health had become fully restored—finally—after intentionally poisoning himself the year before, and the prospect of a reunion with Kate Padgett, after all this time, filled him with a level of anticipation that made him act, if not feel, young again. Or if not actually young, at least not quite as old.

Jacobus had initially been uncomfortable with the plan for him to stay in the home of a total stranger for such an extended period, especially a home that was so opulent compared to his humble cottage in the woods. For Jacobus, affluence was anathema and almost as great a sin as laziness, the worst of all. But the greater reason for his discomfort, unarticulated, was that the relationship between Kate and her sister, Leonia—as contentious as it often was—brought back memories of his own sibling, his long-lost brother, Eli, and wounded him with a bruising, throbbing, inner pain. How inappropriate it would be to exhibit happiness when his older brother's fate remained unknown. Had Eli perished, as their parents had, in the World War II death camps? Had he survived and wandered off somewhere and died? Was he still alive or half-alive, or infirm, or…? Or what? Year after year, Jacobus had tried to find out. Letters written (with Nathaniel's help), phone calls made, libraries consulted, archives pored through. All of his investigations led to dead ends. What could be concluded from all that? Only that his brother was probably dead. Probably. What good was probably? If someone would only confirm that he was dead, at least he could put to rest all the question marks. Maybe then he could be happy. At least he could die in peace.

So Jacobus would have preferred to stay in some bed-and-breakfast somewhere in London. A little corner room off a side street. Somewhere cheap. Somewhere where the stairs creaked, and the basement dining room served a buffet of fatty bacon, overdone fried eggs, cold toast, and instant coffee. And where the guests would be overweight, budget-minded senior citizens from Slovenia or vacationing students in T-shirts and jeans from New Zealand and Nigeria. Somewhere where he would be anonymous. Just another foreign tourist. Left alone. But Yumi and Nathaniel had persuaded him to be with them. And he had received a letter from Leonia, written with typical self-deprecating English humor, saying that if Jacobus didn't stay at her home and take her wild sister off her hands, she wouldn't know what to do with her. Jacobus acquiesced. His arm had been twisted, probably, in part, willingly.

But now, with Yumi's student's death, that had all changed. Jacobus had never met the young lady. Yumi, his own former prize student, had spoken highly of her, and from time to time, she had asked his advice on how to guide Natasha through the avalanche of concertos and sonatas she had to absorb. Jacobus knew how he would feel if tragedy were to befall Yumi, so it was no stretch for him to understand the depths of her current sorrow and to share in it. He had never been able to convincingly verbalize the extent to which he felt the responsibility to invest his thoughts, his emotions, his understanding, into the empty, willing vessel of a new student. It was, he believed, his sacred obligation as the teacher to pass along the accumulation of centuries of cultural heritage from Bach and Vivaldi, through Beethoven and Mozart, and then Bartok and Stravinsky in a way that would, if at all possible, add to that legacy. Certainly, not detract from it. To detract would be a desecration. Maybe that's why some people—a lot of people—considered him a hardass. Because he refused to cut corners or compromise on his standards or accept anything less than a student's best effort. Not many of them were willing to accept the challenge. Yumi had, even when she had first started with him as a teenager, and, bless her heart, she had thrown the challenge right back at him.

In a way, what Jacobus invested in a student was the essence of his very being. Okay, call it a soul if you believe in souls. He didn't care what you called it. But to then lose the student, to witness the chain violently ruptured, would be, in part, to die oneself. So Jacobus mourned for the young lady, his musical "grandchild," though he never met her. And he also mourned for Yumi, for her loss was almost as great. But he would leave it to Kate to console Yumi, because finding the right words in such circumstances was a struggle for him. If, at that moment, he could only play the Bach G Minor *Adagio* for her, she would understand perfectly how he felt.

Though it was not a requirement, most of the Harmonium musicians opted to stay in the official hotel whenever they were on tour. And why not? They were provided with luxurious single-occupancy rooms in a class of hotels they could never afford on their own, including all the amenities: sumptuous, limitless breakfast buffets (a perk that musicians were particularly fond of), health clubs, saunas, massages, first-class room service, and well-stocked minibars. The orchestra always attempted to book official hotels within walking distance of the concert hall, saving the expense of hiring buses. If that wasn't possible, four or five chartered buses provided door-to-door transportation for the musicians both before and after every rehearsal and concert. Yumi almost always chose to be one of the herd and stay with the group. It was so much easier to have her bags conveyed from the airport and delivered to her hotel room, and to either walk to the hall or ride on the orchestra bus, than to have to book her own lodging and transportation, hire taxis and schlep her luggage and violin from one place to another. On one occasion, when she was of a more adventurous age, she booked a room at a quaint gray stone B&B in Edinburgh, desiring to soak in the city's charms. Though the world-famous festival was in August, it turned out to be a cold and rainy August, not unheard of in those parts. In competition with hordes of tourists trying to stay dry in the inclement weather, she wasn't able to procure a taxi and had to walk two miles to the concert hall, wrapping her violin case in a plastic bag, but otherwise arriving soaking wet. Lesson learned.

On this occasion, though, Yumi had chosen to stay with her grandmother, Jacobus, and Nathaniel at the stately and spacious nineteenth-century home of her great-aunt, Leonia Padgett-Trelawney. Kate's older sister and only sibling, Auntie Leonia was a dowager who lived happily in Victorian splendor in London's elegant Belgravia neighborhood, sharing the premises with her corpulent tabby, Pittums, which, as is the case with so many pets, was reflective of the mien and manner of its mistress.

The master plan had been for Jacobus, Kate, and Nathaniel to remain comfortably ensconced in London after the Prom concert and Yumi completed the orchestra's European tour on the continent. After the tour, she would return to London and spend her three-week hiatus until the start of Harmonium's fall concert season vacationing with her friends and family. She would then return to New York with Jacobus and Nathaniel, and her grandmother, Kate, would return to her home in Japan, where she had resided since the end of the last world war. Now, with Natasha Conrad's death, it seemed likely that plan was about to change.

Kate wrapped her arms around her distraught granddaughter. "Dearest Yumichan," she said, emphasizing the Japanese suffix of endearment, "you must be absolutely devastated! We must get you home for a cup of tea immediately. Nathaniel, please be so kind as to fetch us a cab. And then please call dear Leonia and break the dreadful news. As gently as you can manage, dear Nathaniel."

Sitting in the back of the hearse-like, black London cab, with its fold-down seat, Yumi and Kate faced Nathaniel and Jacobus. It was a subdued drive from Royal Albert. Yumi spent most of it staring out the side window into the darkened streets. What little conversation there was had a hollow ring, and was initiated by Kate, who sought to rally Yumi's spirits as much as she could under the circumstances.

Jacobus, as was his wont, used his ears and nose to understand his surroundings. London sounded and smelled nothing like the woods around his cottage in the Berkshires. That was obvious. But it was also different from New York City. Quieter, calmer. A lower energy level. Traffic flowed more patiently, perhaps because the streets wound like cooked spaghetti rather than dry and straight. Nevertheless, it was an unsettling sensation driving on the left, with the approach of oncoming cars sounding more into his right ear than his left. Inside the cab, he detected three different fragrances. Eliminating Nathaniel and the driver, that left only Kate and Yumi. After Yumi's description of her embrace of her student, the thought of who the third fragrance belonged to depressed him.

They were soon in posh Belgravia. Impressive white townhouses, with cozy, manicured gardens, were interspersed with international embassies and upscale hotels, and catered to by stylish boutiques and trendy eateries. Ostentation was shunned, but wealth, however understated, somehow made its presence felt. Many of the area's vintage mansions had been converted to B&Bs, or these days, Airbnbs. But there were still some, like Aunt Leonia's, which had remained intact, single-family homes, retaining the elegance and majesty of earlier times, before the sun began to set on the British Empire.

Aunt Leonia's four-story, stucco mansion on semicircular Grosvenor Crescent was one of a dozen lookalike connected row houses, each with a second-story balcony in front, supported by a pair of impressive pillars. All was quiet as they passed through the black wrought-iron gate, and ascended six gas-lit granite steps. Aunt Leonia, in a full-length Chinese silk robe, greeted them at the door.

"The poor child!" she said to Yumi as they entered.

"She can use a cuppa," Kate said.

"Surely, brandy would be the more resuscitative," Leonia said.

"Tea, certainly, is preferable," Kate said.

"Brandy will do the trick."

"I think what I really need is to go to bed," Yumi said. "So if you'll please excuse me...."

"Why, certainly dear," Kate said.

"See, you've upset her," Leonia said.

"Don't be dozy!" Kate said.

They had been like that all their lives. Even six thousand miles between the island nations in which they lived had failed to blunt their sisterly barbs. They were so different, it was hard to believe that they could share the same genetic pool. Where Kate was lithe, athletic, and always a bit rebellious, Aunt Leonia was stout, matronly, and proper. It had been Kate who had exhibited the artistic DNA in the family, having become a virtuoso violinist while still a little girl. Sadly, the war and a second-place finish in the infamous Grimsley International Violin Competition had cut off her performance career at the knees, after which she dedicated her quiet life to teaching the violin to youngsters on Kyushu Island.

Aunt Leonia, on the other hand, had a penchant for bonbons and brandy, and had dedicated her life to stuffing her home with Victorian gewgaws, collecting antique Isfahan Persian rugs, attending seances, and making sure Pittums remained well fed. Shaded by dozens of philodendrons in oversized Imari ceramic pots, glossily polished corner tables graced every room and were piled high with boxes of chocolates, pulp fiction, tell-all magazines, and learned tomes "proving" that the mysteries of prehistory, such as Stonehenge, the Easter Island heads, and Machu Picchu, were all constructed by the same advanced civilization of stone masons from another planet.

"Please don't fuss," Yumi said to both ladies. "I'm just tired. And anyway, I need to call Natasha's parents."

She gave her grandmother and great-aunt a hug as Pittums nuzzled his head against her leg. She repeated her good nights to Nathaniel then to Jacobus, who had hardly said a word the entire journey from Royal Albert Hall.

Jacobus could feel Yumi's cheek, still damp with tears, against his as she hugged him. Though he understood perfectly how she felt, he was unable—as he had always been unable—to articulate the words of comfort that so easily sprang from everyone else's lips. That's why he was surprised—more than surprised, mildly astonished—when Yumi whispered into his ear, "Jake, are you wondering about the same thing I am?"

"Yes," Jacobus whispered back. "Why wait?"

"Exactly. Why wait for the third hammer stroke?"

Chapter Three

T he second trombone player nudged the violist with his elbow.
"What's he doing here?" he said, shooting a disapproving glance
to the other side of the ballroom.

The violist, who had no ready answer, shrugged. But even if she had one, there was no time for it, as at that moment, Wendell Barton requested everyone to stand in silence to reflect upon the memory of Natasha Conrad.

Outside the Park Tower Knightsbridge it was a crisp, glorious, autumn Sunday morning, a fortuitous free day on the orchestra's tour itinerary. On the inside, the sun was not shining, as the entire orchestra was gathered for an emergency meeting in the hotel's grand ballroom. The agenda had been determined at a sometimes-contentious conference that had gone late into the previous night between the Harmonium management, the musicians' committee, and DCI Mattheson. The essential question to be discussed and decided upon was: Will the tour go forward?

Moments of silence in orchestras, though always well-intended, were more often than not a pro forma gesture of respect and reflection rather than of genuine sorrow because it was usually an elder member, whose death was sincerely mourned but not necessarily unexpected, who had passed away. The moment of silence for Natasha, though, had more than its share of hand-covered eyes, wet handkerchiefs, trembling shoulders, and muffled sobs.

The object of the trombonist's unanswered question was an unanticipated attendee, Maestro Klaus Kruger. Whereas conductors were undisputed lords of the manor on the podium, they were typically not welcome additions to orchestra meetings, as by instinct and by experience, musicians tended to muzzle the free flow of ideas when in the presence of conductors.

Kruger, pale and white-haired too soon in life, and sustained by the chain-smoking and chain-drinking that were also slowly killing him, was a veteran of decades of conducting major international orchestras, each displaying its own distinctive group temperament. Kruger was familiar with them all, and they with him. Some orchestras adored him for his passion. Others considered him overbearing. Others still thought him a dilettante. *"Herr Kapellmeister,"* one orchestra's concertmaster derisively called him. He was not a great technical conductor. He knew that. But precision was not his goal. His interpretations of "the big" repertoire—Mahler and Bruckner specifically—had earned universal praise. That and the quality of sound he was able to coax from the musicians were his strongest points. His devotees, the self-styled "Krugerites," looked upon him with almost religious awe. He had been deeply distressed, for them and for the musicians, when the Mahler Sixth performance had ended so abruptly and so tragically.

Kruger understood very well how his presence at the meeting would be perceived by some, if not all, of the musicians—an unnecessary and unwelcome intrusion into orchestra affairs. Sensitive to the delicate balance that could so easily be thrown out of kilter by his presence, after the moment of silence, Kruger simply requested that he be permitted to make his views known, after which he would depart and accept whatever result was determined by the other parties.

The chair of the musicians' committee, principal bassoonist Charlotte Sedley, asked if there was anyone who had an objection to Maestro's request. No one raised one, though the trombonist rolled his eyes, his concerns hardly ameliorated.

"Whatever," the violist said under her breath. She shrugged again.

But even the trombonist's concerns were relieved by Maestro's deferential attitude and further assuaged by his message. First, Kruger announced he would support any decision made by all the parties regarding the future of the tour. If it was agreed upon that the tour would go on, he proposed removing the Mahler Sixth from the program and substituting a suitable replacement. The Mahler, even in the best of times, left one physically and psychologically raw and ragged, he explained. Considering the enormity of the current circumstances, he felt it would be cruel and unusual punishment to force the musicians to endure that emotional gauntlet. Even an orchestra like Harmonium, which prided itself on its musical discipline, would balk, with justification, at the three hammer strokes. Kruger thought that the Tchaikovsky Fifth Symphony, which ends in majestic triumph, would make the audiences just as happy without being an emotional ordeal for the musicians, and which, since all the musicians knew it cold, could be performed effectively with little additional rehearsal.

"Tchaikovsky Five is an affirmation of life, which is something we need a little of right now, I think."

With that message, Kruger thanked the musicians for their time and departed to spontaneous applause. In all likelihood, it was his consideration of the musicians' frame of mind that turned the tide of the ensuing debate.

"At least he didn't smoke," the violist said.

Kruger's departure was followed by the chair's open invitation to talk about Natasha Conrad. Several members of the orchestra spoke, including Yumi and Fritz Wohlfart, both of whom interrupted their comments often in order to regain their composure.

Though everyone expressed heartfelt sorrow over Natasha Conrad's death, the respective positions of the musicians, management, and DCI Mattheson over the tour's future were predictably divergent. Management's case was expressed not only by personnel manager Wendell Barton, but also by the orchestra manager and, at the top of the food chain, by the managing director. Their considerations were logistical and financial. The tour had been years in the making, and the concert at Royal Albert, though at the tail end of the Proms season, was the first of the tour. If they canceled the remainder of the performances, they would forfeit substantial fees from two concerts each in Lucerne, Milan, Salzburg, Berlin, and Amsterdam. In addition, the orchestra had received six-figure sponsorships from a number of multinational corporations, so there was the question of whether those would have to be returned. The resultant deficit from all those give-backs would put the orchestra in a substantial hole, discouraging future revenue opportunities and jeopardizing their ability to pay the musicians their full salary.

The musicians' rumbling response was not unexpected, if not yet articulated—traditional mistrust of management, who always seemed to be on the prowl for a way to reopen their contract and extract concessions. This seemed to be yet one more ploy, with the clear inference that if the musicians insisted on canceling the tour, management would place the blame at their feet for cutting their own financial throats.

Management was not finished with its presentation. They went on to state that they would also have to cancel hotel, plane, train, and bus reservations, and whether Harmonium would be reimbursed or even given a credit for those expenses was highly dubious. Then there were the travel agency, the security firm, and the guest artists who had been engaged that would have to be disengaged, but who, no doubt, would demand compensation. If the concerts were canceled, management would additionally have to make new, expensive arrangements for getting the musicians, staff, instruments, wardrobe trunks, and cargo back to New York. Until that point, they would have to find new accommodations for the musicians, because the Park Tower was fully booked once they checked out, and there was little likelihood that a hundred hotel rooms could be immediately found in any decent London hotel.

Management thanked the orchestra for giving them the opportunity to present their position and expressed the hope that there would be an agreeable outcome. The silence in which their words echoed suggested otherwise.

The musicians' position was represented by the orchestra committee chair. Charlotte Sedley had been a member of Harmonium for seventeen years and had been involved in contract negotiations on two previous occasions. In addition to being credited with a keen, analytic mind, her solo at the beginning of Stravinsky's *The Rite of Spring* was generally considered to be some of the greatest bassoon playing ever. It was a solo that required ice in one's veins, which was also no doubt a valuable asset to her negotiating skills.

Standing before the assembly, after acknowledging all of management's challenges, Sedley insisted that the death of *any* of their colleagues should be enough to consider discontinuing a tour. Tours come and tours go, and there would be other opportunities for an orchestra as great as Harmonium. Wasn't there already a Far East tour planned for next year? But this was so much more than canceled performances. So much more than dollars and cents on a spreadsheet. This was a young lady who was playing her first concert, whom everyone was still getting to know, whom everyone liked, and who not only died, but was murdered in her chair while doing the job she loved. It was a devastating, traumatic moment, not only for Harmonium, but for all orchestras. For all musicians. To be sitting onstage, doing one's job, totally exposed, and wondering if you are next on some maniac's hit list. How could there even be any debate on allowing the tour to proceed?

Sedley sat down to the applause of her colleagues and to management's grudging respect.

DCI Mattheson, with DS Littlebank in tow, stood to state law enforcement's case, first thanking the musicians for allowing him to speak and expressing his sorrow at the circumstances making his presence necessary.

Punctuating the air with jabs of his pipe, Mattheson went down his list of points to be made. He and his department were committed to bringing the murderer to justice, which, he assumed, is what everyone wanted. He waited for anyone to disagree. No one did. In order to do so, he continued, he needed the cooperation of everyone in the organization to provide any information whatsoever that could shed light on this heinous crime. He conceded that all the members of the orchestra, but one, had been onstage during the concert, "so you're correct to assume that none of you, for the moment, are suspects." Nevertheless, he strongly urged the orchestra to remain in London for "as long as necessary, but as short as I can humanly make possible," where the musicians would be easily accessible for further questioning, rather than "gallivanting about on the Continent."

When Mattheson made the comment, "all the members of the orchestra, but one," there was noticeable shifting among the group as eyes, if not heads, turned toward Donald Stroud, the violinist who had called in sick for the concert.

Harmonium had a very generous paid sick-leave policy. Depending upon the illness or injury, musicians could be absent for weeks or even months and still collect their full paycheck. Musicians who called in sick were rarely questioned by Wendell Barton, the personnel manager, even when the excuses sounded dubious, though he did maintain careful records. Over the years, only one musician, a horn player, had gotten into trouble for abusing the system. He had called in sick for a morning rehearsal and an evening concert. It was later found out that he had played a non-orchestra recording engagement in the afternoon. Management called him into a meeting. Accompanied by Charlotte Sedley and a union representative, the horn player explained that he indeed had felt poorly in the morning, had recovered sufficiently in the afternoon to play the recording session, and fully expected to show up for work that night. However, his efforts at the recording session gave him a relapse, he said, and he felt miserable again. He confessed that because he hadn't informed management in advance of the afternoon session—something he was contractually required to do—things looked bad for him, but that was the truth.

Sedley, who wasn't convinced it was the truth, knew that if she argued too vociferously in his defense, she could lose credibility in future disputes, so she limited herself to saying to Barton, "You've asked for an explanation, and now you've heard it. It's up to you to decide whether you believe a member of this orchestra is an honest colleague or not." The horn player got off with a warning.

That sick-leave policy, if not the entire relationship between the musicians and management, worked very well from both management's and the musicians' perspective because it was built on an assumption of mutual trust. The musicians were dedicated to their jobs, and, on the other side of the coin, everyone understood that if the policy were taken advantage of, they could lose a very valuable fringe benefit. Almost all the musicians came to work all the time. In every orchestra, though, there were two or three members who seemed to live under a permanent cloud of physical ailments, who stretched the credulity not only of the personnel manager but of the musicians' colleagues as well, who came down with one illness or injury or mishap or emergency after the other, and who claimed to require a period of recuperation more extensive than the supposed calamity would suggest.

Donald Stroud, only in his thirties, of medium height and build—maybe a little overweight but not so much it should have mattered—with an unhealthy, pale complexion, was one of those unfortunates. Prone to headaches, lactose-intolerant, allergic to gluten, peanuts, shellfish, feta cheese, and certain varieties of mushrooms, Stroud had been absent from work for most of the month preceding the tour, complaining of pain in his left hand, the cause of which any number of specialists he had seen were baffled. He had returned to work in the two weeks prior to the tour solely in order to perform the repertoire for the tour, because otherwise, he would not have been permitted to go on it. Then, yesterday, on the day of the Mahler performance, the first tour concert, he had called in sick yet again. The thought might have gone unspoken among the orchestra, but it certainly hadn't gone unthought that Stroud was more interested in a paid vacation in Europe than in playing concerts.

Hypochondriacs don't view themselves as hypochondriacs. So when he saw the sidelong glances come his way, he misinterpreted their intent. He didn't realize it was merely, "Oh, Donald. 'Sick' again." He thought they were questioning his innocence in Natasha Conrad's murder. Either way, it unnerved him.

He stood up.

"Excuse me," he said. "Can I say something?"

Mattheson nodded.

"I just want everyone to know that I thought I was getting another migraine last night. The hotel can confirm that because I ran out of Imitrex and had to go out to a drugstore before it got worse. They saw me leave. I didn't know drugstores aren't called drugstores in England, so I looked all over and couldn't find one. Then someone told me they're called chemists. It took me all night, but I finally found one. They can tell you I was there. I went back to my room after that."

"Thank you, Mr. Stroud," DCI Mattheson said. "Any negative insinuation you may have inferred was unintended."

Stroud sat down.

Wendell Barton, the personnel manager, raised his hand.

"I have a question," he said.

"Yes?" Mattheson said. "Go ahead."

"The musicians had to go through security to get into the hall. Each of them was given an ID that was checked by a guard. How could they have let someone into the concert with a gun?"

Barton's question had no doubt been on many of the musicians' minds, as there was audible support for it.

"Please be aware," Mattheson replied, "that very concern has been uppermost on our minds, not only on how it entered the hall, but also how it was obtained in the first place. Be assured we are investigating it and will continue to do so until we receive satisfactory answers. However, our task here, at this moment, is not how to find the murderer, but how the orchestra is going to proceed."

The discussion, sometimes heated but generally civil, continued for an hour. In the end, a compromise was reached. In management's favor and much to their relief, the tour would continue. However, in order to do so, they agreed to certain conditions to satisfy the musicians: At the beginning of each concert, the audience would be asked to stand and join the musicians in a moment of silence. Natasha Conrad's seat would remain empty for the entire tour, in remembrance. The planned, perky encores they had prepared for the tour—Brahms's Hungarian Dances and Smetana's *Bartered Bride Overture*—would be replaced by *Nimrod* from the nineteenth-century English composer Edward Elgar's *Enigma Variations*, oft-performed as perhaps the most touching musical elegy ever penned. Further, the audience would be instructed not to applaud upon its conclusion. Finally, to placate Mattheson and provide him with instantaneous access to all the musicians, the orchestra set up a WhatsApp contact list, and, in turn, Mattheson provided a direct hotline in case anyone had anything they wanted to tell him privately.

As the meeting wound down, Yumi stood to ask Mattheson if there was any information that he was at liberty to tell them.

Mattheson and Littlebank quietly conferred.

Mattheson said, "This we can tell you. It's more than we would ordinarily divulge, but seeing the extent to which all of you have been affected by this tragedy, we are comfortable that we can provide a bit of transparency without compromising our investigation.

"We found a concert program and a brown paper bag on the floor of the Arena, from which location we have concluded the shot had been fired. There was a bullet hole in each with traces of gunpowder residue. The scenario we envision is that, during most of the concert, the assailant had kept the gun in the bag, in a pocket, perhaps. Toward the end of the symphony, he then removed the gun from his pocket, keeping it in the bag and at his side whilst holding the program in front of him with his other hand, presumably to appear as if he...or she—" (nod to Littlebank) "—were reading the program notes. Just before the third hammer stroke in the finale, he would have had to raise his gun hand and aim almost in one motion; anything of longer duration would have been noticed. He then fired the fatal shot.

"He would have to have been an expert marksman with steady nerves to have hit his target with such accuracy with a small-caliber gun, which is what we believe it was. That type of handgun is typically used for defensive purposes and not to kill, which means concealment was primary in his considerations and, perhaps importantly, that he was confident in his aim. Apparently, he was successful in disguising his act, because, as of yet, no one we've spoken to either saw or heard anything suspicious. It must have been a phenomenal risk, but he took it, and he succeeded. That's all we have for now, but the investigation is only in its initial stages, and we are confident of apprehending the culprit."

As the musicians quietly filed out of the ballroom, Mattheson received his only surprise of the morning. The trombone player—the one who had misgivings about Klaus Kruger—gave him a high-five and said, "Good job, Chief."

Fritz Wohlfart lagged behind the others. He was still emotionally shaken from the previous evening. He approached Mattheson.

"Excuse me, sir," Wohlfart said. "I don't know if it means anything, but you wanted us to talk to you if we had anything to say at all."

"Yes. By all means."

"Can you keep this confidential?"

"Absolutely."

"Well, I just want to say that Donald Stroud, the violinist who called in sick...well, he was the only one on Natasha's audition committee who voted against her. I mean, that's everyone's prerogative, but I just wanted to say."

"Please enlighten me, Mr. Wohlfart. How many members are there on an audition committee?"

"Usually about a dozen, more or less. For this one, that's how many there were."

"And is it rare for there to be only one or two objectors?"

"I'd say it's rarer for there to be a unanimous opinion. Sometimes it's almost fifty-fifty."

"How do you decide in such a case?"

"Oh, *we* don't decide!" Wohlfart said, surprised by the question.

"No? Then how is the result determined?" Mattheson asked, equally surprised by Wohlfart's answer.

"The audition committee's opinion is only advisory. It's up to the music director—the principal conductor—to decide. He's the one with authority."

"Would that be Maestro Kruger?"

"Kruger's only a guest conductor. Guest conductors have no authority for hiring and firing at all."

"I see. At least I'm starting to. Getting back to Mr. Stroud, even with his objection, given Miss Conrad's near-unanimous approval by the audition committee, the music director elected to hire her, suggesting that her employment was never much in doubt. Is that about right?"

"By George, I think you've got it," Wohlfart said.

"Thank you very much, Mr. Wohlfart. And I'm glad to see you smile. We appreciate you stepping forward."

After Wohlfart left and the room was empty, Mattheson said, "Littlebank, find out the exact times that this gentleman, Stroud, was seen in the hotel and claims to have gone to the 'drugstore.'"

"Yes, sir."

"And please give Ms. Shinagawa a call. Tell her I'd like to see her here at the hotel tomorrow morning before her departure."

When, after returning to Auntie Leonia's home the night before, Yumi had called John and Helen Conrad, it was Helen who had answered.

"Yumi! Are you calling all the way from England? It's so nice of you to call! Hold on. Let me get John. How was Natasha's first concert? We haven't heard from her yet."

It had been the most difficult conversation of Yumi's life.

The Conrads drove from Lawrence to Kansas City, where they boarded a plane to Detroit, and flew from there to Heathrow. Yumi and DS Littlebank had met them there. The Conrads were not all that many years older than Yumi, but they seemed to have aged by a generation since she had seen them at Natasha's graduation party only a few months earlier.

Both parents were from thoroughly midwestern stock: solid, honest, churchgoing, hardworking. As they emerged through Customs, Helen Conrad's hair was held firmly in place, as always, with copious amounts of spray, though somehow it seemed to have lost its luster and looked dowdy rather than stylish. John's checkered, short-sleeved shirt's pocket held his customary Bic pen and eyeglass case, but his tie was poorly knotted at the neck and hung too long. Helen was the more stoic parent, or maybe that was just an impression because she was the more solidly built of the two. John, the parent who had been the more enthusiastic in encouraging Natasha to pursue her dream to become a violinist, appeared to have assumed the burden of guilt on his sloping shoulders. Upon seeing Yumi, tears welled in his red eyes. He apologized. No need, Yumi said. No need. We all feel the same. Littlebank handed the case containing Natasha's violin to Helen. So recently purchased with such joy, it had been intended to last a lifetime. So it had, in a terribly sad way. Helen, hugging the case, mouthed a thank you.

With Yumi in the passenger seat and the Conrads in the back, Littlebank drove them to the London hotel that he had reserved for them. Mattheson had provided his personal BMW sedan for the purpose. "Forcing them to sit in a police car simply won't do."

"No, sir," Littlebank said, looking forward to being behind the wheel. "And shall I book them in at the Park Tower Knightsbridge, sir?"

Mattheson had removed the pipe from his mouth and looked at his subordinate in perplexed horror. "Don't be a dolt, Littlebank. How would you like to stay in the same hotel as your child who had just been murdered?"

Very little was said along the way, though the Conrads tried their best to smile through their ordeal. It was their first time in England, they said, and oohed-and-aahed whenever they passed a historic landmark more than a hundred years old. There would be some paperwork, Littlebank told them when they arrived at the hotel. DCI Mattheson would need to meet with them at some point, but only when they were ready. For now, they should get some rest.

Chapter Four

After an early breakfast, which Auntie Leonia insisted must be a full English breakfast with fried eggs, bangers, bacon, kippers poached in milk, baked beans, broiled tomatoes, and toast, Yumi said her good-byes to her auntie with Pittums in her arms, her grandmother, Jacobus, and Nathaniel. With her suitcase and violin, she took a cab from Belgravia to the Park Tower, Knightsbridge, where she would board one of the four orchestra buses that departed at 9:15 for Heathrow Airport, destination Zurich; and from there to Lucerne by chartered coach.

Waiting for her at the hotel entrance were DCI Mattheson and DS Littlebank.

"Breakfast?" Mattheson asked, and was puzzled by the wide-eyed look of horror on Yumi's face. They settled for coffee in the lounge.

The lobby lounge, tasteful and elegant, was dotted with a dozen small, round glass tables, each circled by three or four highly comfortable chairs. Potted palms, subdued hues, and soft, piped-in music completed the ambiance. They chose a table in the corner, far enough away from the front desk where musicians were checking out of their rooms so that they wouldn't be heard, and far enough away from the French pastry display so Yumi wouldn't be tempted.

"I know you haven't much time before you board your coach," Mattheson said, "so I'll get right down to it. DS Littlebank discovered some items in Miss Conrad's wardrobe trunk that were outside the scope of what your personnel manager told us should be in there. It might be of interest to us. Perhaps you could help shed some light."

41

"What items?"

"It appears the young lady was in poor health."

"That can't be true. Natasha was athletic. She was a tennis player and was always going to the gym. She was in excellent health, as far as I know," Yumi said. "What makes you think she wasn't?"

"First and foremost, she had a veritable pharmacy."

"For example."

"For example. Painkillers—"

"Painkillers? Prescription painkillers?"

"No, not prescription. She had a drawerful of Aspirin, Motrin, Tylenol. And Dramamine, Imodium, Dulcolax, antacids of various types, cough drops and throat lozenges, multi-vitamins, something called Inderal, bandages, Calamine lotion, various ointments—"

Yumi strained to prevent her lips from continuing to spread sideways, but she was unable to repress her growing smile. Mattheson looked at her with not a little vexation when she laughed out loud.

"I'm glad you find this funny, Ms. Shinagawa. I, sadly, fail to see the humor."

"I can explain it all."

"Please do."

"This was Natasha's first trip ever overseas, and I would imagine she was a little anxious about it. Wouldn't you be, if you were a twenty-year-old going on a three-week concert tour?"

"Go on."

"And so it would be natural for her to ask her colleagues who have done this for years for their advice on what to pack."

"Yes, that would make sense. And?"

"Look over there at the front desk, DCI Mattheson," Yumi said.

"Musicians congregating. Getting ready to depart."

"How many of them look as young as Natasha?"

"Ah. I take your point."

"There. You see? Almost all of her colleagues are older, *much older* than Natasha, and are no doubt a lot more cautious about travel than Natasha needed to be. So she probably took to heart whatever counsel they gave her, and packed all that stuff. You know, for air sickness, for combating diarrhea and constipation. Things like that."

"Yes. That would explain it. But what's this Inderal? I'm not familiar with that one."

"That's what's called a beta-blocker. I don't know the chemistry, but it slows down the heartbeat. Musicians who are prone to getting nervous sometimes use Inderal to calm them down before a performance so that they don't exhibit the symptoms in their playing."

"Symptoms? Such as?"

"For string players, like the bow shaking, the wild vibrato. Some violinists get petrified they'll drop their instrument when they perform."

"As her teacher, did you recommend Natasha take Inderal?"

"Never! She rarely got nervous. She loved playing for an audience."

"So, how do you account for her having it?"

"Abundance of caution? I bet if you examine the container and all those other medications and drugs, you'll see that they're close to unused. I bet they haven't even been opened."

Littlebank nodded affirmatively.

"Good point. Good point, indeed," Matheson said. "Littlebank hadn't thought of that."

"Anything else?" Yumi asked. She started to get up. Almost all the musicians had left the hotel for the coach. Mattheson rose with her.

"Just one more item. We discovered a box of Cadbury chocolates in her wardrobe trunk."

Yumi looked at Mattheson and Littlebank blankly.

"Can you tell us about it?" Mattheson asked.

"I guess she liked chocolate."

"What I meant was, it is a gift box. Do you think she bought it, or perhaps it was bought for her? From someone who might have been courting her? We found no receipt."

"I have no idea why she had a box of chocolates," Yumi said. "But I wouldn't read anything into it."

"Nor should you. Because that wouldn't be your job, would it? That would be our job."

They walked to the exit, passing the gift shop off the lobby. Yumi grabbed Mattheson by his sleeve. "Come with me," she said. "I still have five minutes."

They scurried into the gift shop. Yumi approached the saleslady, who bore an uncanny resemblance to a young Margaret Thatcher. She was in the midst of the daily morning ritual of cleaning the glass countertop of a gift display case, spray bottle in one hand, cloth in the other.

"Sorry, we don't open till ten," she said.

"We're not here to buy anything," Yumi said.

"Oh." She resumed spraying.

"We don't mean to disturb you," Yumi said. "But do you recall whether there was a young lady who purchased a box of Cadbury chocolates here a few days ago?"

The saleslady frowned.

"Do you mean the young lady who...died at the concert?"

"How do you know that's who we meant?" Mattheson asked.

"We've had the orchestra here for four days, haven't we? Her photo was in the newspaper, and I recognized her. Yes, she was here. She said she was very excited to buy the chocolates, dear thing."

"Did she say why?" Mattheson asked.

The saleslady looked at Mattheson quizzically. "Yes! How did you know?" she asked.

"Conjecture. What was her reason?"

"She said she loves chocolates. Don't we all?"

"I suppose so."

"I do hope she enjoyed them."

Four coaches departed for Heathrow with all the musicians but one. After thanking Yumi for her time, Mattheson intercepted Donald Stroud on his way out of the hotel.

"We need to ask you some questions," Mattheson said.

"I can't. The bus is leaving. If I miss the Lucerne concert, I'm screwed."

"We'll be sure to get you there. It shouldn't take too long."

"But—"

"Mr. Stroud, if you fuss, you'll be even more 'screwed,' so please, just come along."

Mattheson gestured toward the curb, where Littlebank, standing outside a police car, waited at attention.

They drove to the Kensington police station on Earls Court Road, Mattheson's precinct office. On the way there, upon Littlebank's request, Stroud rummaged through his wallet and produced the receipt for the Imitrex he had purchased Saturday night. While Mattheson's interview with Stroud took place, Littlebank did the legwork, tracking down the member of the hotel staff who was on desk duty the night of the concert and the chemist where Stroud had purchased his medication. He also did a quick Internet background check on Stroud. By the time Littlebank returned to the station, Mattheson had completed his questioning, and Stroud was sitting in a waiting room taking his pulse with a tepid cup of tea on a magazine table beside him. The two policemen compared notes and came to the mutual indisputable conclusion that there was no way Stroud could have been at Royal Albert at the time of the shooting. Furthermore, Stroud had never owned a firearm and had no police record whatsoever. Fritz Wohlfart's report that Stroud had been the only one to object to Natasha Conrad's tenure determination might have been accurate, but it was by no stretch of the imagination damning evidence.

Mattheson thanked Stroud for his cooperation and told him there was no further reason to detain him.

"So I'm exonerated?" Stroud asked.

"For the moment, yes. As much as anyone. There's nothing for you to worry about except getting to your concert on time."

Stroud took a cab to Heathrow, paid for by Mattheson, and boarded the next plane to Zürich, where, following in the orchestra's footsteps, he transferred to a coach to Lucerne. Though his head was hurting after the stressful day, and the one-hour coach ride—sitting in a back seat with all those fumes—made his stomach queasy, he made sure to show up for the concert. Desperate not to incur further ire from his colleagues, he rushed to Festival Hall, arriving only a half hour before the downbeat, signaling thumbs up to his colleagues when he entered. He felt his vindication was complete and was therefore taken aback when he was given, if not the cold shoulder, at most, the lukewarm variety. Hoping to rally some enthusiasm for his cause, he approached Charlotte Sedley, who was practicing her bassoon backstage.

"I made it!" he said.

"So did everyone else," she said and returned to warming up. Stroud showed up for all the remaining tour rehearsals and concerts and made no further claims of heroic measures.

After Mattheson excused Stroud, he and Littlebank went to work on Yumi's student list. Their pipedream of a theory was that one of the students had traveled to London, went to the Mahler concert, and would be found to have a compelling motive for killing their former fellow student, accompanied by ironclad evidence. But like most pipedreams, theirs went unrealized. One by one, names were checked off the list until, after several decreasingly optimistic hours, all of Yumi's students' whereabouts were accounted for. Most of them were still in New York City, waiting for the fall semester to begin, and those who weren't—the students from Shanghai, Taipei, and Seoul—were eventually traced to their respective homes, enjoying the end of their summer holidays.

If the Lucerne concert was a hill to climb for Donald Stroud, it was Mount Everest for Fritz Wohlfart. He said that sitting next to the empty seat onstage made him feel naked, as if everyone's eyes were on him. "It was almost like how I felt when I played my very first concert," he confessed to Yumi. "Look at me. I'm shaking like a leaf."

It wasn't much easier for the rest of the musicians. Most of the audience had heard of the tragedy that had befallen the orchestra, and for those who hadn't, the moment of silence before the concert and the empty chair left no doubt. But somehow, the orchestra made it through, as professional musicians know how to do, and as the days passed, one concert piling on top of another, the familiar routine dulled their pain. After London, the ensuing two weeks became an anticlimax of sorts, an emotional letdown. Yes, the performances went predictably well. The halls were full, and the audiences were enthusiastic. The Tchaikovsky Fifth turned out to be a more-than-adequate substitute for the Mahler. A much more easily digestible meal than the Mahler—"There's no such thing as a bad performance of Tchaikovsky Five," Jacobus was known to utter—if anything, it was more warmly received than the Mahler would have been. The audiences were particularly appreciative, as they understood fully what the musicians had had to go through emotionally just to sit on the stage and play.

What interest there was in sampling *foie gras* in Paris or hiking up Mount Pilatus in Lucerne, or seeing the Vermeer exhibit at the Rijksmuseum in Amsterdam was the product of habit more than desire and certainly done with less *joie de vivre*. No one had the will to visit the Anne Frank House, a pilgrimage that was typically a "must" destination for many of the musicians. None of it seemed important anymore.

Though it wouldn't be fair to say that Harmonium simply went through the motions, the orchestra performed as well as it did because the musicians were professionals who understood their obligation to their craft and to the audiences. But even if they had merely dialed it in, they were such a finely honed ensemble that only the most discerning of listeners would even have guessed their playing was distracted. And if the musicians' general state of mind was somewhat disinterested during the greater part of the performances, it certainly was fully engaged during Elgar's *Nimrod*. Many members of the audience and several in the orchestra openly wept. From one city after another, critics lauded the orchestra for the quality of its playing. Harmonium had given a tour it could be proud of, but the murderer of Natasha Conrad remained as elusive as ever.

Chapter Five

The morning after the final concert at the famed Concertgebouw in Amsterdam, most of the musicians boarded the plane for the official orchestra flight back to JFK, planning to decompress in their New York homes or to vacation in the country during their three-week break before beginning the grind of the winter concert season in early October. Others, taking advantage of their proximity to Europe's popular tourist destinations, dispersed throughout the continent, hoping to recharge their batteries among the countless art museums, galleries, restaurants, and *haute couture* boutiques. Life went on.

After two weeks on tour, Yumi had had enough of arriving at airports hours before flights and slogging through interminable security. She opted for the Eurostar, the high-speed train from Amsterdam to London, a trip of less than four hours that was quiet, scenic, and civilized. She read, she watched fields and towns pass by in a flash, she took off her shoes and stretched, she had a Stella Artois and crisps in the café car, and when the train pulled into St. Pancras Station, she woke up to find that she had drooled in her sleep.

Upon arriving back at Auntie Leonia's Belgravia home, she encountered an implausible scene of domestic bliss. Leonia was in the kitchen, as usual, humming an unidentifiable tune as she prepared a dinner of an English-style pot roast seasoned with sage and mint, boiled potatoes, and mushy peas. Nathaniel was in the parlor, sprawled on an embroidered Victorian divan like a shameless odalisque, fast asleep with an open book on his chest and a smile of sheer contentment on his face. His substantial belly, a testament to the good life, expanded and contracted in smooth, easy rhythm, like a large bubble at the La Brea Tar Pits as it escaped from a half-opened bathrobe. *Obaasan* Kate, her gray hair held in a bun atop her head with a pair of chopsticks, sat next to Jacobus on the cushioned window bench overlooking the street, the sun shining upon them. Pittums lay on his back between them, all four legs stretched out, making sure he received his fair share of the sun's warming rays. Kate was reading to Jacobus, and they were both laughing uproariously. Kate and Jacobus looked up when they heard the front door open and close.

"Yumichan!" Kate exclaimed and jumped up. "Welcome home."

She ran to Yumi and ensnared her in a tight embrace.

"Do put your things down and join us! We're having the most wonderful time!"

"I can see that," Yumi said.

Jacobus called from his seat.

"Your grandmother was just reading me one of her sister's books. About how noteworthy scientists now agree that the pyramids could only have been built by aliens from another planet. Live and learn."

Yumi had rarely seen Jacobus so happy.

"Just make sure you don't tell Auntie you don't think it's serious," Yumi said.

"We don't?" Jacobus replied.

"Of course, we won't tell her, dear," Kate said. "We wouldn't want to be booted out of such comfortable lodging, would we? Mum's the word!"

Kate invited Yumi to join Jacobus and relax, and went to the kitchen to bring back tea and biscuits. After such an exhausting tour, she surmised correctly, Yumi must be absolutely fagged, and there was nothing more reviving than a hot cup of tea.

While Kate was gone, Yumi quickly dispensed with idle pleasantries, not only because she knew that idle pleasantries made Jacobus cringe, but also because she was eager to ask him if he had heard anything more about the murder investigation. Yumi had tried to find out what was happening on the Internet and in the newspapers while she was in Europe, but there was scant mention of the murder, except for the now-hackneyed eulogies for Natasha Conrad. She had phoned Helen and John Conrad often, mostly to console them, partly for information. The medical examiner had completed the autopsy. Nothing was revealed that hadn't been known from the moment Natasha was shot. Her body was released to her parents, who escorted her back to Kansas. The Conrads, who had always been effusive with Yumi, were as polite as ever, but they had become increasingly distant. Yumi understood why. It wasn't just that their connection to each other—Natasha—had been severed. It was the unspoken sense that they had entrusted their daughter's wellbeing to Yumi, that she was Natasha's surrogate parent, especially in strange lands. She had failed in her responsibility in the most drastic way imaginable. The Conrads would never say so out loud and probably not even to each other. But even if the Conrads hadn't felt that way, Yumi carried the moral burden of having failed them.

Jacobus's response to her questions was deflating. He had called Mattheson's office. Trying to be clever, he claimed to know things that he thought might be valuable to the investigation. What he told Mattheson, generic stuff about symphony orchestras and about Conrad's relationship to Yumi, was a cover for his true intent, to subtly mine Mattheson for nuggets of information and discover what progress was being made. To barter.

Jacobus had to give Mattheson credit. He saw through Jacobus's ploy almost immediately and told him in polite but definite terms to go jump in the lake.

"Did you ask him why he thought the murderer waited for the third hammer stroke?" Yumi asked.

"I didn't have a chance. I was already in the lake."

"Well, what do you think?"

"That depends. I suppose it's possible the murderer knew in advance that Kruger was going to—"

"No, that's not it, Jake. I know what you're thinking. That if he did know in advance that Kruger would give the cue for the third hammer stroke, he could be certain the noise would cover up the gunshot."

"Right."

"Wrong. I asked Maestro Kruger about that. He swore that it was impossible for him to have told anyone what he was going to do because he didn't know, himself, until that very moment in the performance there would be a third hammer stroke."

"Huh. That's interesting."

"Why do you say so?"

"Because if the murderer didn't know for sure, could that mean if there had been no third stroke, he wouldn't have shot?"

Yumi sighed. "That's the same question I've been asking myself for the past two weeks."

Over the years, ever since she first started studying violin with Jacobus as a raw teenage talent, Yumi had learned from him not only how to be a musician, but how to think like him. To question everything, to examine everything from every possible angle, whether it was Bach, Beethoven, or bedlam. After leaving him as a student and venturing off on her own as a professional musician, there had been long stretches when she and Jacobus had been out of touch, and she thought she had everything figured out. But then they would meet again for a dinner, a concert, or, less and less frequently, a refresher lesson. And whenever they would meet, he would have a new insight that had never occurred to her. So, more than anyone else's, she valued Jacobus's opinion, even though most of the time now, his thoughts echoed hers. Most of the time.

"Yes, it's possible," Jacobus said. "It's possible. A variation of Russian roulette."

"Except in Russian roulette, you kill yourself. He wasn't killing himself. He was killing an innocent young lady."

"I think it's a reasonable conjecture he wouldn't have shot if there hadn't been a third hammer stroke, and I don't disagree with it. But, still, it's only a conjecture."

"Meaning?"

"Well, I don't want you to take this the wrong way, but might it be possible there was something we don't know about in Natasha's past that compelled someone to kill her? Justifiable or not?"

"I know how your mind works, Jake. You consider any and every possibility, and only because it's you, I won't discount it or punch you in the nose. But no, I don't think it's possible. And I know you're going to pounce and say, 'Aha! You *think* it's not possible! But do you *know* it's not possible?'"

Jacobus guffawed. "And if I were to say that, what would you say?"

"I'd say you're being a pain in the ass."

Jacobus cackled even louder, which started to make him wheeze, as laughing hard inevitably did, which was one reason he didn't laugh all that often. Yumi waited for him to get his breath back before continuing.

"But even if there was a motive, justifiable or not," she said, "why commit murder in such a bizarre way? In the middle of a huge crowd? In the middle of a concert? Just to be dramatic? It makes no sense."

"You're right. What would that prove? To take a risk like that. Maybe I'm getting senile—no comment, please—but I can't see my way around this one, Yumi. The old noggin is coming up blank. I think we won't know the answers to any of this until the cops figure it out. Hopefully, they'll learn more than we have."

Kate returned to the parlor carrying a silver tray with a porcelain teapot, a plate of digestive biscuits, and all the necessary accouterments. Though Jacobus's boisterous guffawing had been insufficient to rouse Nathaniel from his stupor, the subtle fragrance of Earl Grey bergamot was.

"Ah! The sleeping tiger awakes!" Jacobus said.

"Do join us for tea, Nathaniel," Kate said.

"Yumi!" Nathaniel said. "You're back!"

"Astute observation, Watson," Jacobus said.

As it was a lovely, summery English afternoon, they decided to move to the veranda at the rear of the house. Exiting through leaded-glass French doors, they sat around an antique circular wrought-iron table with a glass top. In the garden, roses of every hue still boasted late-season bloom and sweet scent. Jacobus attempted to identify the varieties by their distinct fragrances: Damasks, Portlands, Bourbons. The Gallicas were particularly assertive. *Who needed to see them?* he thought. *Just a distraction.* He gave up after those and contented himself with identifying the bird species by their calls and songs. In his rough, phlegmy voice, he began to croon, "O willow, titwillow," from *The Mikado*. Kate poured the tea. It was so civilized.

"Shouldn't we ask Auntie Leonia to join us?" Yumi asked.

"I already did, dear," Kate said. "She's still hacking away at her spuds and, like the loyal English soldier, refuses to abandon her post."

Conversation gravitated to the just-completed concert tour. Yes, the hotels were comfortable, Yumi related. The food was wonderful. There was an excellent Miró exhibit in Paris. We were delayed flying to Amsterdam and almost didn't make it in time. One of the cellists got his hand stuck in a door and missed the whole second week. Given their otherwise cheerful mood and the charming setting, the death of Natasha Conrad was a subject Yumi consciously preferred to avoid.

"What were you just reading, Nathaniel?" she asked.

"Whatever it was," Jacobus said, "it did us a favor and put him to sleep."

Nathaniel ignored the remark. "Oh, this?" he said, picking up the paperback he'd brought outside. "Just one of those trashy Jasper Killingsworth true crime novels that your auntie has lying around." Nathaniel looked at the cover to remember the title. "*The Cotswolds Slasher*, from his bestselling *You Be the Judge* series."

"Jasper Killingsworth?" Yumi asked. "I've never heard of him."

"Nor should you have," Kate said. "And don't tell your auntie this, but those books should be banned."

"Why?"

"Because it's scurrilous stuff, that's why!" Kate said. "He feeds the public's insatiable appetite for 'true crime' with raw meat."

"Nevertheless," Nathaniel said to Yumi, with a grin, "your grandmother hasn't had any qualms regaling Jake with some of his recent oeuvres."

"Only because it is too absurd to be taken seriously!" Kate protested in her own defense.

"Will someone please explain what everyone thinks is so outrageously funny?" Yumi asked, in response to general laughter, the cause for which she was being left in the dark.

"Jasper Killingsworth takes what the media reports on current crime investigations," Kate said. "Then he rewrites the news, contorting it into so-called fiction by changing names and details, giving them a cosmetic sheen, and adding a lot of purely imagined color and outlandish, speculative balderdash."

"But isn't that what most crime fiction is?" Yumi asked.

"As far as that goes. But Killingsworth goes further. Too far, in my opinion. Killingsworth is notorious for making a fortune off of others' real life *mis*fortune and distress. It's compounded by his baseless conclusions on who the murderers were, simply with the goal of selling more books. At the end of his books, the last page is what he calls *The Verdict*. That's where *You Be the Judge* comes in. And, of course, throughout the course of the book, he makes the presumed wrongdoer seem more evil than Beelzebub."

"But that has to be harmless," Yumi said, "because by the time the book comes out, the real investigation will have determined who really did it."

"That's the part that upsets me the most, dear," Kate said. "Killingsworth's trick is to get the book out within weeks after a crime, even before the investigation is complete. And from the way he writes, the reading public—"

"Ignoramuses!"

"Thank you, Jake," Kate continued, "the reading public tends to be swayed by his verdicts. Some even believe that his books have influenced the investigations themselves."

"The poor soul who's falsely accused!" Yumi said.

"I must say that his writing style is very colorful and convincing. It's as if he was there at the scene of the crime."

"Auntie's his biggest fan," Jacobus said.

"But that's terrible!" Yumi said, ignoring him. "Hasn't anyone ever sued him?"

"Many times, it seems," Kate said. "It's all a muck, though, I'm afraid. Killingsworth protects himself by changing the facts just enough to call it fiction—which indeed it is!—as I said, by altering the name of the supposed culprit, and then, on his Verdict page, by appending a question mark next to his accused's altered name. It has enabled him to slither through taking responsibility by claiming that he's merely setting forth a possibility. Asking a question. Sometimes his verdicts have turned out to be correct, and everyone cheers and says how astute he is. But when he's been wrong, his victims have had hell to pay."

"Has anyone ever won a suit against him?"

"A few times, apparently. But even when they've sued and won, they're prohibited from saying Killingsworth did anything wrong, and they're forced to sign nondisclosure agreements. So, win or lose, they're still pilloried by the public, and Killingsworth sells all the more books."

"Can't they force him to stop?"

"In a perfect world. But the courts, including the court of public opinion, have chosen to give him a free pass. And his book sales are his publisher's meal ticket, so they would never agree to curtailing the series. The public can't seem to get enough of the trash."

"Like Nathaniel," Jacobus said.

"Well, Mr. Holier-than-thou," Nathaniel said. "Talk about trash. I didn't exactly see you turning your nose up at Auntie Leonia's book that proved the Loch Ness monster was a fifty-foot-long worm."

"Shh! Pipe down!" Jacobus said. "I do believe I heard m'lady's footsteps approaching."

The French doors swung open.

"Dinner is served!" Leonia proclaimed with great conviction.

The next two weeks were idyllic, made so in part by London's unusually cooperative autumn weather. The skies remained unalterably blue during the day, and even at night, a light jumper was more than sufficient to keep them warm. Yumi, determined to slough off the burden of her grief while she was with her friends and family, coaxed them all to indulge her and visit the most touristy London destinations: the Tower of London, Big Ben, Westminster Abbey, the London Zoo, Buckingham Palace, and Madame Tussaud's. She spied Jacobus and her grandmother holding hands at the Sherlock Holmes Museum, which alone was worth the price of admission. Mindless sightseeing was a strategy that she hoped would help her forget. And if not entirely forget, at least not obsess.

They frequented traditional English pubs almost daily, picking them from a tourist guide based solely on the appeal of their names. Anything with Duke or Earl or Sir or Pheasant was included on the list. They inevitably overate, stuffing themselves with ploughman's lunches, fish and chips, and many an Imperial pint. Their few concessions to "culture" were classical music concerts, most of which Auntie Leonia did not attend, and a revival of *Cats*, which Jacobus adamantly refused to set foot in but Leonia adored, and to the rebuilt Globe Theatre for a performance of Shakespeare's *Julius Caesar*.

Simulating Elizabethan England, after the show, they dined at the St. John-Smithfield restaurant where, nibbling on bones of roast suckling pig, they engaged in a lively discussion of the play. Brandishing a rib bone in hand like a classroom pointer, Kate Padgett posed the question: Who is the true tragic hero of *Julius Caesar*, and why?

"I vote for Calpurnia, Caesar's wife," Yumi said, "because she had to endure the tribulation and aftermath of his assassination."

"Brutus," Nathaniel argued. "He had the best of intentions, but history made him a villain."

Jacobus sat there, shaking his head all the while in disagreement as he speared morsels of moist pork into his mouth.

"Why, Mr. Caesar himself, of course!" Auntie Leonia said. "It must be. Otherwise, wouldn't Shakespeare have called the play *Brutus*? Don't you think?"

Pointing her bone in his direction, Kate said, "I sense Mr. Jacobus has a different opinion, and I am inclined to agree with it, if I am not mistaken, what it is going to be."

Jacobus swallowed the pork in his mouth, wiped his greasy lips on his sleeve, and coughed.

"Cinna," he said.

"Yes!" Kate said. "I knew it. Gold star, Mr. Jacobus!"

"The sniveling conspirator?" Yumi asked. "Cinna was a weak nothing. How could he be a hero? He wasn't even tragic."

"Not Cinna, the conspirator," Jacobus said. "The other Cinna. Cinna, the poet, who the mob mistook for the sniveling conspirator simply because they shared the same name. And then, even when he cried, 'I am Cinna, *the poet*,' they tore him apart anyway, justifying their blood lust with the excuse he was a lousy poet."

"I wonder," Kate mused, "if Mr. Shakespeare identified with our poor Mr. Cinna. The poet eternally subject to the fickle whims of the masses."

"I wouldn't be surprised," Jacobus replied, sensing an onset, as irrepressible as it was infrequent, of an attack of barely controllable rage to which he had been subject since his childhood. It was almost like a seizure. He never knew when it would come upon him, but the trigger was always his perception of injustice of one sort or another, and he was helpless to repress it. Intellectually, he told himself these attacks could have been the result of the sexual abuse he had suffered at the hands of the judge of the violin competition he had entered as a young boy or his guilt at the death of his German parents in the concentration camps after they had sent him to the US for his safety, or the sudden blindness that struck him the day of his audition for concertmaster of the Boston Symphony. It could be any one of those reasons, or none of them. He would never know, nor would he ever discuss it with anyone, let alone a professional therapist, in order to find out. It was none of anyone's business. So he lived with his rage, convincing himself but not convincing himself that it was part of his nature, and attempted to justify it because, in the end, he believed he was right.

"As far as I'm concerned," he said, "it's no tragedy when power mongers like Caesar or Brutus die, because it goes with the territory. They asked for it, they got it. Whether they live or die, who gives a shit? There's always a despot next in line to take their place. Step right up, Mark Antony. 'Friends, Romans, countrymen, lend me your gullibility.' One's as bad as the other.

"What's tragic is when a poet, or an artist, or a musician is killed for no reason, and the beauty that he or she might have created for the world to have improved itself from is chopped down, prevented from ever coming to pass because of a goddamn anonymous mob."

Somehow, subconsciously, Jacobus had brought them back to the murder of Natasha Conrad. It had been unintentional on his part, at least, he thought it had been, but perhaps it was inevitable that someone would, sooner or later. He felt guilty for being the party responsible for reopening the wound after everything Yumi had tried to do to cauterize it. The rage subsided, and now subdued, Jacobus attempted to change the trajectory with more than his usual deftness.

"Cinna, the poet, is the tragic hero of *Julius Caesar*. He represents the best of humanity, and the mob represents the worst of society. Cinna, the poet, represents anyone who's been misjudged. In other words, all of us. Things haven't changed. Humanity hasn't changed."

No one had a response. He had done his best. He fumbled for his wine goblet and took a sip but found it empty.

"Pass the beets, please," Nathaniel said.

During those two weeks, that had been the only dark moment among the many bright ones for Yumi. Among all the distractions, though, she most relished strolling through parks—every day a different one: Hyde Park, Regency Park, Hampstead Heath, Victoria Park. For everyone but Jacobus, the sights were the enchanting attractions. For Jacobus, it was the sound and the smell, and the feel. Children hooting with pleasure as they dashed across broad lawns. Golden retrievers straining at leads as they sniffed for squirrels in the shrubbery. Ducks squawking as they splash-landed into ponds. Distant tones of someone practicing the Mozart G-Major Flute Concerto. Early autumn leaves, making a final bow in their brief life span, clattered like whispered gossip. The weather remained fine, as they say in England, with only the lightest of breezes to remind them how lucky they were to be alive.

Chapter Six

Poking with her sterling silver spoon at semi-congealed oatmeal and lacking any interest in actually eating it, Yumi stood the spoon up in the middle of the Wentworth bowl like a mast in a British schooner to see what would happen. It stood.

It was the last day before her scheduled departure to the US, and she was too listless to be interested in breakfast. There was one final planned event on their tourist calendar, a concert that evening featuring Vivaldi's *Autumn* from the *Four Seasons* performed by local Baroque specialists, Rosalind Langstone on the violin, and music director, Branwell Small on harpsichord. All hoped it would be a fulfilling way to end their weeks together, and it would have been but for the one obstinate dark cloud hanging over their heads, Natasha Conrad's death.

With nothing factual to report, the tabloids had gone to town, making speculative, scandalous insinuations about the young lady's past, none of which were corroborated and none of which were remotely true. The stories contained titillating factoids about life in symphony orchestras, all of which were intended to lead readers to believe that orchestra musicians do nothing on tour other than drink too much, indulge in illegal drugs, and play games of sexual musical chairs from one hotel room to the other. The so-called journalists had collared a few willing audience members from the Mahler concert along with one or two employees of the Royal Albert, and had paid them very little to say even less, which the reporters nevertheless managed to contort with salacious innuendo. If that didn't suffice, unnamed "reliable sources" fit the bill. (At DCI Mattheson's command, no one associated with

Harmonium or involved in the investigation was permitted to speak to the media.) The general implication of all the tabloid reporting was that Natasha Conrad, "the fair lass with the fiddle," had something to hide and that the assailant's intention had been to put a stop to it.

The more sober media, like the BBC and *The Times*, presented the story once or twice. Their focus was less on the personal aspects of the murder and more on how it had been possible for such a crime to have been committed in England, in general, and at the Royal Albert, specifically. Who was responsible for security, or lack thereof, they asked, and who would be held accountable? What were the ramifications on US-UK relations of an American citizen being murdered on UK soil, and so blatantly? Would extradition be an issue? Every tangential perspective under the sun. But then the story faded, not because there wasn't public interest, but rather because there was very little to report about the central question: Who killed Natasha Conrad?

It was especially vexing for Yumi, who had been closer to Natasha than anyone outside of her family. So close that she felt compelled to talk to DCI Mattheson one last time before departing England. After all, hadn't he given everyone in the orchestra his direct phone number for that purpose? Why not call him? So as not to offend Aunt Leonia, she extricated the spoon from the oatmeal, which came away with a sucking sound, hurriedly took the final sip of her morning coffee and called him.

Mattheson was as polite as ever but, also true to form, revealed very little. Yumi couldn't decide whether he was withholding information or simply had none to share. No clear motive had yet been established, Mattheson told her. His interview with John and Helen Conrad had not led anywhere fruitful. He admired how exceptionally forthcoming they had been, especially considering how painful it was for them. However, other than recalling one time when Natasha jilted her erstwhile boyfriend at her high school's senior prom because he got "too fresh," Mr. and Mrs. Conrad could think of no one who would have wanted to do her harm.

Not one of the thousands of people at the Royal Albert had noticed the shooter. That was the most maddening and confounding part, Mattheson confessed. Not anyone in the audience, among the ushers, the hall staff, security, the orchestra onstage. No one. Everyone's eyes had been fixated on Klaus Kruger to see whether he would signal for the damned third hammer stroke. Mattheson supposed that shouldn't be surprising. Why would anyone, at that pregnant moment, be paying any attention to a single innocuous groundling in the midst of a churning sea of groundlings? Why, indeed?

What other information was there to share with Yumi? The ballistics report confirmed their preliminary assessment that the shooter used a small caliber handgun. Of course, the investigation is still ongoing! No, there's absolutely no consideration of shutting it down. No matter how long it takes, we are determined to find our man.

Yumi asked Mattheson if he had given any thought as to why the shooter waited for the third hammer stroke, even though there was no certainty there would be one. Mattheson said yes, he had given that issue substantial thought, but the question could only be answered when they had obtained more evidence. Because, he added, they could not totally discount a further possibility: that the shooter would have fired even if there had been no hammer stroke. The assumption had been that the shooter had waited for that moment, but in reality, the timing might have been purely coincidental. Yes, more evidence was key. Until they had more evidence, it was all speculation, and he was determined not to indulge in speculation. It could lead them down an entirely wrong path.

But why not *speculate?* Yumi wanted to say. Jacobus was always speculating, and even though ninety-nine times out of a hundred, his speculations were wrong, it was only by speculating that he discovered the single one, the one no one else had thought of, that was right. It wasn't speculation. It was imagination. It was creativity. It was why understanding music made it possible for him to see connections that others couldn't. But Mattheson made it clear he had said all that he was going to say on the matter, and Yumi knew that pressing him further would only stiffen the oatmeal into cement.

"Please keep me informed, if you don't mind," Yumi said instead.

"Of course," Mattheson replied.

"Look, everyone, what I have!" clucked Auntie Leonia. Entering her house after a morning of window shopping for ceramic French hens, of which she was especially fond, she waved a thin paperback over her head.

No one paid her any attention.

Kate and Jacobus were in the parlor, playing checkers. Yumi, who had cloistered herself in her bedroom to study the score of the Brahms violin concerto for an upcoming performance, had come downstairs and was playing the oboe part on the piano, working out an idea for phrasing in the Adagio. Though the instrument, an original George Steck grand, was irritatingly out of tune, and the F above middle C was totally out of commission, Yumi persevered. Nathaniel had made himself busy in the rose garden, snipping the full blossoms to arrange in vases before they began to fade.

"B3 to C4," Kate said.

"Damn it!" Jacobus replied.

"What are you two bickering about?" Yumi asked. "Sorry, I didn't mean to sound irritable, but I need to concentrate for a minute."

"That's how I play checkers," Jacobus replied. "Each row has a letter, and each square has a number. Kate tells me where she's moving her piece. All I have to do is remember where they all are."

"How do you manage to do that?" Yumi asked.

"Can you picture the alphabet in your mind's eye?" he asked.

"Of course, that's easy."

"Then why did you ask such a dumb question?"

"Don't worry, dear," Kate said to Yumi. "He's just grumpy because he's losing."

"Everybody! Look what I have!" Leonia shouted again, even louder. Maybe she thought she hadn't been heard the first time. She couldn't imagine she had been intentionally ignored.

"What's she got this time?" Jacobus groused. "A Ouija board?"

"It appears to be a book," Kate replied quietly to Jacobus. And to her sister, in a much louder voice, "What is it, dear?"

"Only Jasper Killingsworth's latest! *Murder at the Royal Albert!*"

Yumi slammed her hands on the keyboard, creating a horrendous chord worthy of only the most disreputable contemporary composers.

"What?" Jacobus bellowed.

"Let me fetch Nathaniel immediately," Kate said.

Pittums, perturbed at the disturbance, oozed off his window seat like a caterpillar and left the parlor for the friendlier confines of his cushioned wicker basket in the corner of the kitchen.

"I don't see what all the fuss is," Auntie Leonia said as the tumult swirled around her.

The humans found seats in the parlor.

"How dare he!" Yumi said. "How dare he! It's been less than a month!"

"Let us remain calm," her grandmother counseled. "Everyone knows it's a work of crude fiction."

"But writing a book about Natasha's murder? Dragging her through the mud? Just to make money? It's revolting."

"That it is, dear. Sadly, that's what they call freedom of the press."

"But it's not freedom. It's slander. How can he even suggest someone is a murderer when the police don't even have any clue?"

"You just put your finger on it," Jacobus said. Once again, he felt the bile rising inside him, experiencing a blackness that transcended being blind. Kate must have sensed it. She took his hand in hers and held it tightly until he could breathe.

"What do you mean?" Yumi asked.

"That's *precisely* how Killingsworth can do that. He's filling a void. 'The people's right to know!' 'The cops are keeping the truth from us,' they say. That's the kind of crap that people talk about today. Their rights. Their entitlements. They gorge on rumors."

"I still don't know what the fuss is all about!" Leonia said. "Shouldn't we at least read the book first?"

Silence was their answer.

"Well, I don't know about you, but I'm just dying to find out who did it," Auntie Leonia said.

She turned to the back page. In large, black capitals were written the words

THE VERDICT. Underneath was a name with Killingsworth's trademark question mark after it, followed by, *YOU BE THE JUDGE.*

"Yes," she said, "I knew it. It was who I thought all along."

"I imagine you're going to tell us," Kate said.

"I'd hate to ruin the surprise…but I'll tell you anyway. It was the musician."

"What musician?" Jacobus asked.

"Why, the violinist, of course. Ronald Shroud."

"Donald Stroud?" Yumi gasped. "That's impossible! The police investigated him. They interviewed him and checked his alibi. It couldn't have been Donald."

She jumped from her seat.

"Give me that book," she demanded of her great-aunt.

"Why, dear?"

"Give it to me."

Auntie Leonia, shaken, handed it over without further objection.

Yumi stared at the page.

THE VERDICT

RONALD SHROUD?

YOU BE THE JUDGE.

It was horrible. What would this do to Donald's life? What would his colleagues think? What would the public think? He already was prone to aches and pains, or at least to exaggerate them. Everyone knew that about him, and shrugged it off for the most part. This could tip him over the edge. And all because he had called in sick for a concert! If Donald had been there, this vicious opportunist, Jasper Killingsworth, would never even have heard of his name.

It was inevitable Donald, all of their colleagues, and everyone in the music world would find out about the book. It would be repeated in all the music journals and all the media, social and otherwise. And then what? Would anyone believe he was a killer? Or would everyone?

The unfairness! She had never felt so helpless. She was about to hand the book back to her great-aunt when the last sentence of the preceding page—the very last sentence of the text—caught her eye, and she began to tremble.

Chapter Seven

"Dear, what's wrong?" her grandmother said and sprang as quickly as an elderly grandmother could spring to her only grandchild. Jacobus heard the alarm in her voice. Nathaniel rushed to Yumi's side and assisted her to the divan.

Yumi handed the book to her grandmother and pointed to the page.

"'Mahler's ghost has taken his prize,'" Kate read. "How awfully morbid! Vintage purple prose Killingsworth, I'd say. What do you make of it?"

"*Obaasan*, those are the words Fritz Wohlfart whispered in my ear outside of Royal Albert," Yumi said. "The exact words. Just before you found me in the crowd. No one else could possibly have heard them. And I haven't mentioned it to a single person, it was so personal."

"How's that possible, then?" Nathaniel asked. "No way it could be a coincidence."

"Then there's only one possibility," Jacobus suggested. "This Killingsworth character must have gotten to Wohlfart."

"But Fritz would never have divulged that," Yumi said. "He just wouldn't. I know him."

"For money, perhaps?" Auntie Leonia postulated. "People will do anything for enough money."

"Auntie, please!"

"There's one way to find out," Jacobus said. "Call Wohlfart and ask him."

Surrounded by her grandmother, great-aunt, Nathaniel, and Jacobus, Yumi found Wohlfart's number on her phone's contact list and punched it in. As it rang, she considered the best way to ask. As she had never heard of Jasper

66

Killingsworth before coming to London, there was the outside chance his books hadn't been released in the United States. So how would she—

"Hello?"

"Hi, Fritz, this is Yumi."

"Yumi dear, how are you holding up? Are you enjoying your stay in England?"

Yumi let the conversation flow easily. He had been enjoying his vacation, he said. Life returning to normal. Nothing exciting. Hanging around the apartment with Lilian. They'd driven out to Montauk Point for a few days for a little beachcombing and winetasting—fun but tiring; must be getting older, you know—but otherwise had stayed in the city. Our favorite corner Italian restaurant. Absolutely the best veal parmigiana. Listening to music. A little, not too much. String quartets, mainly. Like I said, nothing very exciting. Yumi could detect the fragility behind Wohlfart's effort to maintain buoyancy. As if what had happened had not happened. How could she avoid shattering the man's hard-earned return to stability?

"So, Yumi, do I guess that the reason for this call is more than just a friendly chat?"

"Actually, yes, Fritz. I wanted to tell you how much your words touched me after Natasha's death. It helped me immensely to know that I wasn't alone in my feelings."

"Well, of course! You were her teacher! Her mentor! If there was anyone suffering more than me, it was you. And I knew you were someone—the only one—to whom I could express thoughts like that. I hope I didn't sound too maudlin. I probably did. I was just so overcome. And you know, the Mahler—"

"No, no! Not at all! I was grateful, Fritz. And I haven't told anyone. Not a single person. But I was wondering if it would be all right with you if I shared what you said with my grandmother and Mr. Jacobus and one or two of my closest friends…."

Wohlfart hesitated. Why was it that silences in international calls seemed to last so much longer?

"Well, if you feel you must," he said. "Though I'd prefer it if it remained between you and me. It wasn't intended for public consumption, and I have no intention of sharing it. Actually, I now feel a bit embarrassed having said it. It must have sounded morbidly gothic."

Yumi laughed, more from relief than humor.

"Not at all, Fritz. And I will keep our confidentiality in mind. I promise it will not go any further than that from my lips."

"Very well. I gather that's what you called to ask me about."

"Yes."

"Permission granted, then, if you need to share it."

"What's next?" Nathaniel asked after Yumi hung up. "And what, if anything, does this have to do with Natasha Conrad's death?"

"There's only one way to find out," Jacobus said.

"A heart-to-heart with Mr. Killingsworth?" Kate said.

"Exactly."

"Ooh! How exciting!" Leonia said.

Yumi thought it would be a simple task to obtain the contact information of a notoriously popular author. Why shouldn't it be? His headshot filled the back cover of each of his books. No shrinking violet, he. To Yumi, who freely admitted her bias, the man looked positively villainous. Reptilian. His thinning hair, slicked back, came to an exaggerated V-shaped widow's peak in the middle of his forehead. His squinty eyes, sharp nose, and tightly smiling thin lips all seemed to converge at the same point. The upturned collar of his white polo shirt shortened his neck and accentuated a complexion that seemed too tanned to be natural.

Face recognition. It was all about marketing. The exact same photo on all the books, regardless of when they were published. Perhaps the reason for that was to create, for those who admired him anyway, an age-defying image of wealth, success, and easy power. So why change the image, right? His fans must love it, but to Yumi it was all about arrogance, and it made her sick to her stomach. Could Killingsworth have been at the Mahler concert? It was entirely possible. But if he had been, Yumi hadn't seen him. She would have remembered a snake like that. But how could Killingsworth have overheard Fritz's Mahler comment without her seeing him?

Yumi turned out to be mistaken, though, in her assumption that contacting Killingsworth would be easy. Reluctantly abandoning the piano keyboard for her laptop's, she retreated to her bedroom in order to sequester herself from an excess of well-intentioned but distracting advice from an older generation whose vague comprehension of Internet searches was rooted in phone books. When she typed the name Jasper Killingsworth into her computer's search engine, it immediately responded with thousands of hits, which was very encouraging. But after a half hour of connecting to dozens of the most promising links, starting with his website and then his blog, there was absolutely no lead on how to contact him. In fact, she sensed a subtle but definite strategy to discourage anyone from being able to communicate with him. That seemed odd for someone who was so prominently in the public eye.

Not one to give up easily, Yumi typed in the name of Killingsworth's publisher, Stone Cottage Press, and was rewarded with both an email address and a phone number. Progress! As she wasn't sure how she wanted to word her questions, and thought that perhaps it might be safer not to have anything in writing at this point, she decided that a preliminary, nonconfrontational phone call would be the more productive and judicious option.

She dialed the number, which was answered after one ring by a message machine: "You have reached the offices of Stone Cottage Press. If your call is in regard to the *You Be the Judge* series or to Jasper Killingsworth, please be aware that you will receive a response neither from Mr. Killingsworth nor Stone Cottage Press to your inquiry, either by phone or email. You should hang up now. If your call is in reference to another matter, please leave a message, and we will reply in due course." Not even a thank you.

It was nearing a month since Natasha Conrad's murder. Yumi had spent two weeks on a concert tour and then two more for R&R with her dearest friends and family. They had tried to take her mind off the tragedy, but she was still consumed by it. Still preoccupied and listless, so unlike her usual self. So, when Yumi yelled into the disconnected phone, "Asshole!" Jacobus heard it all the way downstairs in the parlor. He said to Kate, "Uh-oh, she's starting to sound like me," and suggested they forget about going to the evening concert.

He understood. If anything bad were ever to happen to Yumi, he didn't know how he would cope. Not as controlled as Yumi had been, for sure. At least, so far. He would have flown off into a rage and lashed out, which would have been followed by a vertiginous tailspin into self-imposed isolation. A beloved student is not unlike one's own beloved child. The musical DNA passed from teacher to student may not be a biological substitute for the genetic variety, but it is powerful and connective. Natasha Conrad had been Yumi's to nurture. And she had died mere feet from where Yumi sat. Yumi had been unable to protect her. She felt both powerless and responsible. Yes, Jacobus knew exactly how she felt.

"It's okay, Jake," Yumi said, coming into the parlor. "I guess I overreacted. Seeing Fritz's quote in that book just gave me such a shock. I'm sure we'll figure it out."

"I second Yumi," Kate said. "Tonight is our last big event of our lovely time together, and who knows when the next one will be? Let's savor it."

Everyone knew there had been a tag left unsaid: If there will be a next time. Jacobus, Nathaniel, and Yumi would be leaving for the US imminently, and Kate for Japan. Except for Yumi, none of them were spring chickens.

"Should be a sweet performance," Nathaniel added. "Langstone is a fancy fiddler, and I hear this harpsichord player, Small, is one of the more knowledgeable Baroque period musicians in England."

Yumi whispered to Jacobus.

"Let's go to the concert," she said. "I'd rather spend a night in the Tower of London than stay home with Aunt Leonia's piano playing."

Chapter Eight

Centuries before the infant Antonio was even a twinkle in Signora Vivaldi's eye, quaint Saint Albans Church, adorned with paradoxically ferocious gargoyles, nestled on the hilltop overlooking the quietly bucolic market town of Bishop's Stortford, an hour or so north of London. Like so many of its kind in rural England, Saint Albans, constructed of rough, flinty stone and stout oak beams—materials that its builders, devout or not, knew would stand the test of time—was designed to accommodate no greater a number of parishioners than its local flock. Little did its original designers realize that they were endowing the structure not only with the qualities for proper celestial observance but also with just the right materials, size, proportions, and acoustics to house chamber music performances half a millennium into its future.

The evening had turned decidedly cool. The moon and stars were obscured by a cloud-laden sky that produced a light drizzle, offering the first real hints of autumn. Jacobus turned up the collar on his jacket. He and his friends, sans Aunt Leonia, along with many dozens for whom live chamber music was a delightful treat and not a burdensome chore, arrived a half hour before the downbeat in order to hear a pre-concert lecture by the harpsichordist and local Baroque music authority, Branwell Small. Peregrinating up the hill on a well-trod footpath from the town to the church, Jacobus and friends were enveloped by a faster-paced stream of chatty locals, like-minded pilgrims seeking the beneficence of Handel rather than heaven. Outside the little church, a respectful quiet descended as they passed through the churchyard where gravestones, many of whose epitaphs had long weathered into anonymity, bore silent testimony to centuries of pastoral devotion.

Entering the church, they were enthusiastically welcomed by matronly Elizabeth Twitchell—"hello, hello, thank you, hello, welcome, sorry about the weather, hello"—the Aeolian Concert Society's Volunteer of the Year. She informed them as breathlessly as if they were about to witness the Second Coming that they would be in for one of the most rapturous concerts of the season. She asked everyone, very politely, to please place their wet umbrellas in the umbrella stand and then to please slide their posteriors to the middle of the pews so that latecomers won't have to climb over anyone. "And by all means, join us for a jolly reception after the concert!"

As it turned out, the sliding of posteriors on the oaken pews turned out not to have been a serious concern, as only about half the capacity of two hundred seats, give or take, was occupied, which Mrs. Twitchell later attributed to the unfortunate change in the weather. Jacobus sat eight rows back, where experience had taught him he would get the ideal blend of sound without losing the individuality of each instrument, with Nathaniel to his right, and to his left, Yumi and then Kate.

Promptly at seven o'clock, Mrs. Twitchell, undaunted by the lighter-than-hoped-for attendance, made her way to the front of the sanctuary, positioning herself in front of the half-dozen music stands and the harpsichord. Backlighting created by the stand lights bestowed upon her an angelic glow, which, though unintentional, provided a striking, ethereal gravitas not out of place for the setting. Mrs. Twitchell made some thankfully and refreshingly succinct introductory remarks, suffused with superlatives, after which Mr. Branwell Small assumed center stage to polite applause.

"Jake, believe it or not, he looks a little bit like you," Yumi whispered to him.

"Lucky guy," Jacobus said.

Small had the same lined cheeks as Jacobus, but the creases somehow seemed less the result of care and worry, and more of smiling at oft-told jokes. His hair, gray and springy like Jacobus's, had received at least modest attention—maybe because of the concert—whereas Jacobus's rarely received any at all. "As long as I don't feel anything crawling in it, why bother?" was his patented response. There was no mistaking Small's aura of intelligence, which could not be explained by a single feature alone but rather by the sum of them. That attribute both men shared equally.

"But a little more neatly dressed," Nathaniel added, observing the olive-green tweed waistcoat and red plaid tie, compared to Jacobus's threadbare brown flannel shirt and gray corduroy pants.

"We can't all be so lucky," Jacobus said, not clarifying whom he considered the lucky one to be.

He enjoyed Small's talk, though. Because Rosalind Langstone was the evening's featured artist, Small, also the concert series' artistic administrator, had chosen a program of concertos that Vivaldi had written for two extraordinary female violinists.

Vivaldi had spent decades teaching and composing at the *Ospedale della Pietà* in Venice, an orphanage-convent-music conservatory that produced one of the finest orchestras in all of Europe. Vivaldi wrote dozens of concertos for his two most famous protégées, Anna Maria and Chiara. Small explained that the women had no surnames because, as infants, they had been deposited anonymously at the *scaffetta* of the *Ospedale*. The *scaffetta* was a rotating window, "like they used to have at those clever automats in New York City, except they were made of wood, and instead of cream pie, they served children." Hence, no one ever knew what the girls' last names were, a fact which evoked some gasps from the audience. Yet, they became two of the most celebrated violinists of their time, even though they never left the confines of the convent during their long lifetimes. Louder gasps. Though Vivaldi's *Four Seasons* had not explicitly been composed for those two virtuosos, Small expressed scholarly confidence that they would no doubt have performed them.

"He even sounds a bit like you, Jake," Nathaniel said. "Smart. A little pompous. Except with a British accent."

"And he's more polite," Yumi said.

"I can hear that," Jacobus said. "Are you going to tell me how he smells next?"

"I'll let you know," Kate said.

Small went on to speak in some detail about the *Four Seasons*, one of the most popular sets of compositions in the entire classical music repertoire, and about *Autumn* specifically. As it was the appropriate season, the featured concerto of the evening would no doubt be performed in many other concert halls around the world during the next few months. Small read Vivaldi's entire sonnet that described the action of the concerto, "with special apologies to animal lovers. Sadly, there was no PETA in 1720.

"Movement one, *Allegro: The peasant celebrates with song and dance, the harvest safely gathered in. The cup of Bacchus flows freely, and many find their relief in deep slumber.* Movement two, *Adagio molto: The singing and the dancing die away as cooling breezes fan the pleasant air, inviting all to sleep without a care.* Movement three, another *Allegro: The hunters emerge at dawn, ready for the chase, with horns and dogs and cries. Their quarry flees while they give chase. Terrified and wounded, the prey struggles on, but, harried, dies.*"

Small concluded his discussion with some well-chosen comments about musical imagery in the *Four Seasons*, explaining how Vivaldi utilized particular violinistic techniques like trills to simulate birds and tremolos and sharp accents on short notes to reproduce gunshots. He made particular mention that, though the story might have had a happier ending had Vivaldi told only the hunters' side of it, by also portraying the painful demise of the prey, he not only created an added dimension to the music, he used the image of the dying animal at the precisely perfect moment in order to then reemphasize the final joyous cadence of the concerto.

Jacobus nodded in agreement. It was an observation that he found particularly perceptive—indeed, it had never occurred to him, at least consciously—but Yumi's reaction was quite different. She grasped Jacobus's hand and squeezed it.

"But it's not joyous," she said. "It's just not. It's heartbreaking."

Maybe I made a mistake persuading her to come to the concert, Jacobus thought. *Everything's reminding her of the poor girl's death.*

He patted her hand with his free one. "Don't worry," he whispered. "The guy's full of shit."

Small summed up his lecture by pointing out what a revolutionary project it had been for Vivaldi to undertake, to write not only one but four concertos filled with the graphic music imagery of nature. As in so many other instances, Vivaldi led the way. "So now, please enjoy the performance, the products of a brilliant, creative mind," he said.

Small bowed, and as he departed the stage, he was rewarded by another round of polite applause, which crescendoed as a beaming Rosalind Langstone and the eleven musicians of the Smithson Chamber Players—three first violins, three second violins, two violas, one cello, one string bass, and one harpsichord (Branwell Small)—emerged from behind the pulpit and assumed their respective positions onstage.

Langstone, wearing a long emerald green dress that no doubt was intended to show off her brilliant shoulder-length red hair, was a sprite of a woman in her late twenties. The ensemble accompanying her played with vitality and verve, and although not all of them were equally polished musicians, that didn't matter. Langstone, channeling the spirits of her antecedents, Anna Maria and Chiara of the *Ospedale della Pietà*, was, of course, the focus of everyone's attention, and her performance of five of Vivaldi's concertos on the evening's program was dynamic, and convincing.

Yet it was Small who grabbed most of Jacobus's attention. The requirements of the harpsichord player in Baroque music are unique. In a way, the harpsichordist is more like a jazz musician in that the part provided by the composer merely consists of a bass line with various numbers underneath each note, indicating the harmony the composer intends. It's up to the harpsichordist to "realize" the harmony—in other words, fill in all the voices in both hands—for which there is an endless variety of ways to improvise. Jacobus found Small's realization "spot on," as Small might have said. It was not only pleasingly imaginative, it also reacted spontaneously to the solo violin line, creating an ongoing, real-time dialogue. It was the way he suspected Vivaldi's continuo player would have played. There was something distinctly Italian about it, both in its vitality and passion. To Jacobus, Small's playing, in fact, seemed more Italian than his speaking accent sounded English. That's how convincing it was. For anyone who contended that classical music was a static museum piece, they had just lost the argument.

The applause at the end of the concert echoed the energy of the musicians, with shouts of "bravo," "brava," "bravi," and "encore," providing enough time for Mrs. Twitchell to coast back to center stage while the smiling musicians, glowing with equal parts joy and sweat, were still taking their bows. She reminded the audience of the invitation to stay for cheese and biscuits and a glass of wine and to mingle with the musicians. And, if they were so inclined, to make a donation to the Aeolian Concert Society.

"Do you mind if we skip the reception and just go back to Auntie's?" Yumi asked.

"Aren't you feeling well, dear?" her grandmother asked as they made their way from the pews into the aisle.

"No, I'm fine. It's just that the stories about those violinists, Anna Maria and Chiara, cloistered but safe their whole lives in the convent, and then watching Rosalind Langstone play so beautifully—well, I couldn't help but think about Natasha. I couldn't stop thinking about what if. What if she hadn't died. What she might have been someday."

"Of course, dearest Yumichan. We'll go home and have a cup of tea and—"

"Oh, my! Aren't you Yumi Shinagawa?" It was Rosalind Langstone.

"Yes, I—"

"I *thought* I recognized you out there. I'd be *fibbing* if I said you hadn't made me *nervous*! You *must* let me introduce you to my friends. They will be so *excited* to meet you. I can't *tell you* how much I *adore* your recording of the *Four Seasons*. It's hard to *imagine* it any other way."

"Yours tonight was absolutely—"

Jacobus didn't get to hear the rest of the sentence as Langstone dragged Yumi away to meet the band. While she was gone, and taking advantage of the unexpected delay in their departure, Jacobus sniffed his way among the chattering throng to a place next to the food table, where an accommodating volunteer helped him to a thick wedge of aged cheddar. "Don't bother with the crackers," Jacobus said.

"Crackers, sir?"

"Yeah, the little round hard things you put cheese on."

"Oh, we call them water biscuits."

"Then, what do you call biscuits? The things you put gravy on?"

"A scone, perhaps?"

"You must be kidding. What do you call wine?"

"We, too, call that wine."

"Good. I'll have a glass. I need one."

It was a lively reception. Audiences feel a greater affinity to music when they have a chance to engage with the musicians creating it, even though the contact might only be a casual thirty-second how-do-you-do. There was something to be said, Jacobus thought, about having concerts for a hundred people in such a setting rather than for a faceless five thousand at the Royal Albert. On the other hand, if they performed Mahler Sixth in this church, there would hardly be enough room for the orchestra, let alone an audience.

He filched another piece of cheese and was about to pop it into his mouth.

"See what you've done?" Kate said.

"So what? I like the cheese."

"Not that. You have as much cheese as you like. As much as Nathaniel, even."

"Not possible. What have I done, then?"

"You made my granddaughter such a famous violinist that everyone recognizes her. She's a celebrity."

"That's *her* problem."

Kate gave him a peck on the cheek.

"What's that for?" he asked.

"That's for being a genius. By the way, Mr. Small is heading this way."

"Maybe he likes cheese."

"Would you like to meet him?"

"Nah. Not if he looks like me."

"Too late."

"Excuse me, sir. Please allow me to introduce myself."

"Branwell Small?"

"Yes, how did you know? With your dark glasses and cane, I had gathered you're blind."

"Actually, I'm psychic."

"Truly?"

"If you believe that, I've got a bridge in Brooklyn I want to sell you. My friend here told me you were heading our way. And, also, I heard your talk, so your voice is eminently familiar to me."

Kate did the introductions.

"Kate Padgett?" Small said. "I believe I've heard that name in these parts. Aren't you a violinist, too? Yes, I'm sure of it. You—"

"Once upon a time," Kate said. "But that's ancient history."

It was a history that Kate had spent most of her life trying to forget. She had been a child prodigy when her parents entered her in the Grimsley International Violin Competition before her tenth birthday, sending her to New York City from their London home. There were three grueling rounds of competition against dozens of under-thirteen youths from around the world. She came in second place, an astounding achievement as she was one of the youngest contestants, but as she soon found out, second place meant that you've dashed everyone's high expectations and were shortly thereafter relegated to the dustbin of music history. Then the war intervened, and whatever career she might have had was laid to rest. She married and moved to Japan with her entrepreneurial husband, Simon Desmond, who died shortly thereafter. She married again and became Mrs. Hashimoto. She bore a daughter, Keiko, before becoming widowed a second time. Keiko married Mr. Shinagawa. Their only child, Yumi, was Kate's beloved grandchild.

In retrospect, as runner-up, Kate had actually been the lucky one. The grand prize winner of the Grimsley Competition, a timid Polish boy with dazzling technique, whose name Kate couldn't remember except that she couldn't pronounce it, did not survive the war. Daniel Jacobus, whom fate prevented Kate Padgett from meeting until decades later, was also a contestant in the Grimsley. A skinny, awkward ten-year-old, he had been sexually abused by Feodor Malinkovsky, one of the competition's esteemed judges, who had offered him advancement in the competition in exchange for certain favors. So, there were worse fates than anonymity.

Kate bent the arc of the conversation back to the concert they had just enjoyed. Glorious Vivaldi. Charming England. Such a lovely little church.

Ah, the acoustics! The usual idle banter. All very friendly. Jacobus, bored, was ready to leave, and lately, he had been getting tired earlier and more frequently. Autumn. The concerto, the day, his life.

"Before you go, I must ask you," Small said, "speaking of psychic. And this might seem terribly rude. But, is it possible you and I have met before?"

"I doubt it," Jacobus said. "I never forget a pretty face. Where's Yumi?" he asked Kate.

"Why do you ask, Mr. Small?" Kate said.

"Well, it's the strangest thing, but I just have this feeling that Mr. Jacobus and I know each other. I can't really explain it."

While Kate went off to fetch Yumi, who, from her animated conversation with Langstone and her colleagues, had happily recovered from her ennui, Jacobus and Small tried to patch together when and where they might have met. Small worked back in time, starting from the present. Before assuming his current position, he had been the keyboardist with the Liverpool Chamber Orchestra. No, that wasn't it, Jacobus said. Before that, there had been a stint at the British Museum as a musical instrument curator. No, not that, either. Before that, he'd studied at the Royal Conservatory, during which time he had a part-time job delivering flowers for a local florist. "Definitely not that, either," Jacobus said, "though I do have a penchant for irises."

It all came up blank. The conversation was beginning to annoy Jacobus. Memory Lane was not his cup of tea. The past is gone. The future is unknown. Why bother with either? Only the present, the essential quality of the transitory nature of music, is worth one's attention, which is why he found idle prattling so irritating. It wasted the only time of any value. He heard Kate returning with Yumi and Nathaniel.

"Well, Small, ta-ta. Thanks for the lovely evening," he said. Maybe Small would get the hint.

"Yes, lovely," Small replied, sounding distracted. "Lovely, yes. And I can't imagine we'd have met before my amnesia."

Chapter Nine

No one knew for certain which came first, Saint Albans or the Saxon's Arms. There were misty legends galore to support either argument, and which side one took depended more on one's position on the spectrum, sacred at one end, profane on the other, than on any hard and fast data. But, in any event, the two venerable institutions had a centuries-old relationship that was mutually beneficial. The pub was strategically located at the base of the hill from the church, their symbiotic connection evidenced by the tether of the well-worn path between them, etched deeply into the hillside—originally dirt, then stone, then concrete, and now a fashionable brick, which was for some reason considered "traditional."

It was down that path that Jacobus and his friends, filled with curiosity, had followed Branwell Small like the beguiled rats following the Pied Piper, to the Saxon's Arms. If Jacobus had been able to see the interior of the pub in which he was now seated, he would have appreciated it as an icon as authentically English as Big Ben, or perhaps more appropriately for the occasion, steak and kidney pie.

When Jacobus reacted to Small's pronouncement of "amnesia" with one of his own—"You must be pulling my leg"—Small asked if he and his friends would be kind enough to join him in a pint so that he could explain. Jacobus balked until Small said he had noticed Jacobus's penchant for the local cheddar. That got Jacobus interested. "Then you won't want to miss our local double Gloucester," Small said. "I must say, it puts every other double Gloucester I've ever had to shame." Small's offer to pay for everything cinched the deal.

The man's true to his word, Jacobus thought. The cheese was nutty and rich and just the right amount of crumbly. Served alongside a pint of English-style best bitter delivered with care, straight out of the publican's tap, and complemented with pickled onions and homemade chutney and thick slices of crusty, yeasty granary bread, it transported Jacobus to a realm of such gruntled contentment that he no longer cared how tall Small's tale would be. As it turned out, his strange story was worth every farthing.

"It was near the end of the war," Small began. "I had enlisted at the tender age of sixteen. Younger than that, one would have had to lie in order to serve, which many a lad did. Fortunately, I had started shaving, so I passed muster.

"'Kill the Hun!' 'Save our civilization!' I was gung-ho all the way to join the war effort, especially after the London blitz. We had relatives there who hadn't survived, you see. Hell on earth. So I went off to the front along with all the others, and I almost made it unscathed to the bitter end. But almost is not enough, is it? I had one week to go on my tour of duty. But then, as luck would have it, I was shot in the head."

"Oh, dear," Kate said, deeply distressed.

"Yes. It was unfortunate."

"No doubt," Kate replied. "But I say that not just for you, but for Yumi, as a rather tragic event has recently befallen her."

"I'm terribly sorry to hear that," Small said. "Perhaps it would be better to change the subject."

"No, that's okay," Yumi said. "Really. Thanks for your concern, but your story has a happy ending, so I want to hear it." She made a concerted and remarkably successful effort to feign a smile, then returned to her beer, which she dispatched.

"Very well then," Small said. "If you truly don't mind. Where was I? Yes. I had been shot. They found me lying unconscious on the side of the road on the outskirts of Hamburg, evacuated me back to London, and hoped that sooner or later I'd wake up."

"Which you did," Kate said.

"Yes. Eventually. Except, when I did come to, I couldn't recall a bloody thing about what came before. Everything from my past had been wiped out. Everything."

"Then how do you know you enlisted?" Jacobus asked.

"Daniel Jacobus, do mind your manners!" Nathaniel said. "The man's showing you hospitality, and you're trying to prove he's a liar."

"No, no, Mr. Williams," Small protested. "May I call you Nathaniel? Thank you. That's a perfectly valid question. In fact, I asked the very one myself. And the answer is, they told me the whole story, and everyone else confirmed it. The army showed me the military documents. Name, address, serial number. It was all there. Everyone hoped that by showing me all the facts and figures, it would jog my memory."

"Who's they? Who's everyone else?" Jacobus asked. He didn't care for loose ends.

"They?"

"You said, 'they told me so.' Who's they?"

"Why, my family, of course!"

"I have a thought, Mr. Small," Kate said. "If we talked to your family, might it be possible they could shed some light on your feeling that you know our Daniel Jacobus?" Under the table, she found his hand—the one that was not holding the beer—and gave it a squeeze.

"Sadly, that would be next to impossible," Small said. "My parents are gone, and I have no siblings. The only one of Mum and Dad's generation still with us is my Aunt Claudine. She's on in years, and I'm not sure how 'with us' she really is. If you know what I mean."

"Is it possible the two of you met in Germany," Yumi asked Jacobus, "while Mr. Small was stationed there?"

"Nah," Jacobus said. "By that time, I'd been studying at Juilliard for years."

"Ah, Juilliard," Small said and inquired about the Baroque program there, which had only recently gotten up and running. He expressed gratification that major conservatories were finally giving Baroque music the attention it so richly deserved. The conversation then took a logical turn toward teaching and pedagogy. Yumi, having made her second Imperial pint disappear in short order, found herself waxing poetic about her long relationship with Jacobus. How, when she was his student, he had been brutally honest, which at first made her want to rebel, only to find out much later that that was exactly what Jacobus was goading her to do. Because for her to rebel successfully, she knew she needed to raise her game to a level that would enable her to convince Jacobus that she could stand on her own two feet. That her approach to the violin and to music was comprehensive and thorough, both technically and artistically.

Then, as if a switch were turned on, her benign, nostalgic reminiscences ended and a floodgate of words and tears about her relationship with her own protégée, Natasha Conrad, opened. About how Natasha had seemed such a little girl when she first came to Yumi and how she had matured into a beautiful young lady, full of vitality and promise. And then... Yumi shook her head, as if to dispel "and then." Only her deep Japanese reserves of self-control and civility, instilled from birth, moderated her expressions of frustration with the pace and progress of the investigation into the tragedy of her student's death, a tragedy that would stay with Yumi forever.

"Have heart," Small said. "Mattheson is one of the good ones. A bit stodgy, perhaps, carrying on with his pipe. But don't worry. He'll see it through."

"How do you know Mattheson?" Jacobus asked.

"Such an inquisitive mind, yours, Mr. Jacobus. Mattheson? From reading the papers. His name pops up now and then. Would that he had been around in eighteenth-century Venice," Small said, letting the implied question dangle like a worm on a hook.

Kate bit. "Why do you say that?"

Small reeled her in. "To solve the mystery of Anna Maria and Chiara. Wouldn't it have been interesting to know whence those two brilliant musicians came! Most of the foundlings at the *Ospedale* were from impoverished families who couldn't support yet another child, but others were from well-to-do mothers seeking to avoid public scandal or tangled inheritance."

From there, Small maneuvered the conversation back to the evening's sparkling performance by Rosalind Langstone and the Smithson Chamber Players, broadened it to the future of the Aeolian Concert Society's winter series, and concluded it with a sweeping discussion of the small but—"we fervently hope"—significant role of classical music in contemporary society. Though Small's opinions were expressed in a more circumspect tone, Jacobus noted that, by and large, they mirrored his own. There was little for him to add or argue with. That was unusual.

But that was not the only reason Jacobus kept his own counsel. He admired how deftly Small had steered the conversation away from the investigation, but wondered why. Two possibilities came to mind: Small saw how the subject troubled Yumi and was being sensitive to her feelings, or Small knew more about it than he was letting on. He let it ride, for now.

"Well, Small," Jacobus said.

"Call me Branwell."

"Well, Branwell, that's quite a yarn you've told us tonight."

"I dare say. There's no anticipating what tall tales one will hear in our English pubs."

"And thanks for your music and for your company. May we meet again someday."

Jacobus drained what was left in his glass, lowered it onto the wooden pub table with thudding finality, and wiped his mouth with his sleeve.

"And thanks for the beer."

The alcohol, the late hour, the rambling conversation, and now, the lazy sway of windshield wipers all served to induce Jacobus to doze in the backseat, where he and Nathaniel nodded off in companionable comfort. Kate sat in front while Yumi drove. The only thing that half roused him from Jacobus's somnolence was when he managed to overhear Kate say, "And isn't that Mr. Small so debonair?" Jacobus might have grunted his objection, but that was all.

Chapter Ten

By the next morning, the caressing drizzle had turned into a cold, hard downpour. No park outings today.

Yumi's spirits were also dampened by the lack of progress in the murder investigation, but doggedly determined to see it through, called the airline and postponed her departure date. An artificial gesture of hope, perhaps, but a gesture nevertheless.

Kate suggested they go together to the library—it was within walking distance, it would be lovely to stroll in the rain, and Leonia had brollies galore to keep them dry—to see if they could make any inroads tracking down Jasper Killingsworth and his publisher, Stone Cottage Press. It would at least get her out of the house and perhaps even buoy her spirits. "One never knows what one might discover at a library," she offered.

Nathaniel stayed in bed with a pot of Irish breakfast tea and a book of Sudoku puzzles he had brought from New York to occupy himself in anticipation of the legendary English rain that was now slapping at his windowpane. Perhaps because Nathaniel's was the warmest available body, Pittums selected him as his companion du jour, and lay, purring, between his knees. Leonia was in the kitchen, cracking eggs with great zeal for a new quiche Lorraine recipe. Jacobus sat in the parlor facing a wall, intentionally, as he mentally replayed the entire concert from the previous night. That he had never before heard three of the concertos Langstone had performed was no surprise. Vivaldi had composed literally hundreds of violin concertos, each one more brilliant than the other. Jacobus's mental reconstruction, from first note to last, was more than an idle recollection, more than a cloudy reminiscence of last night's pleasantries. When Jacobus listened to music—music that he liked, to be more precise—it was an exercise in concentration, such that if he were not blind, he would be able to write out those three new Vivaldi concertos without flaw. Memorizing music was a discipline all musicians needed to develop; after Jacobus lost the ability to see, it had become an essential one. Thus, the last thing he wanted while so mentally absorbed was a distraction, which explained why he was facing the wall. No one should mistake that message.

But there was a distraction, nevertheless, when Leonia's Westminster chimes doorbell rang, and Jacobus's train of thought was broken.

They hadn't expected anyone. If it was Yumi and Kate returning from the library, they would simply have entered. Leonia went to the door, returning to the parlor, followed by a second set of footsteps. *Definitely a man's,* Jacobus thought. *But whose?* The clear resonance suggested hard soles. New shoes, or just well-cared for. Mattheson, perhaps, with some news about the investigation?

"A Mr. Small is here to see you," Leonia said. Her inflection suggested she did not approve of uninvited guests. But then again, she had not been at the concert or the Saxon's Arms the night before, which might have softened her indignation.

"Small!" Jacobus said. He was surprised, but not as annoyed at being distracted from his concentration as he might otherwise have been. "Tell me, in the B Minor Concerto last night, were those ornaments Vivaldi's originals, or did the girl add them?"

"I invited her to take as much liberty as she thought tasteful and appropriate."

"As I suspected. I'm glad she didn't abuse the license to trill. Much."

"I'm glad to hear you say so."

"By the way, how did you find me? I don't recall anyone mentioning where we were staying."

"Oh, it was nothing. Just a bit of putting two and two together. Miss Shinagawa had told Rosalind that she was stopping with her Aunt Leonia. Knowing that her grandmother was Kate Padgett, I took a leap of faith and did a search for a Leonia Padgett. I was fortunate there is only one Leonia Padgett."

"Amen to that."

"So, eureka. Quite simple, though the hyphen-Trelawny threw me off-track at first."

"Well, congratulations, Sherlock. But why didn't you just ask last night, if you wanted to know? It would have saved you a lot of trouble."

"Good question, Mr. Jacobus. And the simple answer is, I only thought about contacting you after we all said our farewells. And what I would like to propose to you today, after a long night of contemplation, is better said in person than on the telephone. I dislike telephones intensely, especially these ones that fit in your pocket."

"I'm with you there. The only good thing about phones was when they were attached to cords, so you couldn't take them with you."

"Hear, hear! These days, it's almost impossible for one to be alone with one's thoughts. I fear the day when imagination will be as extinct as the dodo."

"Yeah. Well, maybe since we're not dodos, at least yet, there's a *re-re* of hope."

"*Mi-mi* included?"

"*Sol fa.*"

"*Tra-la-la. Ti?*"

"That brings us back to…your proposal. What is it? Corelli trio sonatas? I'm more of a Brahms man, myself."

Small laughed.

"No, nothing like that. Though someday, who knows? What I have in mind is this: Last night, when Ms. Padgett mentioned the tragedy that had befallen Miss Shinagawa, I have to admit I had been aware of the situation with her student, but at that moment, I was a bit flummoxed. I didn't want to create any greater upset. Should I have said that I knew? Should I have pretended otherwise? It really was untoward of me to bring up my own war story considering the obvious parallels. In the end, I decided to say nothing."

"No hard feelings, I'm sure," Jacobus said. "But Yumi's out with Kate at the moment, so you've come a long way for nothing, I'm afraid."

"I'm sorry I've missed them, but there's more. You see, I was very disturbed when I heard of Natasha Conrad's death. Such a tragedy in so many ways. My initial thought was, leave it to the constabulary to sort it all out. I have faith in their professionalism, and so I let it go at that.

"But then, last night, I was touched by Miss Shinagawa's obvious devotion to her protégée and her determination to seek more information that the authorities might let go by the boards, even DCI Mattheson. In a nutshell, I would like to offer my services."

"Your services? What are you, a private dick as well as a longhair musician?"

Small laughed again.

"You have a refreshing way with words, Mr. Jacobus. No, I think only Sherlock Holmes could boast of that admirable combination of virtuosity. I only suggest it because none of you are familiar with our land or local customs, whereas this is my home turf, as they say in America. I know the 'lingo.' I would simply like to make myself available if and when you and your friends might need me."

"We're home!"

Kate and Yumi walked into the parlor. They were, of course, surprised to see Branwell Small. They said their hellos cordially but cautiously.

"Find out anything at the library?" Jacobus asked. "They have any books there?"

"Are you sure you want to talk about it now?" Yumi asked.

"If I wasn't, I wouldn't have asked you. Would I?"

"I suppose not. I did find out something. Just a little."

Jacobus understood Yumi's reticence. It had to do with the presence of the newcomer, Small. So Jacobus explained Small's offer to help with the investigation and left it to the others to decide if they wanted to accept.

"I think it's a lovely idea," Kate said.

"At this point, I don't see how it could hurt," Yumi added.

"Nathaniel's still snoring upstairs, so I'll take that as a yea," Jacobus said. "All right, Small, you're in. For the moment, anyway. Now that that's settled,

Yumi, you want to tell us what you and your grandmother found out at the library?"

"Well, when I asked the librarian how I might get in touch with Jasper Killingsworth, she laughed out loud."

"They don't make librarians like they used to," Jacobus said.

"Shh," Kate said. "Let Yumi talk, please."

"She told me," Yumi continued, "that it's common knowledge among mystery fans that neither Jasper Killingsworth nor his publisher will, under any circumstances, permit contact with the author. I asked, 'But what about all the lawsuits?' The librarian said it's her guess that those are handled directly by the publisher's law firm."

"But what about book tours?" Jacobus asked. "And interviews? That's what these highfalutin authors do. And even the lowfalutin ones."

"Killingsworth, apparently, has no desire whatsoever to be any species of falutin," Kate said. "He is never seen in public. All his interviews are done by email directed through intermediate servers, whatever those are. Not even phones. He appears to be reclusive in the extreme."

"So he ain't all bad," Jacobus said.

"Jake, please," Yumi said.

"Sorry. But the publisher and the lawyers have got to know how to get hold of Killingsworth," Jacobus argued, "if for no other reason than money goes back and forth. They have to know who and where to make the checks out to."

"And no doubt there have been people like you," Small added, to Yumi, "who sought access to him. Perhaps it would be worth finding out the names of those who sued him in the past."

"How might we do that?" Kate asked.

"What about those lawsuits that the librarian mentioned?" Jacobus asked.

"What about them?" Yumi asked.

"Aren't they public record in this country? I know the UK's a monarchy and all, but still...."

"Indeed, they are public," Small replied.

"See? Problem solved."

"But with some obstinate caveats. Either party in a lawsuit may apply for a restriction of public access if, for example, documents involve confidential or commercially sensitive information. Knowing what we know about Killingsworth, I presume that for us to attempt to go that route would lead us to a dead end."

"It all seems such a mystery within a mystery," Kate said.

"Perhaps," Small said, "we can accomplish something by going through his novels to see which characters he wrongly accused of various crimes who were later found to be innocent. They would be the ones most likely to seek him out, don't you think? Maybe one of them discovered a way to locate Killingsworth."

"Good idea," Jacobus said. "Yeah, go through the old books. We can be thankful to Auntie Leonia for stocking her personal library with his entire motley oeuvre.

"Anything else?" Jacobus asked Yumi.

"The librarian managed to find one piece of information that may or may not be useful: a mailing address for Stone Cottage Press."

"That's the good news," Kate said.

"But the bad news is that, according to the librarian, *Murder at the Royal Albert* is selling like hotcakes. It's already catapulted to *The New York Times* bestseller list. Sooner or later, Fritz is going to see himself quoted, and Donald is going to see himself accused of murder."

"That unsavory scrap gives us yet more incentive to 'research' Jasper Killingsworth's previous novels," Kate said. "Maybe we can determine what unfortunate souls, if any, might lead us to Killingsworth."

"But God, there are so many books!" Yumi said. "The librarian told us Killingsworth was wrong with at least half his verdicts, but who knows if any of them actually sued, and if so, lost the suit, and if so, would be able to help us? And we have to go back to New York soon. I wouldn't even know where to start."

"Tell me if I understand your strategy correctly," Small said. "You are trying to seek out the scoundrel who informed Killingsworth of the comment about Mahler's ghost that your colleague, Mr. Wohlfart, made to you in strict confidence."

"That's right," Yumi said.

"And in order to do this," Small continued, "you first hope to obtain access to Killingsworth himself."

"Yes, that's correct."

"But why, is my question. Hasn't he already reached his verdict, which is an incorrect verdict? What do you expect to get from him that might be the least bit credible? And, even if you find out who leaked Mr. Wohlfart's comment, what is the trail from there to discovering the identity of the shooter?"

"I've been asking myself those very questions," Jacobus said. "And there are no concrete answers, Branwell, except that they might lead *somewhere*. Because of the very vagueness of the possibilities, we can't expect the police will have much interest in pursuing that line of reasoning. But there is definitely something underhanded about how Killingsworth got that quote. My feeling is that if we turn over that stone, we'll find a lot more worms."

"Jake has been right on a lot of his hunches in the past," Yumi said to help convince their new associate.

Jacobus proposed they divide the list of Killingsworth's mysteries into four equal groups for Yumi, Kate, Nathaniel, and Small to read. Leonia was wildly waving her hand. *Okay, five.* Jacobus, unable to read, was the obvious odd man out. Once the books had been read, they would determine which verdicts conflicted with actual convictions, and also which cases resulted in no one being either arrested or convicted. That would narrow things down. Then they would each make inquiries. Then they would compare notes. Time-consuming, but at least it was organized.

"May I suggest an alternative?" Small said. "A possible shortcut, as it were?"

"I was waiting for that," Jacobus said.

"This is what I would propose. That one of us visits the Stone Cottage Press office, chats up whoever is there, and finds out if anyone recently made any sort of ruckus against Mr. Killingsworth. 'Recently' being broadly interpreted. Perhaps within the last year or two. If there had been such a one, I would suggest starting with that person. It could save a lot of time."

"And who do you propose," Kate asked, "should be the one to make this inquiry?"

"Why, myself, of course. I may have no recollection of my first twenty years of life, but I've certainly learned a bit in the past fifty."

Chapter Eleven

The image that the name Stone Cottage Press would naturally conjure up, and no doubt the image that was intended, is of a bucolic warren inhabited by industrious elves popping out tiny books on a hand-cranked printing press inside a rustic but cozy miniature hut in a sunny forest glade. Maybe there would be a millwheel. It was not unlike Jacobus's initial image of the world-famous Academy of St. Martin in the Fields until he was informed, to his great disappointment, that the institution did not date back to St. Martin, who was born in Hungary in the year of our Lord, 316, but was founded in 1959, and was not surrounded by a bucolic English meadow, but was smack-dab in the middle of downtown London.

As a result, he wasn't particularly surprised or disappointed when the address to Stone Cottage Press led him and Branwell Small to a fully modern business suite, inhabited by real humans and not anything resembling elves, halfway up a gleaming twenty-story, steel-and-glass office tower. They entered a waiting area suffused with pine scent and a piped-in vocalization of a contemporary but otherwise nondescript nature, somewhere between crooning and wailing.

"One wonders why they even bother," Small said. "One would be hard-pressed to even call it music."

"My sentiments exactly," Jacobus replied. "Sometimes I think I would have been better off deaf than blind."

"Good morning," the receptionist said, interrupting their critical review. "May I help you?" Her voice was equal parts inquisitive and accusatory. No part of it was welcoming.

"Thank you, madame," Small said. "How kind of you to ask. I would like to speak to your acquisitions editor, if I may."

"Have you an appointment?"

"No, but—"

"Have you an agent?"

"No, but—"

"Editors don't meet with anyone who has neither an appointment nor an agent. We're overbooked as it is."

"But I have got a manuscript! It's about seventeenth-century Baroque—"

"I'm sorry. We don't publish nonfiction."

"But it's crime fiction! Surely—"

Jacobus was impressed. Small, without losing his aplomb, was fast on his feet and tenacious. He wouldn't give up. Finally, the receptionist, who apparently decided the easiest way to get rid of Small was to let him be someone else's problem, buzzed him through. He was escorted to a rear cubicle where he was told he would meet with Justin—no last name—a junior editor, to talk about his musical mystery that takes place in seventeenth-century-somewhere.

"Have you any good ideas for a plot?" Small whispered to Jacobus before he was led off.

"How about a harpsichord player who gets his head handed to him?" he replied.

"That's a good one. I'll try it."

With Small gone, Jacobus sat for close to half a minute before impatience began to get the better of him. He heard the unmistakable clack of a coffee mug being placed on a hard surface and decided to take advantage of the opportunity to strike up a conversation with the receptionist, having two reasons to do so: One was to create a distraction from the incessant musical drivel. The other was to pursue the object of their visit, to attempt to find out whether there might have been a prior target, or targets, of Killingsworth's *You Be the Judge* series who stood out from among all the victims.

"Milk and sugar gal, huh?" he said.

"How did you know?" the receptionist said. "I thought you were...you were...."

"Blind? Is that the word you were searching for? Some people try to be polite and call it 'sightless' or 'unable to see,' as if those wouldn't make me feel as bad, but it is what it is, isn't it? I'm okay with blind. Blind as a bat would be a compliment, because I wish I could hear as well as they could. So call me anything you want. Just don't call me late for dinner."

"Well, you're certainly a live one, aren't you? But if you're blind, how did you know about the coffee?"

"Oh, that would be my sixth sense. Uncanny." Actually, it had been an educated guess, the kind of guess which proved him correct approximately fifty percent of the time.

"Wow," the receptionist said. "I've never met anyone with a sixth sense. Guess my name."

"I wish I could," Jacobus said, "but my karmic energy only lasts so long on a given day. Old age, I guess. What is your name, honey?"

"Isadora."

"Very musical, that name. Isadora. I adora Isadora! *Dat-da-dat-da-dat-da-dat.* Isadora, dear, is there any way to turn that shit off?"

Surprisingly, Isadora laughed.

"Don't I wish, love?" she said. "It drives me barmy."

And so their conversation went, bonded by their new common enemy. Small returned fifteen minutes later, accompanied by junior editor Justin.

"Thank you for reaching out to us, Mr. Small," Justin said. "Your story is certainly original. I dare say I've never read a book about a headless harpsichordist, and I'm most certain you'll find a good home for it. It's just that at this point in time, it doesn't quite sing to me."

"Are you sure?" Small asked.

"I'm afraid so. Baroque gothic musical slasher thrillers are not one of Stone Cottage's niche markets."

"Would it sing to you if I made the headless harpsichordist a singer?"

"Sorry."

Small shook his hand.

"Oh, well. Nothing ventured, nothing gained," he said cheerily.

Going down in the elevator, Small said to Jacobus, "Well, I seem to have struck out, old boy. I tried collaring everyone back there—the editors, the marketing people, the people running in circles looking busy, of whose job descriptions I haven't the foggiest."

"You certainly accept defeat with equanimity," Jacobus said.

"We're British. I daresay we've had to get used to it, haven't we?"

"So, not even a dent in their armor?"

"I'm afraid not. They were all as tightlipped as MI6 on a rainy day."

"That actually might tell us something," Jacobus said.

"It tells us either they're members of MI6 or, more likely, there is something they don't want to tell us."

"The latter, I'd say. And that ties in with what I learned from lovely Isadora while you were off following your dream."

"Do tell."

"Isadora is a recent acquisition here. She's only been on the job for about a month."

"Which would suggest she might not have much to tell us at all."

"It might suggest that, but then again, it might not."

"Jacobus, have I ever told you I love it when you're coy? Out with it, man!"

"After we discovered that we shared a mutual disaffection for the crap music that was being piped in, I struck up a conversation. That's when she told me she was new. After congratulating her and telling her what a great job she was doing entertaining me, I asked what the circumstances were for the previous receptionist leaving. It turns out that she had been summarily fired."

"A flirtation with Sir Boss?"

"Nothing so juicy. She was fired for the high crime of pawning off the office mail to someone else to take down to the post office. Think about that."

"Intriguing," Small said.

"Quite."

"Do we know the identity of that someone else?" Small asked.

"We don't. And 'we' includes Isadora. But she did know the name of the receptionist she replaced."

"Good work, Jacobus."

"Quite quite."

Chapter Twelve

Jacobus and Small returned from Stone Cottage Press to find Yumi stomping about the parlor in what, for her, was a rage.

"I dare say she's throwing a wobbly," Auntie Leonia confided with alarm.

"I'm so...pissed off!" Yumi said.

" Jake's influence has certainly rubbed off on you," Kate said to her granddaughter from the divan. "On the whole, I'm sure that has been a good thing, though I suppose it's possible one could have too much of a good thing."

Kate was sitting side-by-side with Leonia, both of them feverishly compiling a list of *Verdict* victims. Next to the divan was a pile of Jasper Killingsworth's novels heaped on one side of a folding card table, an incongruous but functional addition to the Victorian parlor. On the other side of the table, the side closest to Leonia, was a box of chocolate creams.

Yumi overlooked her grandmother's inference. So did Jacobus. Nathaniel glanced away from his Internet search of Stone Cottage Press to get his two cents in: "Like mold on bleu cheese?"

Jacobus, likewise, ignored Nathaniel's barb, which typically managed a reference to food.

"What seems to be the trouble?" he asked Yumi.

"While you and Mr. Small were gone, I called DCI Mattheson. I ask him for a simple progress report, and he stonewalls me! 'Progress is being made,' he says. Bullshit."

"Yumi!" Kate said. "You'll offend Auntie Leonia's ears."

"Speak for yourself," Leonia said. "The girl has a right to let off steam. I find Yumi's insouciance refreshing. Besides, it reminds me of Mr. Trelawny, may he rest in peace."

"It sounds to me," Jacobus continued, "that it's more than the stonewalling that's bothering you."

"Damn straight! It's that patronizing attitude. I explained to him why we think there could be a connection between Natasha's murder and Jasper Killingsworth—"

"Wohlfart's comment about Mahler's ghost."

"Exactly. But Mattheson just pooh-poohed it out of hand. Treating me like a little girl. Patting me on the head. It was so...so..."

"British?" asked Branwell Small.

"You said it, not me. But yes. And I don't believe him there's nothing to report. I think he just doesn't want to divulge it. I have a right to know, don't I?"

"Of course you do, dear," Kate said.

"Was there nothing at all to report?" Small asked.

"He told me that all of my students had been accounted for and that I 'need not worry about them further.' I could have told him that a month ago, and I did! What a waste of time. You call that progress?"

"Don't worry, dear. We'll sort it out with or without the detective," Leonia said. "My sister and I have compiled the list of every one of the people who Killingsworth falsely accused. We're not sure of their real names, mind you, just the ones he made up in the books. There are sixteen of them: Morton Duggington in *The Panhandler of Paddington*, Louisa Shankley in *Londonderry Dagger*, M. Foster Carruth in *The Assassin of Albury*, Vincent Colston in *The Malignant Tudor*, Artemus Archer in *The Butcher of Blythburgh*—"

"Wait a sec," Nathaniel said. "That name rings a bell. It's on the tip of my tongue. Hold on. Hold on." He punched some keys on his computer.

"Yes, here it is," he said. "Not *Artemus. Archibald.* And not *Archer. Hunter.* Archibald Hunter. And guess what? He's not only one of Killingsworth's victims. He's an author! He's on the Stone Cottage author roster. Here's their blurb for him: 'Riveting short fiction chronicling the Falklands war, told firsthand through the eyes of a decorated soldier who fought brilliantly...and survived to tell the true story!'"

It took everyone time to process the new information. There was a lot to be digested, but it was Jacobus who asked the essential question that was on all their minds.

"Why the hell is someone, whose name was dragged through the mud, writing for the same goddamn publisher as the guy who did the dragging?"

"That, indeed, is the question," Small said. "You put it so eloquently."

"Maybe, if we read *The Butcher of Blythburgh*, we'll find out," Yumi said.

"Good idea, Yumi," Kate said.

"No need! No need!" Leonia chortled. "I know what it's about! *Butcher* was one of my favorites! I've read it!"

"Did you also knit at the guillotine?" Jacobus asked.

"Whatever for?" Leonia asked, somewhat nonplussed.

"Never mind Jake, Auntie," Yumi said. "Tell us."

"Very well. You see, there was a beautiful London socialite. Her name was Amanda Cooper, and she was having a torrid affair with a sailor from Blythburgh named Artemus Archer, whose real name we now know is Archibald Hunter, and—"

"Clever," Small said. "Artemis is the goddess of the hunt. Artemus would be one of her followers."

"Shh," Jacobus said. "We all went to high school, Small."

Leonia continued.

"Well, whatever his name was, Artemus Archer or Archibald Hunter—it doesn't matter, does it?—had just returned from the Falklands, where he had been a sniper with the SAS."

"What's the SAS?" Jacobus said.

"Shh," Small replied. "We all went to high school, Jacobus."

"But you see," Leonia continued, only mildly perturbed at the interruption, "before becoming a soldier, he had been a butcher. That's where the title comes from. Also, you see, because of the things he does later. That's what makes the title so clever."

"You don't need to keep us in suspense, dear," Kate said. "None of us have the slightest inclination to read the book. Please just tell us what happens."

"Well, the socialite's husband, Reginald Cooper, who is a rich banker, wants to find out why his wife was always going somewhere 'with her friends,'" Leonia said, with a wink, "and hires Mr. Archer—"

"Not Archer," Jacobus said. "His name is Hunter. Just call him Hunter from now on, okay? It's confusing enough as it is."

"Very well," Leonia said. "If I must. Where was I?"

"Reginald Cooper has just hired Mr. Hunter," Kate prompted.

"Yes, thank you, sister. Cooper hires Mr. Hunter, who has recently returned to his butcher shop in Blythburgh after the war."

"And what has Mr. Cooper hired this butcher to do?" Kate asked. "Make him sausages?"

Jacobus laughed.

"Why, once Cooper finds out she was having an affair, to kill his adulterous wife!" Leonia said. "He's very religious, you see. The Ten Commandments. I don't quite remember which commandment that was."

"Honor thy flanken and mutton," Jacobus said.

"Jake, please!" Yumi said. "And does he kill her?"

"I should say so!" Leonia said. "He sliced her up like a side of beef!"

"Thank you for the graphics," Kate said.

"That makes no sense," Jacobus protested. "If this Archibald Hunter was Amanda Cooper's lover, why wouldn't it be Hunter who Cooper wanted to kill, more than his own wife? And why would Hunter ever agree to kill his lover?"

"Because Reginald Cooper didn't know it was Hunter who was his wife's lover," Leonia said. "And Hunter killed Amanda because she wasn't the goody-goody she was cracked up to be and threatened to blackmail him. Because, you see, Hunter was married also, and Amanda was going to tell Mrs. Hunter."

"Why did you say Killingsworth's accusation was false?" Yumi asked her great-aunt.

Small answered for her. "Because the police never did find the murderer," he said. "It's a cold case."

"How do you know that, Small?" Jacobus asked.

"I read the papers. Watch BBC. The usual. What are you suggesting, old man?"

"Only that you certainly seem to have your finger on the pulse of blackmailers and murderers."

"It was a sensational case. It had all the elements, didn't it? Like a soap opera. The public followed it for months, but the murderer was never found."

"Not officially," Leonia said. "But as far as Jasper Killingsworth was concerned, it all pointed to Hunter. The way the book goes, Hunter was a sniper whose mind had snapped in the Falklands, turning him into an unbalanced killing machine. And he was a butcher whose tools of the trade matched the murder, and he did know the cuckolded husband. I love saying that word, cuckold, don't you? I could say it over and over again. It sounds like a hen! Cluck, cluck, cuckold."

"Wait a minute," Jacobus said. "How did Hunter and this cuck...jilted husband in London know each other? It's a long way from London to go for a meat pie."

"One hundred fifteen miles," Small said. "Approximately."

"We're just overflowing with handy information. Aren't we, old man?" Jacobus snapped.

"They knew each other from the service, of course!" Leonia said. "They were both in the Falklands together. That's where they met."

"That was fact?" Jacobus asked. "Or just Killingsworth's imagination?"

"The police said that much was true," Small said.

"Reginald Cooper," Leonia said, "denied knowing his wife was having an affair. He denied having had an arrangement with Hunter and anything at all to do with his wife's murder. He placed the entire blame on Hunter, and then when it turned out she had been blackmailing him... That's terribly suspicious, don't you think?"

"It almost sounds like you believe it," Kate said.

"Now that I think about it, maybe I do. Maybe it *is* true."

"Hmm," Jacobus said. "Well, Yumi, we might not have solved a murder any more than Killingsworth has, but at least now we've got something to trade."

"Trade?" Yumi asked.

"Yeah. We've got a connection from Mahler to Killingsworth, Killingsworth to Stone Cottage, and Stone Cottage to Hunter. We'll give this to Mattheson in exchange for him telling us what he knows. What he *really* knows, not just the pabulum."

"Maybe we can do better than that," Small said.

Jacobus understood he was, by his own nature, suspicious of everyone. Whether that was part of his DNA from birth or whether it was from painful personal experience, he couldn't be certain. What he was definitely certain of was that a major contribution to that predilection was his trauma from the Grimsley Violin Competition. When young Daniel Jacobus's response to Malinkovsky's sexual predation was not as forthcoming as Malinkovsky would have hoped—Jacobus vomited in the oral act—he was eliminated from the competition.

In his adult life, there were only three people whose motives he had never questioned: Nathaniel, Yumi, and Kate Padgett. No, that was wrong. When he first encountered Yumi and Kate, it was the very suspicion he had of their motives that enabled him to discover their involvement in the theft of the "Piccolino" Stradivarius from Carnegie Hall. But since then, the bonds between them had become cemented, and the cement had cured as solid as bedrock. Now, he trusted them as much as he trusted himself. More, actually. It was only Nathaniel, then, who had been his North Star from the get-go and still was.

But now, this newcomer, this Branwell Small, this man without a past, Jacobus's alter ego—*he looks like you, he talks like you, but with a smile*—had injected himself into their lives. He seemed to know more than he should about the police, about investigations, about Killingsworth's victims. About just about everything. Jacobus's suspicious nature was on alert. Was Branwell Small the cure, or was he the cancer?

"You think we can do better?" Jacobus asked. "Like what?"

"We shall hunt Hunter ourselves and get to the bottom of this. First thing tomorrow morning. And then when we go to Mattheson, we shall have that much more collateral in hand."

"Splendid," Kate said and clapped her hands. Jacobus wasn't convinced that it was nearly as splendid.

"Nathaniel, what do you think?"

"Worth a try, I suppose."

"Yumi?"

"Anything that might pry that pipe out of Mattheson's smug mouth."

"All right," Jacobus said. "If it's good enough for you...."

"What about me?" Leonia protested, but received no response.

That evening, after Small had departed, Jacobus quietly proposed to Nathaniel that they remain in the parlor after the women retired to their boudoirs. He wanted to share his concerns and Aunt Leonia's bottle of twenty-five-year-old Macallan with him. It was an invitation Nathaniel had no reservations accepting.

Nathaniel was not surprised at Jacobus's apprehension about Branwell Small. In fact, he said he was coming to similar conclusions himself. They agreed they needed to know more about Small's background. The question was, how to get the information. Jacobus's instinct was to talk to people who knew him. That violinist, Rosalind Langstone, maybe. Or, hadn't Small mentioned an elderly aunt?

Nathaniel counseled against that direct approach. If their suspicions had any basis, it might send alarm bells if he found out, negating any progress they might make.

What, then? Starting the next morning, Nathaniel would do his usual: troll the Internet, make some phone calls. Discreet. Jacobus appreciated Nathaniel's expertise with "discreet." It had enabled him to rise to the top of his profession, investigating and recovering stolen art objects and musical instruments for insurance companies, which had saved them millions in claims. He could use his same skills, honed over decades of schmoozing, networking, and researching, to quietly investigate Branwell Small. So Jacobus agreed to "discreet." At least for the time being.

Chapter Thirteen

The main focus of their attention, though, remained Archibald, aka Artemus, Hunter.

Search as he might, Nathaniel found no telephone listing for Archibald Hunter in Blythburgh, or anywhere else for that matter. According to the recorded message, the phone number for his butcher shop, Village Meats, had been disconnected and was no longer in service, and reported with terse, almost scolding finality that no additional information was available. Nor, as Nathaniel expanded his radius, was there an Archibald Hunter to be found in any of the other butcher shops in Blythburgh village, Blythburgh civil parish, the East Suffolk district, or the entire county of Suffolk.

"What about just trying the last name Hunter?" Jacobus asked.

"There's a pack of them."

"How big a pack?"

"Family-size."

A beaming Branwell Small arrived, bearing gifts in the form of a selection of English cheeses—"a local raw milk cheddar *ne plus ultra*, a Shropshire Blue to die for, and a Caerphilly beyond exquisite"—with a bag of apples.

"Picked them myself this morning. A little early in the season, perhaps. Might be a bit tart."

"Fitting. Someone's birthday?" Jacobus asked. "Or a Trojan horse?"

"Perish the thought, old...Jacobus. A peace offering, if anything. I thought a bit of refreshment was in order," he said. "We've a long row to hoe."

Jacobus explained their current roadblock. Small had an idea. *Leave it to me.* He dialed a number while Jacobus and Nathaniel helped themselves.

"Hello, Justin? Branwell Small here. Yes, he of the gothic Baroque murder thriller slasher. Fine, thank you. So sorry to be a bother. Yes, I know how busy you must be. Aren't we all? Sign of the times. No, don't hang up. It's not about my manuscript.

"See here, Justin. I was wondering what you could tell me about these Archibald Hunter stories. *Tales of the Falklands*, I believe they're called. You see, I've finished all the Patrick O'Brians, and to be quite honest, eighteenth-century British naval has become a bit ho-hum. 'Not a moment to lose,' and all that flapdoodle. I'm looking for something a little more contemporary, if you know what I mean. More…lethal."

"Sorry to disappoint you. Hunter is no longer on our roster."

"No longer on…? Why, how is that, Justin? The catalogue's précis was so, so positively glowing!"

"We're in the business of selling books. What would you expect us to write?" Justin replied, in the same passive-aggressive monotone as the recorded phone message that had defeated Nathaniel's efforts. "Look, Archibald Hunter provided us war stories that were serviceable at best. Certainly not inspired. As the fee, he readily accepted for his stories was modest, Stone Cottage was amenable to helping out a former soldier in need. Even so, it took some convincing by him—I don't want to use the term 'begging'—before we agreed to take him on as a client, but as he delivered his stories on time we kept him on."

"And then?"

"And then we parted ways. No relationships last forever, even the best ones. You can probably find some of his backlist on the Internet. Is there anything else I can help you with?"

Justin hung up before Small had a chance to answer.

It seemed they were at a dead end, with so many questions unresolved. What circumstances would have prompted Archibald Hunter, a butcher by trade, a soldier by training, to have taken on a third career as an author? Why had the butcher, having become an elite and decorated Special Forces soldier, then returned to his original, mundane occupation? And what of the murdered socialite, Amanda Cooper, if that was her real name? How did that fit in, if at all?

But those were secondary questions compared to the original ones, which continued to nag them: What did Archibald Hunter and Jasper Killingsworth have to do with the death of Natasha Conrad, if anything? Their goal seemed so far removed, like washing a murky window in order to reach for a star. Might this entire exercise be a total waste of time?

Nathaniel and Leonia voted for abandoning their efforts and leaving the investigation to the police. If there was anything the tragic death of the young lady taught us, Leonia conjectured, it was that we must enjoy life while we can, for there's no telling what might happen the next instant. For once, she sounded serious, perhaps reflecting upon the memory of her long-deceased, affectionate husband, who left her his entire substantial fortune.

Branwell Small sat on the fence, and in this instance, Jacobus tended to perch uncomfortably beside him. The two had developed a level of mutual respect, if not trust, so when on this occasion, Small hesitated, it was no surprise that Jacobus followed suit.

It was Yumi who broke the logjam with a sledgehammer.

"Absolutely not!" Yumi insisted. "We are not going to give up now. At least, *I'm* not."

"But what is there left to do?" asked Kate, who had not yet expressed any opinion. It was not that she was an indecisive sort, only that she had the admirable habit of thinking things through.

"I'm going to Blythburgh and find Archibald Hunter."

"But how?" Nathaniel asked. "If there's no contact information...."

"How you'd do it in any small town in England. I'm going to whatever pub in Blythburgh is closest to where Village Meats used to be and have a beer. I'm guessing Mr. Hunter might have had a pint or two there, wherever 'there' is. And, as Mr. Small said at the Saxon's Arms, there's no telling what you can find out in an English pub. If anyone wants to come with me, fine. If not, enjoy Auntie Leonia's bonbons."

"Did you say beer?" Jacobus asked.

Yumi, Jacobus, Kate, and Branwell Small made small talk at The Cock's Comb bar with Tom Dredge, the publican whose main feature was a frighteningly black toupee, slightly off center. On London Road, The Cock's Comb was three doors down from Village Meats. In between were a National Trust retail shop and a Barclay's Bank. On the High street, alive with foot traffic, Archibald Hunter's shuttered butcher shop, its front window covered in plywood, stood out like a rotten banana in a bowl of otherwise fresh fruit.

Nathaniel and Leonia would have joined the chase, except there hadn't been enough room in Small's vintage Morris Mini to fit them all. They decided the wiser option was for them to stay in London, where Leonia suggested she and Nathaniel indulge in the world-famous Harrods cream tea as they continued to scour the *You Be the Judge* mysteries. Nathaniel, never one to decline an invitation involving pastry, happily acquiesced, as long as he could do some Internet research first.

The Cock's Comb wasn't as antediluvian as the Saxon's Arms, but it had all the same prerequisites for the iconic English pub: the gleaming brass bar, the dark, polished woodwork, the Tiffany-style glass light fixtures, the heavy, floral-patterned carpeting, and the indefinable community coziness that oozed out of the ether. There were, lining the paneled walls, autographed photos of local football teams, rugby teams, cricket teams, and military squadrons dating back to Alfred the Great, or so it seemed. Strikingly, the athletes' mien tended to be heavy and determined, the soldiers' gallantly sunny as they marched off to slaughter and to be slaughtered. The semi-legible chalkboard boasted daily specials of Fried Plaice & Chips, Mulligatawny Stew, and Corned Beef with 3 Veg. Off to the side, at a safe distance, was a dartboard with a posted tally of the year's best scores. No one was playing at the moment. The telly, on low volume, broadcast a football game from Serbia that none of the six or seven other mid-afternoon patrons paid any attention to.

"We heard that Village Meats had excellent pork," Yumi said after the discussion with Dredge about England's debacle in the World Cup had come to a head-shaking conclusion. "We thought we'd pick up a roast there for dinner."

"Well, you heard right," Dredge said, wiping the bar counter with a damp rag, though the counter was cleaner than the rag, "but you thought wrong. They've been shut down for over a month now."

"Board of Health?" Jacobus asked. "Bad pork. What's it called? Stafficoculus? Understand it can kill 'ya."

"No! Nothing like that," Dredge said. "They had the best meat in the district. Everyone would agree. Just ask around if you don't believe me. It's only that the man just went to pieces. He couldn't cope."

"Please, Tom," Kate said, "I can't bear hearing stories like that. They break my heart, when these big-box supermarkets swoop in and put the little man out of business. All they care about is the bottom line. They don't give a fig about community or tradition."

"Wasn't that way, either, ma'am. It was *The Butcher of Blythburgh* that finally got to him. You might've heard of it. One of Killingsworth's masterpieces." He uttered the name "Killingsworth," as if it was an opprobrium. Jacobus waited to hear the follow-up sound of spitting, but was not rewarded with any such dramatic exclamation point.

"Scurrilous accusations, they were," Dredge continued. "And false. False as my dentures." Though he might also have pointed to his hair to make his point, Tom displayed a mouthful of unnaturally white teeth, which would have more closely aligned with a more youthful and vital person, such as the buxom young lady featured in the calendar on the wall behind him.

"NHS," he said. "Didn't cost me a farthing."

"But, Tom, that book was just fiction," Yumi said. "Did people really believe it?"

"Believe it? People stopped going to his shop, didn't they? They stopped buying his meat, didn't they? He got death threats, so help me. And him, who served his country in wartime. You'd think people would take that into consideration, wouldn't you?"

With his rag, Dredge took out his pique on the countertop, which he rubbed with a vengeance, as if to remove a stain that wasn't there.

"Yes, I understand he was a war hero with the SAS," Small said.

"SAS, my arse! Archie was a Tommy as much as I'm a Tommy."

"Translate, please," Yumi said to Small.

"A Tommy is an infantryman. A plain soldier. Infantry. SAS are our Special Forces."

"That business about Archie being a sniper on some kind of elite unit," Dredge continued, "that was all made up. He was no sniper. He was a normal bloke, like everyone else."

With his thumb, Dredge pointed backward to a photo on the wall.

"See there? That's Archie with his mates in the Falklands. Bottom row, second from the left. Defending the Empire."

Archibald Hunter was kneeling, his rifle butt on the ground with the barrel pointed heavenward. Dressed in fatigues, like all the others. Crew cut, confident smile, thumbs up, like all the others. A soldier, yes. But a murderer?

"But even so, Tom," Small said, "wasn't that years ago when the book came out? You said the shop's only been closed for a month."

"You've got that right for a change. At first, when the book came out, Archie lost almost everything. They treated him like a leper, I tell you. He used to be a regular here, but after Killingsworth's lies, Archie'd stop in for a pint, and the tables would clear 'round him. No one wanted to be near the 'butcher of Blythburgh,' and I can't say I blamed them, true or not. He saw he was hurting my business, and, bless his heart, he stopped coming. After his friends deserted him, he took it out on his family—wife and two kids—'til they couldn't take it anymore, and they left him for parts unknown. Can't say I blame them, either. Archie, he was a strong man, and he could get rough, especially when he'd been in his cups. Mind you, I never let him go over the edge, even though I could've paid the rent from his drinking, alone. I tell you, he was in a bad way.

"But then he started writing his stories. About the war. The Falklands. Wasn't much of a war, was it? Good old Margaret Thatcher. She needed something to boost her ratings, didn't she, after she trashed the coal miners and broke the union? Who needed a war for a worthless rock of an island on the other side of the world, I ask you? No one I know ever went there for holiday. Let Argentina have the bloody island, I say. But for Archie, I guess it was therapy for him."

"The war?" Kate asked.

"The writing. Maybe he only made a few quid on the side, but it made him feel good, he said. Got it off his chest. And his business, which had been hanging on by a thread, it picked up again, too. Things were looking up."

"Tom, I don't want to know what changed for the worse," Kate said. "I can't face sad endings. May I have another pint, please?"

Far more fussy with his record-keeping than with his tonsorial taste, Dredge entered a tidy checkmark into his ledger's detailed account of their running tab.

"That's the mystery," Dredge said, opening the tap. "One afternoon, not that far back, he comes in and goes off on a bender like I'd never seen him, even on his worst days. I had to forcibly remove him from the premises, didn't I? Everyone will say I did right by him. Ask anybody. 'Go home, Archie,' I said. I called a cab myself and loaded him in it, and paid the driver. Four quid, mind you! And did I ever ask him to pay me back? He didn't show up at his store the next day, with customers waiting and trucks delivering. I tell you, I like the man, but it's bad for business all around when there's angry people in the neighborhood."

"That was very kind of you," Kate said, "and very wise."

"Another pint, please," Jacobus said.

"Yes, sir. Coming right up."

"You know where Hunter lives?" Jacobus asked.

That brought Dredge's smooth, practiced motions toward the tap, in-grained from years of practice, to a jerking paralysis.

"Whatever do you want to know that for?" Dredge asked. "Like I said, he's in a bad way."

"Because I've been in a bad way before," Jacobus said, working his hands over his beer glass for effect. "And when I was, it was nice to know that someone cared."

He didn't actually mean that, because when he was in a bad way, the last thing he wanted was for someone to try to make him feel better. Because then he'd be responsible for making sure that person didn't feel bad when they failed in the attempt, and he was unwilling to accept that responsibility. Whenever a friend tried to help, Jacobus usually ended up with one fewer friend. In bad times, what he wanted was to be left alone. But he knew the line he delivered to Dredge would have a good ring to it, and it worked.

Hunter lived out in the hinterlands, Dredge told them, and provided landmarks to keep an eye out for in order to find his property, with the postscript, "Just follow your noses. You've got four of 'em. You're sure to find it."

As they left The Cock's Comb, Jacobus had a spur-of-the-moment thought. He asked Dredge, "Does Hunter, by any chance, like music?"

"I suppose. Who doesn't?"

"Give me a f'rinstance, what kind."

"I suspect he'd be keen on Mick Jagger."

"What about Mahler?"

Dredge stopped wiping the counter.

"Yeah, yeah. Archie would like his Mahler, wouldn't he?"

"Really!"

"Oh, sure! Sure! And I'm the Queen Mum."

Chapter Fourteen

"It looks like a disaster area, Jake," Yumi said.

The drive from Blythburgh Centre along narrow hedge-lined roads would have been picturesque if the purpose of their journey had been a carefree jaunt into the countryside, or if the overcast sky hadn't darkened into a threatening coal gray. The faint salt smell of open sea, invisible though not so many miles away on the other side of the rolling hills, taunted them with a vision of expansive, limitless freedom, a vision that seemed to be receding from their grasp even as they pursued their goal. They shared an unspoken disquiet, a disturbing sense that what they didn't know could indeed hurt them.

Yumi, sitting next to Small in the front seat, had given up trying to decipher the landmarks and simply stared out the side window. Behind her was Kate, and next to Kate was Jacobus, who wished he hadn't given up smoking. They had followed Dredge's directions, getting lost twice—*only* twice made it feel like a moral victory—once because Dredge had neglected to tell them "the ancient oak" at which they were to bear left had a grove of close relatives vying for the honorific. Ultimately, they relied on Dredge's only dependable instruction: "Follow your noses. You've got four of 'em. You'll be sure to find it."

They rounded a bend between two tree-covered hills, and suddenly, like mist-enshrouded Brigadoon, Archibald Hunter's secluded homestead was upon them. Small pulled into a pitted dirt drive that accessed the property, made a neatly executed U-turn, and parked. It started to rain.

"We're about fifty feet from the house," he informed Jacobus.

"Why did you park so far away? Trying to make life miserable for me?"

"One never knows when one will need to make a fast getaway," he said.

The property probably had once been tidy. But no longer. Now, like gray-green mold on soggy, week-old bread, encroaching weeds had overtaken whatever lawn and garden there might have been. An undernourished goat, showing its ribs, and a flock of scrawny chickens roamed the yard, scrounging for a meal. Three mangy mongrels, viewing the car's arrival, crouched with suspicion and snapped at each other's rumps. On one side of the brick-and-stucco cottage, a climbing rose vine, more thorn than blossom, shot groping canes off its trellis. Windows, through which no light shone, had gone unwashed, and dripping moss grew heavily on the north side of the sagging, shingled roof. Next to the rocking chair on the unswept front porch, the mound of empty cans and bottles provided the corroborating evidence for, if not the explanation of, the sad state of the property and its inhabitant.

They got out of the car, Small and Jacobus on the driver's side, Yumi and Kate on the other, and cautiously began to pick their way along damp paving stones obscured by the tangle of weeds.

Nodding toward the pile on the porch, Small said, "I presume it's not tonic water."

His wry quip, whether heard by the pile's creator or not, was rebuked by a gun blast. Small wrapped his arms around Jacobus in a bear hug and took him heavily to the ground. Yumi grasped Kate by the hand, and crouching low, dashed back to the car, using it as a barrier between them and the house. The blast panicked the animals, which clucked, bleated, and howled, and dashed in random patterns over the yard.

"Is everyone all right?" Small asked in a judiciously low voice.

"Yes, we're okay," Yumi answered.

"Perhaps it was just a warning shot," he said.

Silence followed, a silence that was as enigmatic, if less perilous, as the shot had been. They waited.

"Hunter!" Small called out. "Archibald Hunter!"

No response.

"We just want to talk."

The next shot blew off the Mini's passenger-side mirror.

"Back in the car, everyone," Small said. "Quickly does it."

As they crawled back in, Jacobus yelled out, "Hunter, you like Mahler?"

A third blast demolished the mirror on the driver's side.

"I think that answers your question," Small said. "Now would not be too soon to leave this place before he destroys the rest of my car."

Small revved the engine, and they drove back toward the town, silent and severely shaken. After Hunter's first shot, Jacobus's reflex had been to crouch down. Not that doing so would protect him. It was a matter of instinct. What he hadn't anticipated was the jolt of Small tackling him and tossing him to the ground like a sack of potatoes. Though he had fallen heavily, he was uninjured. Hardly less of a shock was his realization that Small might have saved his life.

They passed Village Meats and The Cock's Comb and had almost entered the motorway from London Road when Jacobus said to stop.

"Whatever for?" Small asked. For once, his voice was not pleasant. Being shot at and having your car used for target practice might do that, Jacobus thought.

"Just stop for a minute, Small," Jacobus repeated.

Small pulled over and set the brake, but kept the engine running.

"Didn't the bartender, Dredge, show you a photo with Hunter in it?" Jacobus recalled. "I gather you all saw it. Let's get it and take it to Mattheson. Maybe he can find out if anyone saw Hunter at the concert."

"Is that why you asked Dredge and then Hunter about Mahler?" Yumi asked.

"Precisely."

"I was wondering why you did that. But why would he…?"

"How the hell do I know?" Jacobus said. "All I know is that this guy, Hunter, is crazy as a loon, and he's got a happy trigger finger to match. We think—we pretty much know for sure—that there was some connection between him and Killingsworth at Stone Cottage."

"Speculative," Small said. "And tenuous. Don't mean to piss on your parade, mind you, old boy. Go on."

"And Killingsworth wrote the comment about Mahler's ghost in *Murder at the Royal Albert*. So if A equals B, and B equals C, then A equals shit, the way I see it."

"Your syllogism is far from airtight, but I see your logic, old boy," Small said. "I'll grant that. But how do you propose we get the photo?"

"What's with this 'old boy' crap? You're older than me, old boy."

"Let's not get into that, old boys," Kate said. "I have an idea for Branwell to get that photo, keeping in mind Mr. Dredge's predilection for the pecuniary."

A half-hour later, they left The Cock's Comb ten quid lighter but with the photo in hand.

"Tom, I usually don't share this, but I'm an ardent collector of Falkland War paraphernalia," had been Small's opening gambit. "You know, memorabilia, helmets, firearms, documents. The usual. We're all a bit daft. No, not you, Tom. You're a sharp one. By we, I mean we collectors. Becomes a bit of an obsession. I was admiring your collection. Couldn't help it. Top-of-the-line stuff. Tops. And you've got so much of it. Was wondering if you'd be willing to part with one item. Just one. Your photo of the Falkland Tommies. Yes, the one with Hunter. That's the one! If I could only add it to the Wall of Fame in my sitting room. Before anyone else gets their hands on it. The Wall? Yes, exclusively devoted to honoring the Falkland war heroes. No, seriously. Very little space left. No, none of the Argentinians. No worries, there."

That line of persuasion did less to convince Tom to part with the photo than the five pounds sterling Small gladly donated to the local Blythburgh junior rugby team's bake sale and the additional five that Jacobus grudgingly forked over for Dredge's personal rainy day fund.

Chapter Fifteen

T hey braved soggy rush hour traffic into London, minus side-view mirrors, found the Kensington police station on Earls Court Road, the precinct which oversaw law and order in the geographic area encompassing Royal Albert Hall and Belgravia, and, worn out and impatient, parked illegally in a Police Only spot. Surrounded by the buzz of activity typical to an urban police station, they gave their names to a person at a desk, were ignored for a half hour, and were finally noticed by DS Littlebank, who ushered them into DCI Mattheson's office.

Glancing up at them from whatever was occupying his attention at his desk, Mattheson said, "Small," with poorly disguised irritation. "You again?"

Though the question was directed at Small, it was enough to revive Jacobus's suspicions, which had ebbed and flowed like the tide under a full moon. Suddenly, the tide was again in its flood stage.

"Not *just* me this time, DCI Mattheson," Small replied, ignoring the caustic overtone. "I've brought my friends along, with whom I understand you're familiar. May I impose upon you to first listen to their story, after which, if you still think we have wasted your time, you may feel free to boot me out on my arse? I will even turn 'round and bend over for you."

"You're providing me with a powerful disincentive to believe them," Mattheson said.

"On the other hand," Small continued, still unperturbed, "if you find our information valuable to your investigation, you bring us up to snuff on said investigation?"

Mattheson filled his pipe, tamped down the tobacco, and sat back in his chair with a sigh, a gesture of acceptance if not of surrender. To Jacobus, it seemed a well-practiced pantomime between two old adversaries. Something definitely worth relating to Nathaniel.

They left it to Yumi, their moral North Star in the ongoing search for the truth of Natasha Conrad's death, to tell the story of their Blythburgh misadventure, from the time they arrived at The Cock's Comb to the moment they fled from Archibald Hunter's gunshots to their return to The Cock's Comb to obtain the photo of Hunter. Yumi spared no detail, no matter how insignificant, except for Dredge's toupee. When she finished, Small handed Mattheson the Falkland War photo of Archibald Hunter. Mattheson studied it methodically, presumably thinking thoughts more coherent than the nondescript tune he hummed as he did so.

He placed the photo flat on his desk and continued to look at it, drumming his fingertips on the desktop as he did so.

"Thank you for this," he said at long last. "It could be significant, indeed."

"Really?" Yumi said, reflecting her surprise, pleasure, and renewed hope all in that single word.

"If you had thought I am a stickler for procedure," Mattheson said, "you would have been correct. I am aware that I've been tagged with the moniker—by both my subordinates and my superiors, and ostensibly behind my back—the *Pirate of Pedants*. However, being a proponent of an orderly investigation does not preclude one from keeping an open mind. Does it, Small?"

"By no means, sir. No, not at all."

"Good," Mattheson continued. "You know how meaningful your approbation is to me."

Jacobus covered his mouth with his hand to hide his smile. He was beginning to have a better appreciation for this cop.

"Now that I've gained your hard-won validation," Mattheson continued, "this will be my strategy. I will have my constables disseminate copies of Hunter's photo at and in the vicinity of Royal Albert Hall. If we get a match, I'll then notify DCI Levin, my counterpart with the East Suffolk district police, and have Littlebank meet up with his officers posthaste to pay a friendly visit to Mr. Hunter. Blythburgh is out of my jurisdiction, as I'm sure you will recognize, but as this has potential bearing on the murder of Natasha Conrad, I'm sure we will receive the cooperation we require."

"And now it's your turn," Jacobus said.

"My turn, sir?"

"That was the deal when we sat down, Mattheson. We gave you a lead. It sounds like it's vital information. So, you tell us what you've learned. We might speak different versions of English, but I believe it's still the same basic lingo."

"Very well. Though I prefer to call it a gentlemen's agreement rather than 'a deal.'"

"Pardon my French."

"This is what we know," Mattheson said, "and of course, you understand the need to keep it amongst yourselves. Ballistics tell us that the gun used to kill Natasha Conrad was, as Littlebank immediately suspected, a Ruger LCR 22. If you're not familiar with firearms, all you need to know is that, though a .22 does indeed have the capability to kill someone, it is not a weapon that is likely to accomplish that immediately unless it is a head shot at fairly close range."

"In other words, it is a lightweight weapon," Small interjected.

"Just so. It could certainly incapacitate a person handily enough, but if the other person is also armed, it had better be a well-placed shot. It would not be a weapon of choice in a gunfight or an assassination attempt. Unless it is a heart shot or a head shot, the victim is more likely to bleed to death, or not die at all."

"The firearm Hunter used on us for target practice was no small caliber gun," Small said. "It sounded more like a Browning Hi-Power. Semi-automatic."

This Baroque harpsichordist certainly was full of surprises, Jacobus thought.

"That wouldn't surprise me," Mattheson replied. "It is what our infantry used in the Falklands. It can do considerable damage."

"Absolutely."

"So that's what accounted for our hasty retreat?" Jacobus asked.

"Quite so. Discretion being the better part."

Mattheson paused to give the discrepancy in weapons some thought. He also seemed to be undergoing an internal debate: Had he divulged enough, or would be worth his while to throw them another bone? Well, they've been good dogs, all things considered. Why not give them another treat?

"You may recall mention of the paper bag we discovered on the Royal Albert arena floor," he continued. "It contained some crumbs and grease residue, which appeared to be from some sort of pastry. We have undertaken a chemical analysis of those components in an effort to determine the product, then the manufacturer, and then the purveyors closest to Royal Albert Hall of said product. Once we get the laboratory results, which, with hope, will provide us with serviceable information, we will interview those vendors, show them the photo of Hunter, and from there, trace his movements.

"Now, regarding the bullet holes in the bag and concert program. There are a few things we can surmise with some confidence. Because the holes were very small and neat, it would indicate the shooter inserted his gun hand all the way into the bag, probably to disguise the fact that he was indeed holding a gun and that the bag was held close to the program."

"I would think shooting a bullet through a bag would rip it apart," Jacobus said. "Or ignite it into flames."

"You wouldn't think that if you knew anything about firearms," Small said.

Kate gave Jacobus's hand a meaningful squeeze. It said, *Yes, I agree Mr. Small has a tendency to put himself on a soapbox and be quite full of himself when he has a captive audience.* It also meant, *Jake, now is not the time to open your mouth.*

"If the gun were held as DCI Mattheson conjectures, the bullet would have just punched through the paper, and the energy of the shot would most likely happen *outside* the bag. In my humble opinion, even gun residue would be forced outside the bag. If there had been much space between the muzzle and the paper, you'd probably have more paper damage—a bigger hole and perhaps some residue on the inside."

"Thank you for the tutorial, Small," Mattheson said. "It's evident Mr. Jacobus appreciates your expertise. I would only clarify what you said by adding that most of the energy of a gunshot blows out of the muzzle, along with the projectile. The closer the muzzle is to the paper bag, the less the damage to the bag."

Mattheson stood up from his desk. Time to wrap things up. Promised the wife to be home for tea.

"Again, I say thank you for the information you have brought me. Whoever killed Natasha Conrad was an expert marksman, as our Mr. Hunter seems to be. And if it turns out that he was at Royal Albert for the Mahler concert and that the bullet that killed Ms. Conrad came from a weapon he owns, it will all but put a well-deserved noose around the man's neck."

Yumi rose from her chair, as much to block the doorway for Mattheson's exit as to prepare to leave.

"But why?" she asked, not ready for the interview to be over. "There's no connection between Hunter and Natasha that we know of. What can his motive have been?"

"To be very honest, I haven't the foggiest," Mattheson said, "but once we have him sitting down with us, it shouldn't take long to elicit an answer. An hour, a day, a week at most. We'll find out, one way or the other. That's all I have to say. Are there any more questions?"

"Tom Dredge said Archibald Hunter was merely a regular infantryman," Kate said. "That he really wasn't a Special Forces soldier. But now you're saying he was an expert marksman?"

"May I remind you, madam, who this Tom Dredge is?" Mattheson said, with some heat.

"The publican at The Cock's Comb. Who sold us the photo."

"That is correct. Tom Dredge is wrong. He should stick to the occupation for which he is qualified, pulling pints. Any more questions?"

There was silence.

"There being none, I wish you all a very pleasant evening. I will inform you of developments as they may occur. And, Mr. Small, may I say you are extremely fortunate."

"Really? Why?"

"There will be no need for you to bare your bottom. At least, not today."

"Ding-a-ling-a-ling! Dinner is served!" Auntie Leonia held a tiny dinner bell aloft and shook it vigorously, as unnecessary as it was annoying for Jacobus, who simply wanted some peace and quiet. *"Ding-a-ling-a-ling!"* she repeated, just in case no one had heard the actual bell.

"Welcome, amateur sleuths!" she proclaimed. "Your good Mr. Williams and I have spent the day diligently preparing for your return."

"'Good' is relative," Jacobus said. "As is 'diligently.'"

"I gather what you mean by that," Kate said to Leonia, "is that you're dying to hear the progress of our investigation."

"Dear sister, why would I even—"

"Let's eat," Jacobus said.

After returning to the house from the police station, he had conversed privately with Nathaniel, providing a summary of the long day's drama, including being wrestled to the ground by Branwell Small, and Small's curious familiarity with DCI Mattheson and with firearms. Nathaniel's report on what he had accomplished during the day was not nearly as noteworthy. As far as the results of his snatches of research were concerned, the intended hours for which had been stolen by Auntie Leonia's insistence she accompany him for a tasty visit to Harrods (to which he easily acceded) and with helping her prepare dinner (to which he was more resistant), Branwell Small was no more or less than what he appeared to be: an esteemed amateur musician, well-known for his scholarship and good nature, who had appeared on the concert scene, fully formed, after studying at the Royal Conservatory after the war. His affection for crime and its instruments for carrying it out seemed no more than a dilettante's pastime.

Jacobus had to admit that Auntie Leonia's ham, baked in cider with a honey, orange, and ginger glaze, was as magnificent as she declared it would be. Along with the boiled potatoes in butter and parsley and the steamed Brussels sprouts.

"Speaking of ham," Jacobus said to Branwell Small, "you certainly put on a show at the police station. And why do I get the feeling that you've been around the block with these types of things before?"

"Oh, it really is nothing. We all have our little avocations to take our minds off the weightier issues, don't we? I've dabbled a bit here and there with firearms. They genuinely fascinate, especially when you've been on the wrong end of one, as I have. Perhaps that's why they intrigue me so. Please pass those yummy potatoes. Aren't they exquisite?"

His attempted deflection didn't sway anyone.

"DCI Mattheson seems to know you pretty well," Yumi said.

"Oh, him. Well, yes, I've approached him now and then with ideas about crimes I've read about in the papers. When one lives in a small hamlet, it helps keep one entertained on those long winter nights."

"Considering your interest and how much you know of the subject, might it be possible that before your war wound, you were an arms expert?" Kate asked. "Or an intelligence officer?"

"Those have been two theories bandied about, yes," Small replied. "But, alas, no one has been able to prove or disprove them. So for me, investigation remains a hobby, like stamp collecting or butterfly catching. I'm a mere dabbler."

"That sounds a little like you, Jake," Nathaniel said.

Before Jacobus could respond that the difference was that Small seemed to enjoy the "hobby," Kate said cheerily, "I'm sure that between the two of you, we will wrap up this mystery in two shakes."

Jacobus heard something slam on the table. A glass, perhaps.

"I can't believe this!" Yumi cried. "You all make this seem like a child's game! Don't you understand you're talking about my student—*my student!*—as if she were some character in an Agatha Christie cozy. Natasha is dead! She's been murdered! As far as I'm concerned, you're all as bad as Jasper Killingsworth!"

Jacobus heard Yumi push back her chair and stomp off.

"Oh, dear!" Kate said, and went after her.

There was a long silence at the table. The ham no longer tasted quite as magnificent or the potatoes as exquisite. The only taste that lingered was bitter.

"Well," Leonia finally said. "I'll just straighten up here. It was a lovely dinner while it lasted, wasn't it?" No one answered.

With Leonia back in the kitchen, Small said, "Well, Jacobus, I guess we've outdone ourselves this time."

"She's right, you know," Nathaniel said.

"We have to make it up to her, don't we?"

"No shit," Jacobus said.

"Next step?" Nathaniel asked.

"We wait. Wait until we hear back from your buddy, Mattheson," Jacobus said to Small. "Then we'll know where to go from there."

"There's something I suggest we could do before that," Small said.

"Why am I not surprised?" Jacobus said. "What is it this time, Sherlock?"

"An idea that I believe you'll be amenable to. I spied a bottle of twenty-five-year-old Macallan on dear Leonia's sideboard. I suggest I pour us each a rather large tumbler."

"Now you're thinking," Jacobus said. "Nathaniel and I are familiar with that bottle. There might still be enough left."

After lubricating themselves sufficiently, which didn't take very long, Jacobus popped the question he had been ruminating upon ever since Nathaniel had reported back to him with his research into Small's background.

"So, Small, how did you get into music?"

"One follows one's passion, in a nutshell. Isn't that what you did?"

"Well, I mean, I started when I was a little kid, listening to my parents play records on their phonograph. Playing music was as much a part of my life as walking or reading. But, as far as we know, you weren't involved in anything musical until after the war. Kind of late for a professional musician of your caliber to start, wouldn't you agree?"

"'As far as we know?'" Small replied. "Oh, dear! I see. Have the two of you been vetting me? Yes, you have. Haven't you?"

"I wouldn't go that far, Branwell," Nathaniel replied. "Simply that you've had such an intriguing life. Renowned musician, war veteran, the amnesia, weapons expert, on easy terms with the police. Not many people sport a resumé like that. We're just interested, s'all."

Small drained his glass.

"Fair enough," Small said. "Yes, when you put it that way, I can see how one might be curious. Who wouldn't be? In all honesty, my life has been like this bottle of scotch. Very tasty, rich, intense perhaps, distinguished, some might even say. But half-empty. Or half-full, depending on the mood one is in at the moment.

"The half-empty part is, of course, before the war. As you've apparently determined, there is no record to indicate I had an affinity toward music. Sports, yes. Maths, somewhat. Art and music, none whatsoever. That's what I've been told, anyway, and what few remaining records indicate, as I have no recollection.

"Yet, upon returning from the war, it was as if the tap had been turned on full measure, unlike Tom Dredge's at The Cock's Comb. I learned to play the piano with ease, to study Mozart scores, to communicate in the language of music with facility. My parents called it a blessed miracle. Doctors said that my head wound might somehow have recircuited the neurons in my brain. Probably the truth lies somewhere in the middle.

"As to my association with the forces of law and order, let me assure you that it is only in the capacity of an amateur attempting to do good. Over the years, there have been a number of cases over which highly qualified, but uncreative professionals like DCI Mattheson have, at least in my humble opinion, stumbled like a blind man in the forest. Sorry, Jacobus, no offense intended.

"Because I like to see wrongs righted, I have, from time to time, provided the authorities with what I believed were valuable insights. And because I don't want to be thought of as a crackpot conspiracy theorist, I've studied. I've read everything I can get my hands on that's pertinent, whether it's about firearms, statistics, criminology, or whatever. Nevertheless, as you can imagine, professionals don't often demonstrate a great deal of appreciation or respect for the opinions of amateurs. It is no different which profession it is. Take music, for example. I'm certain you'd agree that the last thing you'd want to hear is advice about how to play the Beethoven violin concerto from the back row second violinist in your local community orchestra."

"Yet you persevere in it," Jacobus said, neither agreeing nor disagreeing.

"Just as you have!" Small said.

"What do you mean?"

"I hope you'll forgive me, but I have to confess that even as you and Nathaniel have been investigating my past, I have taken the liberty of doing so with yours. I have had some delightfully entertaining and revealing conversations with Yumi and Kate about the many 'capers'—as you Americans call them—that you have solved over the years. I am highly impressed, almost as much as they are, with your accomplishments. You are clearly a tandem to be reckoned with, and, if I were on the other side of the law from the two of you, I would tremble in my boots."

"Nathaniel," Jacobus said. "Tell me, is Small trembling?"

"If he is, I don't see it."

"That's a relief. Pour us all another round of Auntie Leonia's finest."

Chapter Sixteen

The next morning, Yumi was back in DCI Mattheson's office, accompanied by Jacobus and Small. Kate graciously stayed home with Nathaniel and Leonia. "Too many cooks," she said.

It had been a long night. Ever since Jacobus's first violin lesson with Yumi, one of the qualities he had admired in his young student was her stubborn, steely determination. Maybe Jacobus appreciated that trait in her because it reflected his own tenacious tendencies, or maybe it was because even in his position as her superior—which he was in all ways, at one time—she had stood up to him on occasion, infuriating and gratifying him simultaneously. Her doggedness had not ebbed over the years, though she had learned to put it into abeyance, only bringing it to the fore when necessary. Clearly, at least in her own mind, this had been one of those times. After she had lambasted them at the dinner table, Kate and Leonia tried to console her. Consolation was not what she needed, she insisted. Jacobus, Nathaniel, and Small, in their Macallan-klatch, maintained what they had hoped would be a safe distance, waiting out the storm. It didn't work. It erupted upon them with the knife-edged fury of a North Sea gale.

Marching back downstairs into the living room, she chastised them, all of them, without reservation. This wasn't a game, she reminded them, as if they should have needed reminding. This wasn't you, Daniel Jacobus, in your dotage, playing checkers with my charming grandmother, and it wasn't a hobby to keep you, Branwell Small, sufficiently entertained or to inspire your witticisms, and it wasn't a means to keep you, corpulent Nathaniel, occupied between meals, and you, Auntie Leonia, it sure as hell wasn't the mindless make-believe of extraterrestrials coming to this planet to teach earthlings how to build the pyramids.

A young lady—a talented, beautiful, breathing young lady—had been shot in the head with a bullet that exploded in her brain and in a split second, had erased all that talent, all that beauty, and all the breath of life. Yumi was determined to find out not only who, but why.

"And if anyone wants to help, fine. But if it's going to be a game for you, then go home. I'll do it myself. Have a good sleep."

She left the living room without waiting for a response, which was just as well because no one had anything to say.

"We have made progress." Mattheson addressed his comment to Yumi, observing that she had taken the chair opposite him, the two gentlemen seated behind her. *She has exerted her authority over her elders, or so it appears. An impressive achievement for the young lady.* Seated at his desk, the smoke from his meerschaum drifting in lazy patterns, Mattheson was at ease. DS Littlebank, standing to his side and behind, seemed less so. Listless, perhaps. Or, as so many seconds-in-command are, uncertain about disseminating information to civilians.

"The crumbs and oil in the brown bag we found on the arena floor have been analyzed," Mattheson said. "They are the remains of a meat pie made by a national firm, Patsy's Pasties. They sell all over the UK, with the vendor nearest Royal Albert in very close proximity. Not a particularly sexy clue, but potentially a highly significant one. Tell them, Littlebank. Go on. Out with it."

"Yes, sir." Littlebank cleared his throat. A formal pronouncement forthcoming. "The vendor, a Mr. Rajiv Singh, manages a snack stand just across the street, at the base of the steps to the monument to Prince Albert. Do you care to know his home address?"

"Is it important?" Yumi asked.

"No, I don't think so."

"Then why would we?"

Mattheson removed his pipe and covered his mouth.

"We showed Singh the photo of Hunter," Littlebank continued, "and he confirmed immediately that Hunter had been a customer."

"But there must have been a thousand customers at that stand," Yumi said. "How could he possibly recall one particular person on one particular day who had only been there a minute? How could he be sure?"

"Good question. Ours as well," Matteson replied. "Tell her, Littlebank."

"We also distributed the photo of Hunter to the box office staff and to several Arena ticket holders whom we tracked down from their purchase receipts. We received corroboration on all counts. In addition, the box office describes Hunter as arriving at the last moment, out of breath, and being in a rush."

"So, you're certain, then," Jacobus said.

"We are certain," Littlebank said. "Hunter was there."

"Chilling," Small said.

"Indeed," Yumi said. "What else?"

"Go on, Littlebank," Matteson said. "Don't be shy."

"Yes, sir."

There was a long pause.

"Come, come, Littlebank! They're not the enemy. We owe them."

"Yes, sir. We have further ascertained," Littlebank continued, finally getting into a flow, "that on the day in question, Hunter boarded a coach from Sydling St. Nicholas. He took the coach—"

"What?" Small asked, sounding very surprised. "A coach? From Sydling? That's nowhere near Blythburgh. It's almost in the opposite direction from London."

"You don't need to give us a geography lesson, Small," Matteson replied, somewhat testily. "You can give us more credit for intelligence than that."

"But what could he have been doing there? And to go from Sydling to London for a concert? The coach takes an entire half day. I presume one must change at Dorchester and thence to Belgravia, Victoria Coach Station. It's twice as fast if one drove."

"Why he was in Sydling," Matteson said, "and why he went to the concert remain to be discovered. But I have received authorization to send in the

SCO19 unit to apprehend Hunter—"

"SCO19? What's that?" Yumi asked.

"The Metropolitan Police elite, special firearms unit," Small said. "Like your SWAT team in the US. Necessary when confronting a highly armed, highly dangerous adversary."

"Quite," Mattheson said. "And it shan't be long before we have the answers to Miss Shinagawa's questions. Our Mr. Hunter is now Mr. Hunted."

Chapter Seventeen

"It's for you," Leonia said, shaking Yumi awake in the middle of the night. "It's DCI Mattheson. I think it's very rude to call at this ungodly hour, and was tempted to tell him so. In fact, I did tell him so—I do hope that wasn't the wrong thing—but he said it was urgent."

"Thank you, Auntie," Yumi said. "Don't worry. You did the right thing. I'll take it from here."

Yumi fumbled in the dark for her own phone, which she had turned to *Do Not Disturb*. She checked recent calls. Yes, Mattheson had tried her number and then, as she hadn't answered, must have decided to call her aunt.

Yumi didn't know what to think. She might not go so far as to say it was rude, but it was certainly unexpected. And because it was unexpected, it filled her with apprehension. *And why call me?*

"Hello," she said into the phone.

"Good evening, Miss Shinagawa. I realize it is out of the ordinary, to say the least, to call at this hour, but as you were personally attached to Miss Conrad, I wanted to talk to you before you read it in the newspapers in the morning."

"Thank you. That's very thoughtful of you."

"I'm glad to hear you say so. I was half expecting you'd bite my head off for calling this late."

"I understand my aunt already did that. No need for me to rub it in."

"Just so."

"So, go on. Read what?"

"You see, there have been developments."

131

"Developments?"

"Yes, and it's a bit of good news, bad news."

Yumi remained silent. Waiting.

Mattheson cleared his throat.

"As you know," he continued, "we sent in our SCO19 team to apprehend Mr. Hunter at his home in Blythburgh, fully expecting he would be heavily armed and would greet us in a similar manner as he had you and your friends."

Yumi had a premonition she was about to be told that all had not gone well. That Hunter had either escaped and was headed toward Belgravia, or worse, had already killed again. The seed for the premonition, sown by the silence on the other end of the line, grew larger the longer the silence lasted.

"DCI Mattheson, please, tell me," she said.

"Indeed," Mattheson said, as if her three-word demand—politely conveyed, but a demand nonetheless—had recharged a rundown battery. "Indeed, it is true that Hunter was heavily armed. And I use the word 'was' with intent, as we discovered upon arrival at his home that Mr. Hunter was not only heavily armed, he was also dead."

"Dead!"

"Yes, I'm afraid so. It is evident that, after consuming a substantial amount of alcohol, he shot himself in the temple with the type of weapon with which Miss Conrad was killed. Perhaps the same one. Of course, we will wait for an autopsy for confirmation, but from experience I am confident enough to suggest that will be the medical examiner's official conclusion."

Yumi was more confused than ever. Other than confusion, though, she didn't know what to feel. So many questions. Where to start? Maybe with the simplest, if only in order to get her bearings.

"DCI Mattheson, do you believe Hunter was the man who murdered Natasha?" she asked.

"I have no cause to doubt it. I believe that's the reason he took his own life. He knew he had been found out. He knew he was trapped, and there was no exit strategy for him, but one. The one he took. Maybe he believed it was the most soldierly, the most honorable way to end it all. Better than a sordid trial and a life in prison. I think you can put your mind at ease that justice has been served. Miss Conrad's killer is no more."

"Thank you, DCI Mattheson. There's so much to absorb. Can I ask a question?"

"You may ask, and if I can, I will answer as candidly as possible."

"Are you certain that it was suicide and that he wasn't killed by someone else?"

"That is, of course, the first question we asked ourselves. Everything at the scene indicated suicide, and nothing indicated foul play. It is as definitive a case of suicide as one can envision unless one were there to witness it oneself."

"Including a suicide note?"

"Yes, that as well, though its text was somewhat inconclusive. Otherwise, all the classic elements of suicide were present."

"Are you at liberty to tell me what the note said?"

There was an edge to his reply, as if he felt she hadn't trusted his judgment or she had not appreciated how far he had extended himself to answer her questions.

"Why is that important to you?"

"You know why. I would feel better if there was a confession."

"I see." He paused. "That is understandable. All right. It was a very brief, very concise note, and you may take it for what it is. The note read: *'I didn't kill her. I didn't mean to kill her. I meant to kill her.'* End of note. It was handwritten and signed, by the way, in case you were wondering whether someone else might have written it. And yes, it is Hunter's handwriting. It matches other written documents of his that we found on the premises, in case you were wondering that as well."

Yumi repeated the text out loud. *"'I didn't kill her. I didn't mean to kill her. I meant to kill her.'"*

"Yes, that's correct," Mattheson said.

"Don't you find that bizarre, DCI Mattheson? For someone's final message to be a puzzle?"

"The man's judgment had been impaired with alcohol. He was overcome with remorse for his actions, and was in the final throes of deciding whether to end his life. Given those circumstances, my feeling is that it would have been extraordinary if his note was *not* cryptic."

"But have you determined a motive?" Yumi asked. "Or any connection at all to Natasha?"

"I'm afraid we haven't. Mr. Hunter has taken the answer to that question with him to the grave. With his death, that door seems to have been shut. Regrettably so."

"So, are you telling me that, at this point, you consider the case closed?"

Mattheson chose his words carefully. "Archibald Hunter was our one and only suspect, thanks to you and your friends. As I said, we have no doubt he was the man who shot and killed Miss Conrad, and you should be comforted by that fact. I see no other conclusion to which the investigation could conceivably lead us."

"I see."

"Is there anything else I can do for you, Ms. Shinagawa?"

"No, thank you."

"Well, then—"

"Yes! Yes, there is. I assume the former Mrs. Hunter will be asked to identify the body."

"She already has. It was less difficult to find her than we thought it would be. She lives not far from Blythburgh. But why do you ask?"

"I would like to meet her."

"Why, may I ask?"

"To express my condolences."

"That's somewhat out of the ordinary, but I don't see why not. After all, you were kind enough to relieve me of the burden of notifying Ms. Conrad's parents, and Hunter's obituary will no doubt include enough public information for someone of your determined nature to piece together how to find her, anyway. Yes, I'd say this quid pro quo is reasonably in order."

Mattheson gave Yumi Audrey Hunter's address and phone number.

"Thank you. I'm grateful," she said.

"Good night, then."

"Yes. Good night."

What a cliché: Good night. There was nothing good about it. Though Yumi turned the lights out and lay back in bed, sleep wasn't a remote possibility. *I didn't kill her. I didn't mean to kill her. I meant to kill her.*

It was a clear progression, starting from denial and evolving into an admission of premeditation: I didn't, I didn't mean, I meant. A confession? Seeking absolution? Yes, it was clear. Or was it?

That's what kept her awake. The note didn't actually say he killed her. Just that he *meant* to. And now that she thought about it, "I *didn't mean* to kill her," sounded more definite an act than "I *meant* to kill her." But what was the motive? The statement was frustratingly moot on that subject. It still didn't make any sense. No matter how Yumi reasoned the suicide note, it lacked the finality she so desperately sought. Closure continued to resist her grasp.

"You look absolutely out of sorts," Auntie Leonia said to Yumi as they sat around the breakfast table. Pittums, unconcerned, was its centerpiece. Yumi was by far the youngest of the group, but it seemed as if she had aged overnight far beyond her years. "You must have more toast. I've got some lovely homemade greengage jam to go with it."

Yumi tried to smile. If only all problems could be solved by one's stomach. She had filled everyone in about Mattheson's phone call and expressed her intention to pay a condolence call on Archibald Hunter's widow. No, thank you, I want to go alone, she insisted, declining all offers to accompany her.

"What is it that's troubling you, dear?" Kate asked. "We know now who killed the poor girl. As you told us, DCI Mattheson said he was certain they got the right man. Why doesn't that settle things satisfactorily?"

"But why?" Yumi asked the universe, not expecting any more answers from it than she did from Pittums. "Why did he do it? It makes no sense."

"Yes, you've been saying that," Jacobus said. "For weeks. And you're right, it didn't make sense then, and it doesn't make sense now. But what good does it do to drive yourself *meshuga* over it? Some questions never get answered, and sometimes it's best to leave them alone." He was, of course, thinking about his own unanswered questions: What would his life have been like had he not gone blind? What would have happened to him if he had stayed in Germany with his parents, as his brother had, during the war? What had happened to his brother? He had tried to put those questions behind him. But had he? Maybe he was, in fact, *meshuga*.

"I can't believe I have to go back to New York so soon," Yumi said. "I just feel like this is going to hang over my head for the rest of my life if I can't find out why."

"Dear Yumi," Kate began, but was interrupted by her sister.

"Oh, pooh! There must be a clue somewhere," Leonia said. "There's always a clue in the suicide note. Why, every mystery I've ever read where there's a suicide note, it was a clue. Agatha Christie, Dorothy Sayers, P.D. James—"

"Jasper Killingsworth?" Jacobus interrupted.

"Well…"

"Enough said. As Yumi said, no more fiction."

"I'd like to make a suggestion," Nathaniel said to Yumi. "We'll think about what we can do to help you. Honestly. And maybe we'll come up with something. But if we can't, let's at least make the end of your stay here in London a happy one. So it won't hang over your head forever."

"Ooh, I like that idea," Leonia said. "What did you have in mind?"

"Music! It's what we all have in common. A soirée. After Yumi returns this evening from seeing Mrs. Hunter."

"Poor Mrs. Hunter!"

"And let's invite Branwell Small so we'll have a pianist to play some Corelli trio sonatas with us, and Auntie Leonia can make us a big going-away dinner."

Auntie Leonia clapped her hands.

"What do you mean by 'play with *us*'?" Jacobus asked.

"You and Yumi and me and Kate, if she wants," Nathaniel said. "I'm sure you've memorized at least a few of those sonatas. Haven't you?"

"Of course, I've memorized the damn trio sonatas, but—"

"No buts, Jake," Kate said. "The important thing is to have a little fun. It doesn't have to be Carnegie Hall. I think it's a lovely idea, Nathaniel. And before you create problems, Mr. Jacobus, like asking where we would get the instruments and the music, I'm sure the answer is that Branwell will easily be able to accommodate us in that regard."

"Branwell this, Branwell that," Jacobus chided. "Is there anything our good Branwell can't do?"

"Why, Jake, I believe you're jealous!" Kate said.

Even in his blindness, Jacobus could feel himself blushing.

"Forget it," he said. "What do you say, Yumi? It's up to you."

"I think Nathaniel's right," Yumi said. "It may be we never find out why Hunter killed Natasha, but we're all still alive, and, well, life goes on. And maybe it's best to remember Natasha with a smile."

"That's my girl!" Auntie Leonia said. "Now, have some more toast, dear."

Chapter Eighteen

The parish of Walberswick, population three hundred eighty and a short stretch down the road from Blythburgh, was an unhurried shadow of the Suffolk port it had once been in its fourteenth-century heyday. In recent years, bemusing the locals, an influx of actors and writers, and other artistic types decided it was an in-thing to be attracted to Walberswick's leisurely pace of life, its protected marshlands, and scenic beachy seaside. Audrey Hunter found herself among that crowd, but only in the physical sense, as a server within it, surely not as an equal.

She lived alone, two blocks from the sea. Audrey kept her windows spotlessly clean in the upper storey of a stodgy, nineteenth-century brick house that she rented and worked five days a week scrubbing some of the town's more elegant ones. The income from those labors, plus the modest monthly payments she had received irregularly from her ex-husband, Archibald, had sustained her. With her two boys, Artie and Alexander, having grown up and flown the coop to spread their wings, she could now afford not to work on Saturdays as well as Sundays.

What she was worried about, she told Yumi, was that now that her ex was dead, of course, the alimony would stop. Was there any life insurance? Yes, but she had heard that insurance companies don't pay out if the death was ruled a suicide. Would the government provide something in consideration for his military service? There was so much red tape. No one seemed to have an answer.

Other than financial concerns, she hated to admit it, but it was true: Audrey Hunter felt a sense of relief. Not just for herself that she didn't have to worry ever again about Archie breaking down the door in a drunken rage and brandishing his belt or his fist. But she also felt relief for Archie. For his suffering. Her bruises had healed. His never had, nor could they ever. Except now. Now it had come to an end.

"Can you tell me more about that, Mrs. Hunter?" Yumi asked. They were seated on opposite sides of a round table with a plastic tablecloth in a small but functional kitchen, sunlight and salt air pouring through dancing diaphanous white voile curtains from open, east-facing windows. Yumi would like to have been one of the seagulls whose cawing mocked her for being inside on such a spectacular day. She accepted Audrey Hunter's invitation of homemade blackberry jam and white bread, fresh out of the oven, which accounted for the warm, damp, and yeasty kitchen. A simple pleasure, home-baked bread, and jam. Maybe not being a seagull had its compensations.

"What do you know about Archie already?" Audrey Hunter asked.

"Only from what the publican at The Cock's Comb told us—"

Audrey laughed an unhappy laugh. "Tom Dredge," she said, shaking her head. "That Tom. He is one to stretch a tale. As real as the mop on his head. And always manages to end up the hero, doesn't he?"

"And from that terrible book by Jasper Killingsworth."

The laughing stopped.

"If there were ever two more unreliable sources," Audrey said, "I wouldn't know where to look. What either of them says is the truth are lies, and maybe Tom Dredge is well-meaning, or maybe he isn't, but there isn't any maybe with Killingsworth.

"Let me say first that I had issues with Archie. Serious ones. Like him laying his hands on me and the boys when he came home, night after night, soused from The Cock's Comb. And then him having his little fling with that London hussy."

"Amanda Cooper?"

"It was Amelia Carpenter, and we don't speak her name in this house, if you'll be so kind."

Yumi apologized.

"But I'll tell you one thing: Archibald Hunter did not have PTSD from the Falklands. He was not mentally damaged by that war. He served with distinction. He put his guns away when he came home and, for years, never took them out. He returned to his butcher shop because he was proud to be the fourth generation to carry on the tradition of his family's trade.

"Archie did not murder that woman. God knows who did it if the police don't, but I'll be honest with you: Good riddance to bad rubbish. It was she who ruined our marriage more than anything or anyone else, but the idea that Archie killed her is a fairytale trumped up by Jasper Killingsworth to sell books and nothing more. Nothing more. It wasn't the war that destroyed Archibald Hunter. It was Jasper Killingsworth."

Audrey Hunter stopped herself abruptly and spooned jam on her bread. Maybe she was just pausing with her indictment, or maybe she was finished with it. Yumi went to the window to give both of them time to think. Below and to her right was the village green. Though it was still morning, it was a warm day, and people were still dressed for summer. Mothers in light skirts and dark sunglasses wheeled their toddlers in pushchairs. An elderly bearded gent in a gray smoking jacket and red ascot brandished his walking stick to emphasize what was clearly an important point with a crone, similarly attired. A younger man with long hair and short pants held a piece of driftwood aloft, teasing his border collie, which was quivering with anticipation. Life is out there, Yumi thought, and Audrey Hunter is in here.

Living alone in this little corner of the world, without her children, without real neighbors, cloistered in this little flat, who did Audrey Hunter have to talk to? Who did she unburden her fears and apprehensions to? Maybe that was why Audrey had been more forthcoming than Yumi had expected, and though a total stranger, fate had selected her to be an unwitting confidante. It wasn't a role she was entirely comfortable with. She had wanted only to find out if there was a piece of the puzzle that would enable her to solve what seemed insoluble, but now, here she was, feeling a responsibility to offer comfort to a grieving widow whose husband had murdered her student.

Yumi had only one question left unanswered—the essential question—and maybe Audrey sensed what it was. Maybe that's why she had paused to spread her jam. To wait and see if it would be asked. Should Yumi wait as well? Should she even ask it? If not now, when? She turned from the window.

"Mrs. Hunter, there is one thing that is not a fairytale, and it's what I still don't understand but want to understand. Your ex-husband shot and killed Natasha Conrad in cold blood."

Audrey Hunter sighed deeply. She gently placed her bread and the knife on her plate. She rose and walked to the window, standing next to Yumi. She looked out in the direction of the ocean, which she would have seen but for newer, taller, more expensive buildings that had stolen her view.

Not looking at Yumi, she said, "I don't understand, either. And I'll never understand. All I know is, Archibald Hunter was an honorable man."

Leonia's roast leg of lamb, rubbed with fresh rosemary and garlic, served with buttered mashed potatoes and lima beans and sweet carrots from the garden was a smashing success. They all, even Yumi, ate so much that they insisted upon a break to play music for as long as it might take to regain enough appetite for their pudding: a humongous trifle that Leonia had spent the entire day preparing. "Every going-away party absolutely must have a trifle. I shall brook no argument." The trifle was from a secret family recipe that Leonia claimed had originated with their grandmother, Millicent, and had been passed down from Victorian times. It was so secret that Kate had never heard of it and, though she kept it to herself, suspected that her sister had gotten it from the baking cookbook in the kitchen that was covered with incriminating cream fingerprints.

"I daresay," Branwell Small said, unbuttoning his waistcoat and patting his stomach, "that if we're to earn our keep for a dinner such as that, we shall be here for some time to come."

Yumi, Jacobus, and Kate alternated playing the two violin parts to the trio sonatas that Small had brought. Nathaniel was the dependable continuo player, doubling the keyboardist's left-hand part on the cello. It would have been more appropriate to have a harpsichord, and Small was clearly less at home playing on a grand piano, a square peg of an invention that arrived on the concert scene a century after the round hole of Baroque music had been composed. Whereas the piano has hammers that strike the strings, the harpsichord strings are actually plucked by plectra so that the manner in which the keyboard player presses the keys on the two instruments is entirely different. In the beginning, Small found the challenge daunting, and his unease with the variations in touch evoked grunts of dissatisfaction. It wasn't long, though, before he settled into a comfort level—it was surprisingly quick, in fact—much to the admiration of his friends.

Yumi had her violin, of course, and Small had borrowed the remaining string instruments from Rosalind Langstone and generous members of the Smithson Chamber Players, who graciously donated them for the evening. Because Jacobus, Kate, and Nathaniel were also playing on unfamiliar instruments, they, too, were somewhat less at home than they would have been playing their own. But no one was looking for an "authentic" performance, simply one that would disperse the dark cloud that had been hovering over them for so long.

Though Jacobus's violin technique had begun to show the effects of the ravages of time, a condition to which no musician is immune, his memory remained uncannily sharp, for which he received unanimous kudos. Kate, who had for many years restricted her musical activities to teaching, and Nathaniel, who had switched professions altogether, were the rustiest. Small, though the eldest, was still an active performer whose technical facility playing Baroque music was almost faultless. Yumi, who was at the top of her game as a violinist, was clearly the superior performer of the entire group, though, to be the good colleague, she occasionally chose to play a note out of tune, "accidentally on purpose."

Small had brought trio sonatas by Arcangelo Corelli and George Frideric Handel. It was music that was in equal parts familiar, accessible, and of unrivaled quality. At first, they played nonstop from beginning to end, one after another, pausing or commenting infrequently, except when one of them made an inadvertent mistake or missed an entrance, upon which they would go back to a reasonable starting place and give it another go, or stop for a moment for a sip of an after-dinner glass of port or something stronger. The result was, the longer they went on, as one would expect, the more frequently they had to stop. Small, as the Baroque expert, was the one who most often declared a point of order, offering helpful hints which were at first appreciated, but over time, also as expected, began to grate.

"Mr. Jacobus," he said at one point in the Corelli Trio Sonata in F Major, "would you be kind enough to back away from the cadence?"

"Why?"

"It's fairly standard practice to relax on the resolution. More on the dominant harmony, less on the tonic."

"That may be standard practice," Jacobus replied, "but it's not a law. Besides, don't you think it would be boring to do it the same way every time? Rules were made to be broken. I think, in this case, the resolution is the climax. It's an important arrival, so I say, less on the dominant, more on the tonic."

As they discussed, Aunt Leonia struggled to carry in the huge glass trifle bowl through which you could see layer upon layer of strawberries, custard, raspberries, gateaux, and whipped cream. All told, it must have weighed twenty pounds.

"I'm sorry to take exception, my dear man," Small replied, "but to do as you suggest would have been blasphemy in Corelli's day. It puts the em*pha*sis on the wrong syl*la*ble, you see. The accent must always be on the note of greater harmonic tension."

"Bullshit, Small. The damn accent should go on the note of tension release. The arrival at the tonic is a triumph. Show it off. That's where the accent should go."

There was a crash. Pittums screeched and hissed and raced from the parlor as if shot out of a cannon, impressive for an animal carrying that amount of weight on its slight frame.

"Oh, dear! Oh, dear!" Leonia cried.

"What the hell's going on?" Jacobus asked, aware only of the sound and not the sight.

"It appears," Kate said, "that my dear sister, Leonia, has dropped Grandmother Millicent's trifle on her priceless Isfahan."

"Don't worry, Auntie!" Yumi said. "We'll clean it up."

"We weren't hungry anyway," Kate added, to comfort her. "Were we?"

"Oh, who gives a fig about the bloody trifle!" Leonia exclaimed. "I know what the clue means!"

"What clue? What are you talking about?" Yumi asked.

"The clue! I knew it was a clue! I knew it!"

"Please, Auntie—"

"A clue, sister?" Kate asked, clearly unconvinced, suspecting that Leonia's diversion was primarily intended to distract their attention from the mess on the floor. "And what clue might that be?"

"What Mr. Jacobus and Mr. Small were just arguing about. The accent, of course!"

"You agree with me, then?" Small said, gratified that even a dilettante could see his point.

"No, no, no! Not that! Not that at all!"

"What accent are you talking about, Auntie?" Yumi asked.

"Why, the suicide note, of course! 'I didn't kill her. I didn't mean to kill her. I meant to kill her.' You've been saying the accent on 'didn't,' 'didn't mean,' and 'meant.' You've got it backwards. The accent should be on 'her'!"

"What difference does that make?" Nathaniel asked.

"Why, all the difference in the world! Don't you see?"

"I see!" Jacobus said. "You're right, Leonia. It makes all the difference if the 'hers' refer to three different people."

"Yes! Yes! That's it! You understand!"

"Three 'hers'? Who would the three 'hers' be?" Yumi wondered. "Natasha Conrad must be one of them, for sure. But which?"

"And that socialite in *Butcher of Blythburgh*, Amanda Cooper, aka Amelia Carpenter, certainly could have been another 'her,'" Kate said.

"Who would be the third, though?" Nathaniel asked. "Hunter's wife?"

"I doubt it," Jacobus said. "She's still alive. But that's the right question. Who's the third? Natasha and Cooper are the only two, at least the only two we know about. We'll need to put our heads together to figure that one."

"Auntie Leonia," Small said, "has anyone ever told you that you are absolutely brilliant?"

"Actually, yes. One time, when I was seven. After my very first Stilton soup."

"I suppose that proves it," Kate said.

Not to be outdone by Branwell Small, Jacobus rose from his chair to embrace Leonia and congratulate her for her epiphany.

"Watch your step, Jake," Nathaniel cautioned. "Sad to say, but our dessert is spread out on the floor like a Jackson Pollock."

"I'm heartsick," Jacobus replied. "It was no mere trifle."

"Whatever appetite I had," Small said, "that attempt at humor just quenched it."

Jacobus was inclined to tell Small where he could put the trifle, but considering the important breakthrough that had just occurred, declined to sour the moment.

Pittums, braving the potential peril of another crashing object, cautiously slunk on his belly back to the scene of the calamity. Once confident there would be no further mishaps, he took upon himself the awesome responsibility to singlehandedly cleanse the priceless Persian rug of Grandmother Millicent's trifle.

Chapter Nineteen

What a difference a day made. Yumi had not only regained the energy of youth, she was absolutely hyperactive. The first thing she did upon awakening was call her employer, Harmonium, even though it was six hours earlier in New York, and pleaded to be excused from the first week of upcoming concerts. Wendell Barton, the personnel manager, balked—Yumi was the concertmaster, after all, and it was the opening of the season. There was the gala, too, where she was expected to be there to schmooze with the rich patrons. The conversation went back and forth, but Yumi arrived at the breakfast table imbued with the glow of victory and a healthy appetite.

"Pass the French toast, please," she said.

"How did you talk them into it?" Jacobus asked. "Call in sick?"

"I would never lie like that, Jake."

"Sugar in your coffee, Mr. Jacobus?" Leonia asked.

"Sugar? Blasphemer!" Jake said to Leonia. And to Yumi, "What do you mean, 'I would never lie *like that*'?"

"I told them *you* were sick and that I had to take care of you."

"Me! Sick? I've never felt better. I'm not sick."

"Yes, you are. I could have sworn last night I heard you say you were heartsick. Over the trifle. When it fell on the floor."

"As I said, you've had too much influence on my granddaughter, Jake," Kate said. "You've corrupted her."

"Me?" Jacobus protested. "What are you blaming me for? Who, do I recall, masterminded the plan to steal the 'Piccolino' Strad out of Carnegie Hall and recruited her innocent teenage granddaughter in the effort?"

"Touché, Kate," Leonia said.

"Please stay out of this, sister," Kate said. "It was all for a good cause. As you well know."

"Pass the marmalade, please," Nathaniel said.

"But there was one piece of news that our personnel manager shared with me that really bothers me," Yumi said.

"You were fired?" Jacobus asked.

"Worse. Donald Stroud has been getting death threats."

"Because of Killingsworth's book?" Jacobus asked.

"Uh-huh. He's gotten calls, letters. All anonymous, of course."

"How people can believe that trash," Nathaniel said.

"And then to behave so abominably," Kate added. "What's to happen with Mr. Stroud?"

"The orchestra's granted him leave with pay and has instructed him to remain out of sight."

"From what I understand about Stroud," Jacobus said, "that shouldn't be too difficult for him."

"Not funny, Jake. They don't want the same thing happening to him as what happened to Natasha."

"Not unreasonable," Small said.

"That's simply despicable," Kate said. "Death threats! And even now, when we know the actual killer, they still believe Killingsworth. But what can be done about it?"

"Find Killingsworth," Jacobus said through a mouthful of bacon. "If we can find Killingsworth, we can get to the bottom of this. And by 'this,' I mean everything."

Small, who had become as much a fixture in Auntie Leonia's house as her teapot, said, "An intriguing hypothesis. Explain, sir, why you believe it to be so."

"Think about Aunt Leonia's revelation that 'her' refers to more than one person. If we assume for a moment that Hunter was telling the truth in his suicide note—"

"Which is almost always the case with suicide notes," Small corroborated.

"Then let's say the first 'her,' the one he said he *didn't* kill, was Amelia Carpenter. The fact that the police never found the perpetrator doesn't either exonerate or incriminate Hunter. And it's also a fact that he was never arrested for it and continued to deny he did it even after Killingsworth incriminated him."

"*Especially* after Killingsworth incriminated him," Small added. "Go on, sir."

"The second 'her,' the one he *didn't mean* to kill, could have been Natasha Conrad. Since no one has come up with any connection between Hunter and Natasha, let alone a motive, let's say 'I didn't mean to kill her' meant it was an accident."

"An accident!" Yumi said. "Is that possible?"

"For the purpose of argument, let's say that's true," Kate said.

"Then the question remains—"

"Who is the third 'her'?" Small said.

"Exactly. 'I *meant to* kill her.' By 'meant to,' he couldn't be referring to Natasha because he had just said he 'didn't mean to kill her,' which would make it a contradiction. Nor is it likely it refers to Carpenter, because if he didn't kill her it hardly makes any sense for him to then say he 'meant to kill her.'"

"For the sake of argument, Jacobus," Small said, "it might not be likely, but it is possible. As in, 'I didn't kill her *though* I meant to kill her.'"

"Yes, I thought about that, Small," Jacobus replied, "but it's all about geography."

"Geography?" Leonia exclaimed. "I'm afraid you've lost me."

"I'll show you," Jacobus said. He took his coffee cup and slid it to his left as far as he could, spilling only a few drops on the linen tablecloth. Next, he moved his bowl of oatmeal that he had hardly touched because he hated oatmeal as far to the right as he could.

"Somebody pass me the sugar," he said.

"You said you don't take sugar," Leonia said.

"Just pass me the damn sugar."

Kate handed him the sugar bowl. He slid the sugar bowl until it clicked against the oatmeal bowl.

"Okay," he said. "You see the setup. What does it look like I'm planning to do with the sugar? Sweeten the oatmeal or sweeten the coffee?"

"Sweeten the oatmeal," Small said. "That's obvious. And it can certainly use it."

"Exactly. Now let's call the coffee, 'I didn't kill her.' The oatmeal is 'I didn't mean to kill her.' And the sugar bowl is 'I meant to kill her.'"

"Ah, I begin to see your point, Jacobus. If Hunter intended those two statements—'I didn't kill her' and 'I meant to kill her'—to be related, they would have been contiguous. The intervening 'I didn't mean to kill her,' diminishes the probability of that argument to near nil."

"So, in my humble opinion, to say 'I meant to kill her' can only mean one thing. It means he tried to kill someone but didn't succeed. Which must mean that the third 'her' is still alive."

"Alive!" Yumi, Kate, and Leonia cried simultaneously.

"I daresay you're on to something, here, old boy," Small said. "But couldn't it have meant something else as well?"

"Like what?"

"You've explained how the sugar and the coffee are unrelated. But the oatmeal is not an independent entity. It is subject to the influence of the sugar. So perhaps that while meaning to kill number three 'her,' he accidentally killed number two 'her.' In other words, it was a shorthand way of saying, 'While intending to kill number three, I killed number two by mistake.'"

"Maybe that's why he killed himself," Kate mused. "He made a mistake he regretted to the core."

"One way or the other, there's a number three 'her' we have to find," Yumi said, "and what better way than through Jasper Killingsworth?"

"Exactly," Jacobus said. "That's where all roads seem to lead."

"And how do you propose we do that?" Small asked.

"We're going to go back," Yumi replied, "not all the way to square one, but almost. Jake, what was the name of the receptionist again? The one you flirted with at Stone Cottage Press."

"Isadora. Why?"

"Because you were on a trail to find Killingsworth at that point, and then we got sidetracked. Now we're going to get back on track."

"And what is the next station on the track, if I may ask?" Small asked.

"As I recall, Isadora's predecessor was fired after giving the mail to someone else to put in the post. We're going to pick up that trail and see where it leads, and the first step is to find out who it was that had Isadora's job before her, and then to find out from that person what was really behind her getting fired."

"I second the motion," Jacobus said.

"All in favor?" Kate asked.

It was unanimous.

"Just one more question," Nathaniel said.

"What now?" Jacobus barked.

"Could you please pass the sugar?"

After the table was cleared and the dishes were washed, Yumi called DCI Mattheson. The first order of business.

"Ms. Shinagawa. What can I do for you?" he asked. Though the words were civil, their tone suggested he was leaning back in his chair with his eyes closed, pipe in hand, and wishing it had been anyone other than she who had called.

"My colleague, Donald Stroud, is getting death threats because of Jasper Killingsworth's libel."

"I'm truly sorry to hear that."

"What can you do about it?" Yumi asked.

"You may recall that after we questioned and released Stroud, we made it clear to him that he was exonerated. That was weeks ago. More recently, we held a well-attended press briefing and issued an official statement affirming our conviction that Archibald Hunter was the killer of Natasha Conrad."

"But Donald is still getting the threats! People still believe he did it."

"I'm afraid there's little we can do about what people choose to believe or disbelieve."

"But he's innocent!"

"Everyone is innocent, my dear, except for Archibald Hunter. What do you suggest?"

"Issue a public statement saying that Donald Stroud is an innocent man."

"I regret to say that's not going to happen, Ms. Shinagawa. Not only is it out of the purview of this department to provide personal support to private citizens, it is a futile use of valuable resources to repeat what we have already made clear. Furthermore, it has been our experience that such a statement would put even more of a bull's eye on Mr. Stroud's back. Plus, with Mr. Stroud now in his home country, he is out of our jurisdictional reach, regardless of whatever repercussions there may be. It would be up to American law enforcement agencies to protect him further."

"This is all Killingsworth's fault," Yumi said. "If he wasn't able to write this trash, people wouldn't be in this position."

"I couldn't agree with you more."

"Then shut him down!"

"I wish we could. But, like you Americans, we English have something we cherish, called freedom of speech."

"For your information, I'm not American. In fact, I'm a quarter English!"

"Rule, Britannia."

"That's insulting!"

"My apologies, Miss Shinagawa. Sincerely. It's frustrating for all of us."

"Oh, I'm sure it is. I'm sorry to have bothered you."

"Is there anything else I can do for you?"

"Thanks. Maybe another time."

Since he had made such a splash with her the first go-round, Jacobus was elected by consensus to make the next call, to Isadora, the receptionist at Stone Cottage Press. This time, Isadora wasn't nearly as cooperative. It wasn't exactly the coldest of shoulders she displayed, but the warmth of their initial camaraderie, spawned by their shared detestation of the piped-in music, had fallen well below room temperature.

"And the reason for your inquiry?" she asked when Jacobus asked for the name of the previous receptionist.

He improvised.

"You remember that snooty Brit I brought along with me? The author wannabe?"

"Him. Mr. Full-of-himself. Who can forget?"

"Yeah, him. Well, he's looking for a secretary. Someone to keep his house in order, as it were. He can't even keep track of his appointments because he always loses his appointment book. Head in the clouds. You know what I'm sayin'?"

"I see." She sounded unconvinced. "But they've got a strict policy here. We're not at liberty to divulge employee contact information to strangers," she said, which sounded as much of an improvisation as his own had been. "You know, liability and all that."

"Look, honey," Jacobus said. "First of all, I'm not exactly a stranger. You and I, we're more…soulmates. We could make lousy music together. Hell, I might even be your best friend. Second of all, we're not talking about an employee. We're talking about an *ex*-employee. Third of all, what if the poor gal is out of work and desperate for her next paycheck? You don't want that on your conscience, do you? Fourth of all—"

"All right," Isadora said. "I get the message. You're going to be a pain in the arse until you get what you want. Is that it?

"You're a mind reader!"

She finally laughed again.

"Hold on."

Jacobus waited, listening to a tape loop of some atrocious arrangement of some atrocious British rock group. *What is that supposed to accomplish, making me listen to that crap?* Jacobus asked himself. *To get me to hang up?* To block it out, he began to sing *Là ci darem la mano* from *Don Giovanni* in full voice. Nathaniel called out, "I wish you wouldn't."

"Her name is Halima Danjuma," Isadora said, finally, rescuing him from the tape loop and Nathaniel from Jacobus's guttural baritone. "I never did meet her. In person, that is. So I can't really recommend her."

"Recommend her?"

"In fact, it would be better if you don't even mention my name."

For a moment, Jacobus had forgotten what it was that Isadora didn't want to recommend her for, and then recalled that bit he had made up about her being Branwell Small's secretary. Now, however, Isadora's reluctance piqued his curiosity.

"Why not?" he asked. Was this woman, Danjuma, an issue? A security risk? A liar? A drug addict? A felon? Maybe there was a good reason she had been fired. Jacobus began to wonder if their plan to track down Killingsworth might already be fatally flawed from the get-go.

"Because she's from Nigeria."

"Nigeria?"

"Yes, Nigeria."

"What does she have, Ebola or something?"

"No. Nothing like that. You know what I mean."

It took Jacobus a few seconds to understand "what I mean," which once again reinforced his low opinion of humanity. How could the same race that produced a Mozart also have such an indelible stain of racism? The best of human nature and the worst. It was no wonder that when he and Nathaniel had been in Japan together, tracking down the "Piccolino" Strad, Nathaniel refused to bow to Jacobus's friend and colleague, Max Furukawa, in the Japanese tradition. Jacobus totally understood. His own people shared a history of persecution with Nathaniel's. He already liked this Halima gal, however, the wheels of fortune turned.

"Yes," he said. "I guess I know what you mean. You've got a phone number and address?"

After listening to it once and memorizing it, Jacobus said, "Thank you, Isadora, and may our paths never cross again."

Halima Danjuma lived in a walk-up, fourth-floor flat in a nondescript concrete apartment block in Barking, a low-income suburb in East London inhabited by a patchwork mix of Pakistanis, Africans, whites, and Indians. If "drab" ever became a fashion statement, Danjuma's neighborhood would be near the top of the list of desirable real estate.

Balconies in her building, railed with some kind of cheap, white synthetic material and overlooking a treeless parking lot, served double-duty as outdoor recreation areas with charcoal grills and for the occasional housebound dog, cat, or caged canary and also as makeshift storerooms for secondhand toys, cleaning supplies, drying laundry, and dented bicycles.

Yumi, who had called in advance to make an appointment, knocked on the unpainted, hollow-core plywood door of Danjuma's flat. She had decided to go to the meeting solo, calculating that the likelihood of a successful outcome was greater with a one-on-one than having a group of intimidating and mostly lily-white strangers descend upon this woman. Nathaniel, most assuredly not lily-white, offered to accompany her, but Yumi politely declined, her intuition telling her that it would be better for a first encounter to be between women only. Her visit to Audrey Hunter had reinforced that opinion.

While she waited for someone to answer, she examined a scrawled, multi-colored crayon line drawing on a sheet of white, lined notebook paper of two children holding hands with two adults that was thumbtacked to the door. At least, that's how Yumi interpreted the drawing. It could also have been a still life of a fruit bowl. When she heard two children crying inside the apartment, it confirmed her first interpretation of the drawing and also gave her a warning of what to expect. The word "futility" lit up in bright neon in her mind, not of her own situation, but of this woman's.

A bolt from within slid free. The door, still chain-locked from the inside, opened a notch, revealing a left eye, bloodshot and half-closed, set against a sliver of a deeply dark-complexioned cheek and forehead. If the vignette had been a photograph, it would be in a gallery exhibiting the dire, exhausting plight of immigrant communities. It might even win a prize.

"You are Yumi Shinagawa?" the woman asked.

"Yes. And you must be Halima."

"Wait."

The door clicked closed. The chain was released from its slide bar, and the door reopened. Halima Danjuma was younger than Yumi, though Yumi didn't know how she came to that conclusion because Danjuma looked older than her years. Or how she could tell that Danjuma was now unhealthfully pale even though she was dark-skinned. Or how she knew at one time Danjuma's eyes were bright, her hair had been cared for, that she had once been neatly dressed, and there had once been a smile on her lips. None of these things were presently evident, yet Yumi knew they were once the case.

"Come in," Danjuma said. "The place is a mess. Sorry."

Yumi entered, and Danjuma locked the door, sliding the bolt back into place.

It was a one-bedroom flat. Yumi couldn't see into what was probably the bedroom on the left more than she had been able to see through the one-inch crack in the front door, but the main room in which she found herself had enough chipped and scratched secondhand furniture to classify it as the living room. Cheap toys and games and coloring books and decks of playing cards, and discarded pajamas were scattered everywhere. There was an unmade mattress in the corner by the sliding door that went out to the balcony. Plastic pots of dying philodendrons and coleus sat neglected on the one window sill.

Dirty dishes were the common denominator between the living room and the kitchen, which was the flat's epicenter. The two crying children, one of whom was a girl about four years old and the brother who was closer to two, both light-skinned, were trying to rip a Spiderman blanket out of each other's clutches. The brother was losing the battle and, as a result, was the louder screamer. Upon Yumi's entrance, they both ran behind the frayed couch which, at least, quieted the room.

"I can't offer you anything," Danjuma said.

"That's all right."

Danjuma invited Yumi to sit on the couch and used the sweep of an arm to scatter an assortment of toy trucks and dolls onto the floor to make a space for the two of them.

"What is it you want to know?"

Yumi began to explain that she understood Danjuma had been let go by Stone Cottage.

"Let go! Is that what they called it? They fired me. And I tell you, it was for no reason. And with no notice. I have not been able to find a job since, and I have two children."

"What does the father do?" Yumi asked.

"If I even knew where he was, do you think I would be living like this?"

The little girl behind the couch jumped up and grabbed Yumi by the hair. The brother, still hidden, giggled. Yumi smiled and gently extricated her hair from the girl's sticky Nutella-laden grasp.

"I'm sorry," Danjuma said. "I don't know what to do with them. They are a handful."

"Very playful," Yumi said. "That's a good thing. Why do you think you were fired, then?"

"Because they are racist. That can be the only reason. They think they can treat immigrants like furniture. Especially Africans. They use us, then they dispose of us."

"I was led to believe it had something to do with giving the mail to someone else to deliver to the post office."

"That's what they may say, but it was only because I am Black and African, I tell you. That was just an excuse. Who would fire someone for that? Tell me that."

"So it's not true you gave the mail to someone else?" Yumi asked. Another dead end, she began to think.

"That much is true. I did. But so what? It was just mail. It wasn't a package or special delivery. It wasn't anything valuable. It was just mail."

"Do you remember who you gave the mail to?"

"Yes. I remember because he was the only nice man, even when he had too much to drink. Which was often."

"Someone who worked there?"

"No. It was that soldier who always came around with his war stories."

"Archibald Hunter?"

Danjuma eyed her cautiously, as if she was wondering if Yumi might be trying to trap her.

"Yes, that was his name. Do you know him?"

It was apparent Danjuma had no idea Hunter was either a murderer or had killed himself.

"We've met, once," Yumi said, "but I don't know him well."

"Yes," Danjuma said, weighing how much Yumi could be trusted and deciding a little more information was not dangerous. "Mr. Hunter came to the office every few months with a new short story. We told him he didn't have to do it that way."

"What way?"

"To bring it in to us. He could mail it in. But he said he preferred to hand deliver it. 'Just to be safe, you know,' he said. 'Can't trust those posties.' He was old-fashioned, he said."

"And he wasn't...you know...a mean person?"

"No, not at all! He was always very polite. He always took an interest in what I was doing. In a good way. He didn't put his hands on me, like some of the others who work there. Yes, he is a good man."

Yumi tried to think of what question to ask that might be meaningful. Random facts might not necessarily be helpful, but enough of them, strung together, might form a comprehensible picture.

"Just so I understand, am I correct you asked Hunter to deliver the mail for you?"

"No, that is wrong, lady. I asked no one and would have done it myself. That was part of my job. He offered to do it. And I thought, why not? I could stay here in the office and get more work done. Maybe they would see how hard I was working and give me a raise. But no. They told me I was lazy and had disobeyed their rules. They gave me ten minutes to get out."

Danjuma's tired eyes filled with tears. Yumi found herself wiping her own.

"Did you try to explain?"

"I tried. They would not let me. It was as if I were a leper or had killed someone."

"Had Hunter ever offered to do that before? To take the mail for you?"

"No, that was the first time. And the only time, because I was fired."

"Do you remember what day that was? The day you gave Hunter the mail?"

"Of course. It was the last Friday of last month."

"You sound sure about that."

Danjuma laughed for the first time.

"That is easy. It was payday."

"For you?"

"For me, for people who work at Stone Cottage, for the authors. For everybody. You see, that is when all the royalty checks go out also."

Yumi thanked Danjuma for her time and got up to leave. The two children wrapped their arms around her legs and begged for her to stay. She removed a hundred pounds from her purse and held out the notes. Danjuma refused. "I am not a spy." When Yumi assured her that it wasn't for the information, it was for the children's next birthday, Danjuma relented and thanked her for it.

"Of course! Of course!" Small said, pacing on the same rug which only a day before had been victimized by Auntie Leonia's calamitous trifle. "Follow the money. What they always say in the cinema."

"You're saying that you think Hunter offered to take the mail to the post office simply so he could see Jasper Killingsworth's address on the envelope?" Kate asked Yumi.

"Precisely!"

"And that he spent all that time building Danjuma's trust just so he could get his hands on it?"

"Yes, I'm convinced of it. It was Stone Cottage's most closely guarded secret."

"And look where it got *her*," Jacobus said. "Fired."

"And she's never understood the real reason why," Leonia said. "Oh, dear."

"What's our next step?" Yumi asked no one in particular.

"It's obvious," Jacobus said. "Do what Hunter did and what Small said. Follow the money."

"But how?" Nathaniel asked. "Sounded like your honeymoon with Isadora is over, so you can't just go back to Stone Cottage and ask her to hand you the envelopes."

"Yumi," Kate said, "hell hath no fury like a woman scorned. Perhaps if you called Miss Danjuma back…."

"Yes," Yumi said. "Yes. She may still have access to the mailing list."

"Precisely," Kate said.

"I have a better idea, I think," Jacobus said, "if you really want to be sure to get the addresses from Danjuma."

"And what is that?" Small asked.

"I told Isadora that I wanted Halima's address because you were looking to hire a secretary."

"An artful tale," Small said. "Clever. Not as creative as a gothic musical slasher thriller mystery, but clever."

"You wouldn't want to make a liar out of me, would you?"

"Of course not. But I don't see... Do you mean?"

Jacobus erupted in laughter.

"She could really use the job, Branwell. She really needs the money. You said it. Follow the money!"

Chapter Twenty

"Damn!" Small said upon his return from a certain disheveled flat in Barking. The change in scenery from Belgravia had been striking and depressing. Sitting in the opulent comfort of Leonia's parlor, sipping coffee from antique china demitasse cups, didn't seem fair and not nearly as enjoyable, having just experienced "the other side of the tracks."

"No joy, Branwell?" Jacobus asked.

"No joy, indeed. Not only have I just hired an unnecessary assistant at a usurious rate, I daresay we have nothing to show for it."

"So, would you say, Barking up the wrong tree?"

"That's unforgivable, Jacobus."

Small summarized. In the few minutes after Halima Danjuma was fired from Stone Cottage, she had taken it upon her own initiative to forward a small storehouse of their internal documents from her office computer to her personal one. Her "rainy day fund," as she referred to it. Just in case. In the unexpected event... While in their employ, she also had ample opportunities to overhear negotiations between literary agents and Stone Cottage bosses.

Small's fatal mistake with her had been to show too much interest. When it became apparent that he was anxious to get his hands on the Stone Cottage authors' mailing list, Danjuma put her innate skill and training to good use and bargained for a salary that would enable her to put food on the table for her two children for the foreseeable future. Though she knew nothing about classical music, she insisted she was a quick learner—Small already had his proof of that—and had the office skills necessary to keep Small's

160

musical life in order without him having to give it a second thought. As they shook their right hands to seal the deal, she handed Small the printout of the mailing list with her left.

"So what's the problem?" Jacobus asked. "You've got a secretary, and you've got the list, don't you?"

"Yes, we do. It is a long list."

"So what? We only need one name."

"Yes, but not just any name. And the one we want happens to be curiously absent."

"Oh, no!" Yumi said.

"Oh, yes, I'm afraid," Small replied. "One Jasper Killingsworth."

"Oh, pooh!" Auntie Leonia said. "Give me that list. Surely his name is on it somewhere. How could it not be? After all, he did write all those books."

Leonia snatched the list from Small's hands.

"Oh, dear. Heavens, you're right."

"Well, I don't need to see the damn list," Jacobus said. "Killingsworth is on it, and I know which one he is."

"How so, my dear man?" Small asked. "Clairvoyant, are we now?"

"I'm trying to think like Hunter did when he tracked down Killingsworth. We know Killingsworth has done everything possible to hide his identity, right?"

"Right."

"So I imagine he instructed Stone Cottage not to put either his name or home address on the list."

"But then, how to send him his royalties?" Nathaniel asked.

"Elementary, my dear Watson. His mail would have been addressed to a post office box."

"That's possible, Jake. But that could be anywhere," Yumi said. "Couldn't it?"

"Could be. Doesn't matter."

"Why not?" Nathaniel asked.

"Because wherever it is, he has to pick up his mail somehow. But from what we know about Hunter's movements, we do know it's not just 'anywhere.'

In fact, we know exactly where it is."

"Blythburgh!" Leonia said, clapping her hands. "Brilliant!"

"No, not Blythburgh!" Jacobus barked. "I thought you were a mystery buff!"

"Where, then?"

"Sydling St. Nicholas! Hunter followed Killingsworth to Royal Albert Hall by bus from Sydling St. Nicholas to London, remember? He must have tracked Killingsworth to his home there by using his post office box address, which is what got Small's brand new assistant fired from her old job. That's clear as a bell."

"Brilliant!" Leonia said, clapping her hands once again.

"Good thinking, Jacobus," Small said. "I must say."

" Mind if I channel my inner Watson," Nathaniel said, "and ask if there's a post office box address for Sydling on the list, then?"

"Sadly, I'm afraid there isn't," Leonia said, clearly deflated. "Pooh times two."

"Perhaps because there might not be a post office in Sydling," Small conjectured. "It's a tiny speck on the map. But if there are post box addresses on the list and one of them is close to Sydling, that would indicate we're on to something."

"Aha!" Leonia said. "Cerne Abbas! Yes, Cerne Abbas! I went there once to see the Giant on the hill. It's just a few miles from Sydling."

"What giant?" Nathaniel asked. "Is this another of your 'alien' theories?"

"The Cerne Abbas Giant is a national landmark," Small answered. "He's an ancient hundred-eighty-foot naked gent etched into the side of the hill and backfilled with chalk, which has kept his outline intact over the centuries."

"And no one knows how it got there!" Leonia added. "It could be—"

"He's particularly famous for his rather impressive ten-foot erection."

"Which no doubt was what caught my dear sister's attention," Kate said.

"And many before her," Small said.

"Giants aside, we're making progress, putting all our heads together," Nathaniel said.

"But it doesn't all fit together as tidily as one would hope, does it?" Small added.

"Meaning?" Nathaniel asked.

"Small is right," Jacobus said. "Meaning that even if we assume Hunter shot Natasha Conrad by accident, his confession was, 'I meant to kill *her*.' Not him. Not Killingsworth, no matter how shabbily he treated Hunter. We still don't know who 'her' is."

"Perhaps," Kate said, entering the fray, "Hunter was hoping that by following Killingsworth, he would lead him to 'her.' Or could it be that Killingsworth was a decoy of sorts?"

"Possible," Jacobus said. "Possible."

"So what's next, Sherlock?" Nathaniel asked.

"Something I can't do," Jacobus said.

"Is there such a thing?"

"Unlikely as that may be, yes. We need someone with eyes."

"Just so," Small said. "We shall take turns waiting."

"Take turns waiting for what?" Leonia said. "I'm getting so confused!"

"Simple, dear sister," Kate said. "Following Jake's thinking, once upon a time on a certain Friday, Archibald Hunter arrived at Stone Cottage Press, maybe to drop off another story or to pick up his monthly royalty check. There was nothing new or unusual about this. We know that Hunter was a familiar presence there.

"The overworked secretary, Halima Danjuma, whom he had slowly but surely befriended, was only too happy to accept Hunter's offer to take the other authors' checks, in addressed envelopes, to the post office. When Hunter discovered that the envelopes had every author's name but the one he wanted, Jasper Killingsworth's, he was devastated. There was one envelope, however, that was addressed only to a post office box in the small town of Cerne Abbas. I am betting that Hunter posted the letter, went to Cerne Abbas, and waited inconspicuously until someone came for the check. He prayed it would be Killingsworth."

"And his patience pays off," Jacobus said. "I'm sure of it. Once Hunter sees Killingsworth, with his Special Forces skills, he would not have difficulty keeping his prey in his sights, waiting for an opportunity to gain his revenge."

"Revenge for what?" Leonia asked.

"Obviously, for being falsely accused of murdering Amelia Carpenter and having his life ruined," Kate said. "Please don't interrupt, dear sister. Proceed, Jake."

"So Hunter follows Killingsworth to Royal Albert Hall and attempts to kill him there. But something goes terribly awry, and it's our poor Natasha who falls victim to his scheme."

"Is that now clear, dear sister?"

"I should say so! Terribly so!"

"Therefore," said Branwell Small, "I propose we shall all have a splendid family outing to Cerne Abbas, taking turns keeping an eye on post office box number...what box number did you say it was, Leonia?"

"Let me see. It's number 182."

"And the name? They wouldn't deliver it without a name."

"All it says is 'Current Resident,' Post Office Box 182."

"That would do it, I think. So much of my rubbish mail is similarly addressed. One only wishes they would stop sending it. Current Resident, Box 182, it shall be then, until our dear Mr. Killingsworth arrives to pick up his misbegotten paycheck."

"Since when are you family?" Jacobus asked.

"No need to become territorial, Mr. Jacobus," Small said. "If I have my genealogy correct, neither are you a family member. In any case, I speak only in the general sense, the extended family. I would be overjoyed to be embraced to the bosom of the Padgett clan even a fraction as much as you have been."

"I'm sure you would," Jacobus said. "But maybe 'the Padgett clan' should have a say in how close to their bosom they want you to get."

"Before we get overly stimulated here," Nathaniel said, "what do you say we ask Mattheson first and let him handle this? It's the man's job, after all, and he's got the manpower and the resources. I mean, a stakeout, for us to do...."

"I don't think so," Yumi said. "As far as Mattheson is concerned, the case is closed. And as far as I'm concerned, good riddance."

"It wouldn't hurt, though, would it?" Kate said. "I don't think it's a bad idea."

"I tend to side with Yumi here," Small said. "I know DCI Mattheson. I know what he'll say. That they found their man. That he has urgent, open cases to attend to. That their resources are stretched to the limit. Yes, it's exasperating to us. It sounds like an excuse, but it's reasonable. He would decline, politely no doubt, but he would decline."

"Nevertheless," Kate said, "I wouldn't want any of us to run afoul of the law, especially those among us who are not UK citizens. And then, of course, if he says no...."

Mattheson, behind his desk, removed the pipe from his mouth and carefully placed it on its silver tray, folded his hands, and leaned forward. These gestures, as opposed to when he reclined with his hands behind his head, were not a good sign.

"I would strongly urge you not to undertake the action you suggest."

"And why not?" Yumi asked, who once again took the leadership role.

"Because in the event that you are successful in intercepting Killingsworth—an event for which I estimate the chances are close to nil—knowing his litigious track record, he would file a complaint with the police for stalking and/or harassment and/or any number of other offenses, and chances are that not only would he win, he would be in the right. With you, Mr. Jacobus, and Mr. Williams as temporary visitors to our cherished island nation, I would be remiss if I didn't also remind you that such a complaint could have international repercussions."

"How can I rest, though, when I don't know why this happened to Natasha? And what about her parents?"

"I don't mean to sound coarse, but what about them?"

Before Yumi could express her indignation, Mattheson continued.

"Last year in the UK, we had approximately seven hundred homicides. I understand that such a figure pales in comparison to the US, where there were over fifteen thousand. Nevertheless, for each of those deaths, there are friends, there are loved ones, there are family members, all of whom ask the same question you are now asking: Why?

"Why did it have to be my brother? My daughter? My mother? My best friend? Why? And let me say, it is a question that never is satisfactorily answered. It is never laid to rest. Yes, we, the police, gather evidence. Enough to convict—at least, we try our best to do so. But no amount of evidence is ever sufficient, is ever satisfactory, for those who grieve. Even when we do know the reason! And that is because the real impetus behind 'why' is the desire to bring the dead back to life. And, sadly, that will never happen.

"Thus, my advice to you and your friends, Miss Shinagawa, is to let it rest. You and Miss Conrad's family can take solace in the knowledge that not only did we find their daughter's murderer—thanks in great part, truly, to you and your friends—he was brought to justice more efficiently and with more finality than if he had been arrested, tried, and convicted."

Chapter Twenty-One

I t wasn't too early for a pint and a sad imitation of a pepperoni pizza at the Sir Winston, the pub nearest to Mattheson's police station. The watering hole bustled with the upwardly mobile, oozing with profit-spiked adrenaline from their cyber-connected cubicles of surrounding office buildings, and not yet ready for the commute back to the boredom of suburban domesticity.

Mattheson's oration had given them pause, Yumi included. Not necessarily to abandon their plan. That possibility was quickly dispatched. After all they had gone through, abject surrender was not an option. No, they had merely to refine the plan. To be careful. No stalking, that was for certain. No harassment. Of course not. Nothing to inflame Mattheson's wrath. What, then, was left?

Waiting. Waiting wasn't against the law, was it? Everybody waits, don't they? Wait for friends to arrive, wait for the server to bring their order, wait for the electric company to get back to you. Part of life, isn't it.

So, yes, waiting and, if that was successful, following. What's the difference between following and stalking? No one knew for sure, but they'd know it, certainly, when they saw it. Are we agreed, then? Waiting and following? Good, it's unanimous. That would be their immediate objective.

The main conundrum they needed to sort out was what their goal was. They conceded it was undeniable that Jasper Killingsworth had not broken any laws—technically, anyway—so what could they realistically hope for? What could be the best of all possible outcomes that they could envision? To knock on his door and inform him that they now knew where he lived? That

167

would be a moral victory, surely, but what good would it do? Just to be able to say "boo to you"? He would laugh in their faces. What if they expose him to the public for being a rabble-rousing charlatan? Shame, shame? Would that end his career? Probably not. Mightn't the notoriety even enhance it? Good point. It's possible. Happens with politicians all the time. In summary, any outcomes they could foresee from their plan were not spectacular, but what else could they do to him as, to repeat, he hadn't committed any crime?

"Jake will think of something," Yumi said. "He always does."

This time around, they drove in two cars, Branwell Small's Morris Mini, mirrors repaired, and Auntie Leonia's majestic Jaguar sedan, and booked rooms in Cerne Abbas at The Rosery, so named for its century-old garden, but otherwise a somewhat long-in-the-tooth local B&B that was the only lodging left in town with enough available vacancies to fit all six of them. Upon checking in, they set a timetable for taking turns surveilling the post office and awaiting Killingsworth's anticipated arrival to pick up his mail. Their one advantage was that he would be easily identifiable from the headshot on the back jacket of all of his ghastly books. Even though the photo had not changed over the years, it was not difficult to imagine what his predatory mug would look like ten or twenty years older.

So as not to appear suspicious, they promptly became ensconced at, and soon became regular patrons of, Crosby's Fine Teas & Coffees, est. 1825, next door to the post office, where, soaking up the salubrious early autumn weather, they sat at outdoor umbrellaed tables with at least one pair of alert eyes fixed on the post office entrance at all times. The shop manager was not at all displeased to have a group of international visitors providing a free advertisement for Crosby's famous raisin scones and tea sandwiches on a more-than-daily basis, and made sure their stakeout, which they called "absorbing the local culture," was well-catered to. As long as they supported the local economy, how could anyone accuse them of stalking? If anyone asked, they were in Cerne Abbas on family holiday, and in reality, it almost felt that way.

From time to time, one or another entered the post office, as if on an errand.

Yumi bought sheets of postage stamps for her nephew back home in New York for his British Royalty stamp collection. "What's your nephew's name?" asked the postmaster, delighted that a youngster across the pond would have an interest in his profession and his country's proud philatelic heritage. "Harry William," Yumi said, improvising reflexively, the enterprising nephew having been a spur-of-the-moment product of her imagination. When the postmaster raised a questioning eyebrow, she shrugged her shoulders and said, "The whole family's like that—Anglophiles. They have a bulldog named Winston. Go figure."

From the Crosby's gift shop, featuring the image of the Cerne Abbas Giant—he of the engorged phallus—on every gewgaw known to man, Kate purchased several pairs of Giant-embossed teacups and made several trips to the post office to ship the parcels, one at a time, to various crones back home in Japan. They would never show such salacious things to their husbands, but then again, there were many things they didn't share with their husbands. "Not that it's any of my business," the chagrined postmaster asked, "but why don't you ship them all at once?"

"It is a bother, isn't it?" Kate replied with a sympathetic smile. "But my friends just can't get enough of them and keep asking for more."

Branwell Small's preferred tactic was to assiduously study the flyers of local interest on the post office bulletin board and meticulously jot down the details on a notepad, even though the expiration dates of some of them had long come and gone: *Hedgehog Protection Fund. Holiday Accommodations for Rent or Lease. Bake Sale to raise money for Maud Raspenwall's New Wheelchair! Concert on Saturday to Raise Money for the Preservation of our Beloved Giant. Charming Chapel—gently used—For Sale.*

Small's practiced eyes couldn't help themselves. They instinctively wandered back to the concert flyer's small print: *The Queen's Consortium. St. Mary's Church. This Saturday. 19:00. Local retired amateur musicians. Annual concert. Bach, Handel, and...*he groaned...*Vivaldi's Autumn. Autumn* yet again. Shoot me.

Nathaniel and Leonia also took turns watching, but less than the others. Nathaniel, conspicuous by his color and size, would have aroused suspicion if he spent too much time loitering in the post office. As far as Leonia was concerned…well, it wasn't stated in her presence, but it was agreed she would too easily give the whole game away if she started talking to the postmaster, so she was appointed to the critical post of keeping an eye on things from their table at Crosby's and informing them if she noticed anyone who might be onto their scheme.

Their waistlines expanded along with Crosby's Coffee's coffers as they waited and waited on their stakeout. But, as far as spotting Killingsworth: nothing.

"Of course, he won't come!" Kate declared in the act of spreading apricot jam on her flaky butter croissant. "He wouldn't come in person, would he? If his goal has been to remain anonymous—"

"He would send a go-between," Jacobus said, finishing her thought.

"Exactly."

"We're screwed," Yumi said.

"Maybe not."

Plan number two.

Knowing Jasper Killingsworth's box number, and now, considering the possibility—the likelihood in fact—that he was sending a surrogate to collect his mail, Kate went to the local library, typed a letter, unsigned, saying that "we"—also unspecified with names—have tracked him down and are aware of where he is, and that it would be in his interest to contact them, and that the way to do so is by pinning a flyer on the post office bulletin board, saying, "Looking forward to seeing you soon," and for Killingsworth to name the time and location.

It was now Jacobus's turn. He took the letter to the post office.

"Can you put this in box number 182 for me?" He handed the letter to the postmaster.

"I mean no offense, sir, but someone seems to have taken advantage of your disability."

"Meaning?"

"I took the liberty of looking on the envelope to see to whom the letter is

170

addressed."

"Yes. Jasper Killingsworth. Is it not clear on the envelope? It was typed, wasn't it?"

"Yes, that much is clear. And, of course, I know who Jasper Killingsworth is. Who doesn't?"

"What seems to be the problem, then?"

"Well, it's just that Jasper Killingsworth hasn't got a box in this post office."

"No? But we thought...."

"Doesn't really matter what you thought, then, does it? Box 182, that's Edwina's box."

"Edwina? But..."

"Edwina Deveaux. She's come for her mail every Friday since the Giant was a babe-in-arms."

"Are you sure?"

"Not to sound disrespectful, sir, but is it possible someone is trying to pull your leg? Some of these *You Be the Judge* fanatics are known to be up to mean tricks."

Jacobus didn't respond.

"Do you still want me to put this letter in Edwina's box?" the postmaster asked.

"No, thanks."

The postmaster was kind enough to place the letter back in Jacobus's outstretched hand.

Jacobus returned to Crosby's and broke the news. They had failed again. Maybe it was time to give up. They left their savory pasties and fresh fruit tarts unfinished and slumped back to The Rosery, speaking little. They informed the proprietor they would be checking out the next morning, said good evening to each other, and went to their individual rooms to pack.

Yumi lay in bed on her back, her hands behind her head, staring at the peeling paint on the ceiling, when her phone rang. It was Wendell Barton, Harmonium's personnel manager.

"Don't worry, Wendell," Yumi said, preempting the message she was certain was forthcoming. "I'll be there next week for sure."

171

"It's not that, Yumi," Barton said. "I've got some bad news. Sit down."

"What is it?"

"It's Fritz. Fritz Wohlfart. I don't know how to tell you this. He's passed on."

"Oh, my God!" Yumi cried. She was on her feet, pacing. "How? What happened?"

"He over-medicated, Yumi. It appears it was intentional."

Yumi didn't know what to say. If her heart hadn't broken when Natasha died, it had now.

"He did leave a note, Yumi. It was for his family, of course, but he mentioned you in it. He wrote that he could no longer bear the thought of sitting next to where Natasha had been. That it made it impossible for him to continue. But he wanted you to know that he had faith in your strength to be a great leader and that he hoped he hadn't let you down. I'm paraphrasing. It was kind of rambling. But that was the message."

Yumi stared at her phone. If she deleted the call or destroyed the phone, maybe it would take back what she had just been told. She wanted Fritz to be alive. She wanted Natasha to be alive. She even wanted Archibald Hunter to be alive. Tears streamed down Yumi's face. There were no words, none at all, for her, so she thanked Barton and hung up.

She lay on her bed, convulsed in grief, crying in silence so that no one would hear her through the thin walls. When she couldn't cry any longer, she went into the bathroom and showered, as hot as she could stand, until her skin was bright red. It had long been her ritual to purge herself from grief or fear, to cleanse her soul.

After dressing, she knocked on all her friends' doors and asked them to gather in fifteen minutes in the common room downstairs.

"We're not leaving," she said when all had arrived and explained why. "We need to come up with a plan number three. One that's going to work."

"As much as I admire your pluck," Small said, "if the postmaster is to be believed—and there's no reason he shouldn't be—then we have no Jasper Killingsworth in our midst. He has eluded us at every turn."

The conversation continued in hushed tones, so as not to awaken other guests, with little direction and no resolution. It was only a tribute to Yumi's determination, Jacobus believed, that kept them talking, though the talking seemed hardly more than a courtesy to provide moral support. How far into the night, though, would the discussion need to continue to be sufficient to satisfy her need to believe she had done all she could before throwing in the towel?

With that objective and little else in mind, Jacobus talked and talked, almost babbling at times. It was the least he could do for his beloved Yumi, his spirit daughter. She deserved so much more. But as he talked, his idle words coalesced into an idea, and from there, into a plan. Would it work? Probably not. But he did it for her.

Jacobus suggested that since Stone Cottage mail had been going to Box 182 in Cerne Abbas and that the box belonged to this Edwina Deveaux, and that all other Stone Cottage addresses were accounted for, logic dictated that the old lady, unlikely as it may be, could be the go-between Killingsworth was using. Maybe, he conjectured, since Killingsworth went to extreme lengths not to be seen (or sued) by the public, it was Edwina Deveaux who was, in fact, the perfect avatar, gathering his mail for him and then delivering it to him. Who would guess that a little old lady would be Jasper Killingsworth's conduit to the real world? Maybe if we trailed her…

But if Killingsworth is that careful, Small reasoned, Deveaux, too, might be wary of being followed, just as a matter of course.

" So," Jacobus said, warming up to his plan as it materialized on the fly, "you keep an eye on the Cerne Abbas post office. And since we know that Archibald Hunter had followed Killingsworth to London from Sydling St. Nicholas, Yumi could be stationed there. It's a crummy little hamlet, right? So that if Small follows Deveaux to Sydling, Yumi can take over, Small keeps right on going, and Deveaux won't have any idea she's being followed."

"But couldn't that be construed as stalking?" Kate asked. "I thought we had decided to refrain from pressing our luck."

"Oh, sister, don't be such a Goody Two-Shoes," Leonia said. "Stalking is when slimy, hulky men in trench coats with hats pulled over their eyes pursue innocent young ladies on dark, wet streets in the middle of the night.

At least most of the time. All the books say so."

On Friday, the day the postmaster mentioned that Edwina Deveaux came for her mail, Kate followed every woman over the age of forty into the post office. She had been selected for the job as she was an old lady herself and would receive the least amount of scrutiny. For fear of arousing the postmaster's suspicion, she no longer sent pornographic teacups to her Japanese friends. Instead, taking Small's cue, she perused the bulletin board and wrote down the information in a notebook as if she was seriously interested in any of it.

Shortly after lunchtime, a modestly dressed elderly woman entered the post office. Kate was impressed—if that was the appropriate word—for how plainly attired the woman was. For some reason, she had expected that someone working at the behest of a super-wealthy author would have a more fashionable, if not ostentatious, appearance. *But, of course!* Kate thought, *If this woman is working for Killingsworth, she'd do her best not to attract attention, wouldn't she?*

Walking directly to Box 182, the woman looked neither left nor right. She extracted a key chain from her coat pocket, inserted it into the box's lock, and removed all the mail, which she slid into her purse.

"Have a good weekend," the post officer said to her on her way out. The woman glanced at him and offered a curt nod and smile, but seemed in no mood to socialize.

Kate, following her from the post office, waved to Small, who was seated in his Morris Mini across the street, with the kind of condensed, surreptitious gesture she thought would be appropriate for spies. The woman, presumably Edwina Deveaux, drove off in her car. Before Small started his engine, he opened his glove box to make sure his Luger was there. *Never know when you'll need it.*

He followed her along the country road at a reasonable distance. As the woman drove at a cautious, senior-citizen speed, it was not difficult for him to trail her on the three-mile drive along High Street to Sydling, passing tidy fields of corn and wheat almost ready for harvest and the occasional paddocks of goats and sheep. He called Yumi on his cellphone to tell her to keep her eye out for a vintage teal 1967 Ford Anglia. *Lovely vehicle, indeed,* he thought. *I might have to trade in the old girl for one of those.*

There being very little traffic, Yumi had no difficulty picking up the slow chase, waiting for the Anglia and then Small's car to pass before entering High Street. As the woman's car entered the hamlet's center and then made its way out again, Small diverged, staying on High Street and leaving Yumi to follow the Anglia a few more winding miles, until it stopped in front of a home nestled in the countryside.

The house was set far back from the road on several acres of meticulously manicured grounds. Beds of late-season chrysanthemums were brimming with bright reds and oranges. A low deciduous hedge, trimmed with military precision, bordered the property. The low-slung, gabled stucco house with its massive central chimney appeared centuries-old, with a thatched roof, increasingly rare due to the fortune that fire-wary insurers charge in premiums. Yes, an expensive home, well-loved and immaculately tended. An original Elizabethan cottage, by all indications. A storybook home. Jasper Killingsworth's home?

Yumi did not stop her car as she passed by, trying to appear as inconspicuous as possible in Auntie Leonia's highly conspicuous Jaguar, but slowing enough to glimpse the old woman's back as she unfolded from her Anglia.

That's where the disconnect started. Her appearance did not fit at all with the artistic, groomed bucolic picture. She was dressed in a nondescript, old woolen overcoat, below which extended brown support hose from a bygone era. Later, Yumi would compare notes with her grandmother, whose impressions of the woman matched hers. But, unlike Kate, Yumi saw the woman's destination. If this was indeed Edwina Deveaux, could it be that she was a servant at this house? Yumi had scant seconds to look. The woman looked vaguely familiar. Where had Yumi seen her before? There had been so many new faces and places over the past weeks. London, Bishop's Stortford, Blythburgh, Lucerne, Milan, Salzburg, Berlin, Amsterdam. Countless pubs, restaurants, concert halls, churches. Where else?

Yumi circled through a maze of country roads with a nebulous sense of the directions to backtrack her route to Cerne Abbas, trying to place where she had seen this woman before. She started from their arrival at Cerne Abbas and worked backward in time. When it dawned on her with the suddenness of an alarm clock unexpectedly going off at four a.m., she momentarily lost control of her great-aunt's car, skidded off the winding land, and missed hitting a tree by inches. She backed the car up onto the road and parked, unable to drive again until she had regained some semblance of composure.

There was no doubt. It had been this woman, this sweet woman, Edwina Deveaux, who, with tears in her own eyes, had consoled her outside the Royal Albert Hall after Natasha was shot. It must have been she who had overheard Fritz Wohlfart's lament, "Mahler's ghost had taken his prize." It must have been. There had been no one else.

What did this all mean? Start from the basics. With what they could be sure of. For one, they now knew where she lived. Or, at least, where she delivered the mail from Box 182. Yumi began driving, the countryside a blur, her hands squeezing the steering wheel, struggling to remain under control. It was hard enough as it was to stay on the damn left side of the road.

The last rays of the setting red-orange sun glowed in fiery brilliance before descending below the hillside overlooking Cerne Abbas, where the club-wielding Giant was either protecting or menacing the little town, depending on which legend you'd heard that day. A light evening breeze had arisen, stirring an ancient apple tree's endgame foliage outside the bay window of The Rosery's common room. Of course, Jacobus, half-hidden by a heavily cushioned loveseat, saw none of this, though he could smell the rancid sweetness of apples rotting on the ground. But even if he wasn't blind, he wouldn't have paid it any attention, as his brain had gone into overdrive, and he was little aware of his surroundings. As the debate swirled around him, he remained silent and immobile. He went into a self-induced trance, closing off to the outside in order to allow the inner workings of his brain free rein to ponder this strange new development. Yumi had recognized Edwina Deveaux.

Over the years, Jacobus's blindness, like the worst house on the nicest street, had become an unexpectedly valuable asset. One of the many benefits was the ease of filtering out extraneous distractions, enabling him to focus his mind ever more inward. Some called it his genius, others his Midas touch. In more prosaic terms, it was his ability to reassemble millions of bytes of seemingly random information into a coherent whole. Referring to his talent more modestly, he described his gift as "putting two and two together that any idiot could figure out."

There was one particular knot in the current tangle upon which he needed elaboration in order to begin to understand the greater whole. The web, as he thought of it. Interrupting the conversation that he hadn't been listening to, he asked Branwell Small to tell him as much as he could about the head wound he had sustained at the end of the war. Small started to talk about its strange effect on him. The amnesia.

"No, no, not that," Jacobus said, irritated that Small didn't understand the direction he was taking. "The circumstances. The circumstances."

"Oh, those," Small said. "Not much there, I'm afraid. All they told me was that the shot seemed to come out of nowhere. That, in all likelihood, there was no particular target. That it was random fire. Maybe even friendly fire."

"Or, what about this for a third possibility? That some retreating Nazi had a bad aim, or his target ducked, or a bird shat on his head when he pulled the trigger. But that the intention was to shoot someone else," Jacobus said.

"I suppose that's a possibility. Good for the bird if that's true."

"That's the possibility I think happened to Natasha. Before, we were just guessing that Natasha's death was an accident. From what you just told me, I'm sure of it now that our assumption was incorrect. Hunter killed the wrong person."

"You say you're sure, old man," Small said. "But how can you be?"

Jacobus emerged from the cushions and sat on the edge of the chair.

"Because this is what happened; here's the whole story. We've got a saying back home: 'the whole shootin' match.' It's particularly appropriate here.

"Picture it: First, let's accept that Hunter is the Special Forces soldier who Mattheson said he was, not the common infantryman Tom Dredge thought he knew. This is important, and I'll prove it in a minute. Hunter tails Edwina

Deveaux to her home, just like you and Yumi did, using the royalty check sent from Stone Cottage to Box 182 as his guide. He thought she was going to lead him to Killingsworth's house, just like you did. As we know, Hunter had long dreamed of killing Killingsworth, but now realizing Killingsworth was a woman—"

"Killingsworth, a woman?" Kate asked. "Do you mean he was in disguise? He looks nothing like—"

"No. I mean the photo of Killingsworth is just as much a fiction as his books. The author of the *You Be the Judge* series is a woman. A woman named Edwina Deveaux."

"Jake, that is a bit of a stretch. Even for you."

"*Obaasan*," Yumi said. "Please. Quiet."

"Yes, I know it's a stretch," Jacobus said. "But the truth isn't always what's most likely. Sometimes, not often, it's the least likely. But understanding that Edwina Deveaux *is* Jasper Killingsworth is the key. That was why her identity was such a closely guarded secret. That's how she so successfully remained anonymous. Who would have guessed Jasper Killingsworth was a woman? No one. So, in a way, this truth is the most obvious."

"You may be on to something, old man," Small said. "Now, convince me."

"Look, there have been plenty of women authors who took male pen names: Amantine Lucile Aurore Dupin as George Sand. Emily, Charlotte, and Anne Brontë as Ellis, Currer, and Acton Bell. Mary Anne Evans as George Eliot. Louisa May Alcott as A.M. Barnard. And what's-her-name as Robert Galbraith."

"J.K. Rowling?"

"Yeah, her. The only difference was that Deveaux added a face to it. A man's face. The same ugly mugshot plastered on the back of every damn book she ever wrote. Everyone thought they knew what Jasper Killingsworth looked like. That's what's thrown everyone off."

"Bloody ingenious," Small said. "Not just her. You, Jacobus! Take us to the next step. You were saying that Hunter realizing Killingsworth was a woman...."

"Once Hunter realizes his quarry is a woman, he doesn't know if he's capable of going through with it. He's a decent human being. He has a soldier's sense of honor. He needs to think. Yes, she deserves to die, many times over, for how she had ruined his life. But it was one thing to kill a faceless enemy in the heat of combat. Can he kill a woman in cold blood?

"Hunter must have followed Deveaux ceaselessly, awaiting the right opportunity, if indeed, it would ever come. Day after day, he tracks her. One day, she gets on a bus—sorry, a lorry."

"Neither. A coach."

"Okay, so he gets on a damn coach to London. Why is she going to London? He doesn't know, but he gets on with her."

"Wouldn't she have recognized him, Jake?" Nathaniel asked. "After all, she'd already outed him in her book."

"Two things to remember, Nathaniel. One, he's Special Forces. He's trained to evade detection. Maybe he wears a disguise. Maybe he stays behind her back. Holds a girlie magazine in front of his face. How the hell do I know? Number two, and this is important, she has no idea he's stalking her. As far as she's concerned, Hunter was just one more loser on her list of flunkies she had taken advantage of over the years. Hunter is ancient history. She no more thought about him than about last year's cabbage. So one way or another, he's able to stay on the scent, and she is unaware.

"They get off the train at Victoria Station. He follows her on the Tube to Royal Albert Hall. Why would Deveaux go all the way to London for a concert, you may ask? She's a music lover, that's why, and Harmonium, the great symphony orchestra from America, is performing the magnificent Mahler Sixth Symphony. Would never happen, could never happen in her neck of the woods down in County Dorset. A once-in-a-lifetime opportunity."

"How do you know she's a music lover?" Kate asked.

"Because she was there, of course! And she told Yumi how much she had been looking forward to the performance. She didn't know before the concert that Natasha was going to be killed and that she would end up writing *Murder at the Royal Albert*. That was all a fringe benefit."

"Hmm. Go on."

"What's the 'hmm' all about? You don't believe me?"

"You're making a lot of assumptions."

"When I'm done with my assumptions, then you can 'hmm.' In the meantime, keep it to yourself. Please."

"Since you said please...."

"To avoid detection," Jacobus continued, "while they're still outside the hall, Hunter keeps his distance. He buys a meat pie across the street as he keeps an eye on her, like we all did at Crosby's. He's still not sure what he's going to do, but while he's chomping on his pie, he has an idea. He's been trained to be resourceful. He can save the bag and use it to help conceal the handgun that's in his pocket, should he need to use it.

"He follows Deveaux to the box office, watches her buy a ticket for the Arena, where she'll stand on the floor along with a thousand other music-loving fanatics. I suppose you're going to ask, why does a person as rich as Edwina Deveaux buy the cheapest ticket? That would be a good question, but there are good answers: It's consistent with her old-lady image. With the clothes she wore that day, she would have been a lot more noticed, i.e., observed, if she had sat in the kind of deluxe seats Yumi got for the three of us. As we now know, Deveaux would go to any lengths to maintain the greatest perceptual distance between the humble spinster and the celebrated popular author. And who the hell knows? Maybe it just gave her a thrill to stand in the Arena with fellow Mahler wackos. There's no accounting for taste.

"So, Hunter makes his way through the line, and he, too, buys an Arena ticket. It must have been easy enough for Hunter to get his gun through security. Maybe it was in parts, and he reassembled it. After all, that was his trade. Small can tell us more about that. Possible, Small?"

"Yes, possible. Especially if the gun was plastic. Metal detectors have a hard time with that. Security personnel do their job, but they would have been up against someone who was well-trained in the art of killing. No contest."

"See? Possible. If Branwell says it's possible, then we know for damn sure it's possible. Yes, Hunter is Special Forces. A sniper, maybe. You and I might think sniper is a coward's profession, staying hidden and picking off the enemy one at a time. But maybe Hunter had a different perspective. Maybe he truly believed being a sniper had been an honorable trade. How many lives—his fellow soldiers' lives—might he have saved with a single bullet on the battlefield? So who are we to judge? But Deveaux-Killingsworth had used Hunter's profession to demean him, making him seem like a common criminal. The truth is, Hunter had been a decorated hero, not the murderer of the socialite Amelia Carpenter. 'I didn't kill her,' he wrote. Even when he tried to escape back to his more humble profession, a local butcher, the fictional past Deveaux had trumped up and sold to the world followed him mercilessly.

"Once Hunter gets past security at Royal Albert, he may well have had a hard time keeping track of Deveaux in the crowd, but he finally pushes his way toward her and stands directly behind her, his gun hidden. 'This is no place to execute someone,' he must have thought. Or is it? Maybe it's the perfect place. But the main question remains: With his code of honor, can he murder a defenseless woman? As he stands there, deciding whether the woman in front of him will live or die, he holds the program book in front of him as if he's as interested in the concert as everyone else. Lo and behold, he reads the program notes about the legend of the three hammer strokes of fate in Mahler Sixth! The three hammer blows of fate. Will the third one fall or not? That strikes a chord, if you will, within him.

"Then and there, he decides to let fate make the decision for him: If the percussionist brings down the giant hammer, he will shoot Deveaux with the bang of his little popgun .22 obliterated by the ear-splitting decibels of the hammer stroke. If the conductor, on the other hand, chooses to forgo the third stroke, Hunter will end his vendetta, and the emotional burden he was carrying for years will be lifted. Either way, there will be finality. Finality is what Hunter was seeking.

"What will the conductor decide? Will he or won't he? Yes or no? If the answer is yes, then there will be death. If the answer is no, then there will be life. Strange juxtaposition, this. Usually, yes is an affirmation. No is a thumbs-down. But on that day, at that moment, yes meant death. There was no other choice.

"Think about the scene as we listened to the Mahler at the Royal Albert. A mass of humanity swaying to the music. The conductor, Klaus Kruger, had been coy. He would determine, as the spirit moved him, whether to instruct the percussionist to come down with the life-or-death hammer stroke, but only at the very last moment. Little did Kruger know that it would be life or death in a very real sense.

"So, here we are at the last movement of the symphony. One gargantuan movement of Mahler has followed the other. Remember that the audience on the floor has been on its feet, immobile, in silence, for over an hour. Yumi, Kate, Nathaniel, you remember what the level of anticipation was like. Minutes before the moment of the third hammer stroke, everyone could sense the crowd becoming agitated and unsettled. At the fateful moment, Archibald Hunter sees the percussionist raise his arm. Hunter raises his gun hidden in the paper bag, holding the concert program with his other hand as if he's reading it, preparing to utilize—for what he hopes will be the last time—the special skills which he thought he had put to bed after the Falklands.

"Think about what's going on inside Hunter's mind: a single bullet to Edwina Deveaux's head. *That's all it will take today to make up for her ruining my life.* A shot to the head he could not miss in his sleep. But still, he doesn't know: Yes or no? Yes or no? Over and over again, the internal debate. If no, she goes free, and so will I. If yes, the hammer stroke will drown out the gunshot. No one will hear. She'll fall. Panic in the hall. I leave unnoticed. Liberation. Either way.

"The moment is coming. Watch the conductor. Will his hand go up? Will he give the cue? Life or death? Which will it be, Mr. Mahler? The moment is upon us.

"The hand goes up. The hammer comes down. The shot goes off.

"But just as Hunter pulls the trigger, with all the people in front of her swaying and jumping up and down in their frantic ecstasy, Deveaux leans one way or the other to get a better view of the stage. Unbelievably, Hunter's shot misses Deveaux. Even more unbelievably, the bullet strikes and kills

CHAPTER TWENTY-ONE

Natasha Conrad."

No one in the room spoke. Jacobus let the weight of his story settle in. Only the ending was left.

"It takes a moment for Hunter to fathom what has just happened. At first, he can't believe it. But because of the tremendous noise of the hammer stroke and everyone's fixation on the music and then on Fritz Wohlfart shouting "Stop!" and then on the murdered young lady, no one notices the inconspicuous man who pulled the trigger. Hunter moves with stealth and by instinct, the result of the training ingrained into his head. In the pandemonium, he escapes, but he makes a single mistake. In order to put the gun back in his pocket, he drops the bag and the program with the hole in it. Yes, he escapes. He thinks, forever. But there is no escape from his conscience. He returns to Blythburgh, but his guilt over killing Natasha Conrad, accident or not, eats him up. He shutters his shop and tries to drink himself into oblivion. Shooting himself in the head was a far easier option than going on living."

Jacobus fell back in his chair, physically and mentally exhausted. It was rare for him to speak in paragraphs, let alone chapters, for the same reason he preferred a twelve-minute Vivaldi concerto to a ninety-minute Mahler symphony. The more longwinded one became, the less people wanted to hear the message. At least in his opinion.

But more than fatigue, he was afflicted by a sense of regret for lives ruined, lives cut short, that settled on his soul like a cold, dense fog. And whenever that sense of irreparable loss crept upon him—as it did from time to time—a sense, which, most of the time, he was able to cram into a small compartment in the back of his mind and lock with a padlock, a vision of his lost brother, Eli, enveloped his consciousness and he was overcome with a desire to die.

Why was he alive when others were not? Why was he alive when Natasha Conrad and Fritz Wohlfart, and Archibald Hunter were dead? He had so much more reason to be dead than any one of them. He had evaded death at the hands of his enemies so many times it had almost become routine, and yet... And yet, here he was, and poor Natasha... There was no explaining it. Life wasn't fair—he had said as much in so many words to innumerable students who had lost auditions they thought they should have won. But death wasn't fair, either. No amount of coaxing or cajoling or humoring or sympathy or reasoning or even offers of pastrami sandwiches from the people who loved him and knew him best could ever snap Jacobus out of his profound malaise. Only time could do it.

So when Jacobus finished his exposition of what happened the day Archibald Hunter shot Natasha Conrad, he could no longer speak, and he could barely listen. His faculties, usually so acute, shut down. What he vaguely heard was someone, probably Small, mutter underwater words that sounded like "Brilliant, brilliant." What was he talking about? Brilliant? What was brilliant? Jacobus wondered. It was just the same as always. Failed humanity.

Then someone else, he thought it was Yumi, say that she forgave Archibald Hunter. That, in a real way, it was Edwina Deveaux, not Archibald Hunter, who had been responsible for Natasha Conrad's death.

The question was posed by someone: But what can we do? What laws had Deveaux ever broken? None. At least none that had been proven. She wasn't even aware the bullet was meant for her.

We must do something. We can't let her get off scot-free, can we?

It was Kate, Jacobus thought, through his cloud, who said, "The best we can do is to publicly expose Deveaux's identity as Jasper Killingsworth, leaving her to a life of public shame and endless litigation from the people she has wronged, thus allowing Mahler's mighty hammer of fate to fall squarely on her shoulders."

Jacobus moved his lips. "How literary," he wanted to say, but could not form the words.

But why hadn't Archibald Hunter done that? Nathaniel asked. Why hadn't he exposed Deveaux as Killingsworth as soon he found out? That would have gotten him some modicum of revenge. Don't you think?

There are several possibilities. It was Small, Jacobus thought, who might be saying this. One is that, having once exposed her, it would have then made killing her more difficult, if that was what Hunter eventually decided needed to be done, because it would have required him to come out of the shadows and into the open. He would have surrendered the advantage of surprise and would have made himself an immediate suspect. And there was no guarantee that exposing her would have made a difference, was there? Who knows, the notoriety might even have helped her sell *more* books. And there was a reason with which Hunter was likely all too familiar. Since Deveaux had been sued before, many times before, she'd have the legal resources to counter any negative effects of the exposure. Hunter had none of those resources. He could have ended up once again the victim. So it all would have been in vain.

Or something like that. Jacobus was having an increasingly difficult time following the thread—it was more convoluted than a cricket match, he thought—as he dozed off into an uneasy sleep.

Jacobus woke with a start the next morning with a rancid taste in his mouth and panic-stricken. He had no idea where he was—not just which room, but which country—or whether it was day or night. He was in a bed—that was easy enough to ascertain—but he had no recollection of having gotten into it or why he was still in his street clothes.

In a supreme effort to gather his wits, he forced himself to lie still and listen. A hint of a cool, moist breeze touched his cheek. That means a window, an open window. Conversational voices, too distant to decipher, outside and below whatever room he was in. A slow-moving truck, stopping and starting—a garbage truck? A faint flush of a toilet. Birds chirping, not flying, in one place, stationary, in a tree? What tree? Apples. Yes, he could smell apples. That rang a bell. A bell. Church bells? No, a clock chiming. Big Ben. The full hour. One, two, three, four, five, six...Six. Six o'clock. Day or night? The clues pointed to dawn. It was starting to come back. England. Cerne Abbas. The Giant with the big dick. Edwina Deveaux. Ah, a rooster crowing! Time to wake up. Yes, it must be morning. He needed to hurry.

Still, he couldn't remember everything. Some things were foggy, like where the bathroom was or pieces of furniture he might walk into. Where was his damn cane? He couldn't remember. But there was no time to lose. He lowered himself from the bed and crawled on his hands and knees until he bumped into the nearest wall and then followed that wall to a doorway. The bathroom. He relieved himself and then lowered his head under the cold tap until he was fully awake. He breathed deeply, or at least as deeply as his cigarette-scarred lungs would allow. *Yes*, he said to himself. *Of course.*

Who's to say whether it had been a dream or his subconscious brain working overtime as he slept, but on that Saturday at dawn, once Jacobus had parted the cobwebs, he had his plan, fully fledged. With his sleep had come clarity. Wearing the clothes he hadn't bothered to change out of, he fumbled his way to the other rooms, banging on doors.

It will end today, Jacobus told them, and explained how.

Chapter Twenty-Two

Too energized even to finish her morning coffee, Yumi dashed off to Edwina Deveaux's home, this time, at Jacobus's suggestion, in Small's Morris Mini rather than Auntie Leonia's Jaguar. She parked the car around a curve in the lane where it was hidden by a tall hedge. Approaching the house silently, she slid a note between two bottles of delivered milk on Deveaux's front doorstep, where she would be sure to see it. The note said, "Hello, Edwina. So looking forward to seeing you at the concert tonight at St. Mary's." Yumi signed her name.

"That should certainly shock the pants off of her," Jacobus had said around the breakfast table. "She'll wonder, 'Shinagawa knows my name! She knows where I live! But how?' No way she won't go to the concert to find out the answer."

After Yumi's doorstep delivery, she returned to The Rosery. The rest of the day was spent planning and planning some more. And waiting.

The bracing aroma of roasting Arabica coffee beans breezing in from Crosby's, just down the lane on the corner, had undoubtedly kept many a parishioner awake, if not alert, during Sunday services at ancient St. Mary's Church on Abbey Street. At the evening concert, there was no need for such external stimulation.

The venue was intimate, with a seating capacity of perhaps a hundred, at most one hundred twenty if enough music-loving ectomorphs were inclined to attend. At any other time, Yumi would have enjoyed sitting there, soaking up the unique *bonhomie* that these little English country churches exuded

187

that made one feel part of something timeless, communal, and awesome. In such a setting, maybe she would even have gone so far as giving Christianity a second thought. But not tonight. Tonight was electric. Tonight was for her. Tonight was now, with only one purpose: redress. Mattheson had been right: They had found the man who had shot Natasha. But where he was wrong was that it was Edwina Deveaux, not Archibald Hunter, who had, years ago, pulled the trigger that ended in tragedy. Mattheson had said that asking "why" was futile. He was wrong about that, too.

Yumi placed her purse on the seat next to her to reserve it, turning a blind eye to the program's explicit proscriptions and nasty glances from the more community-minded. Directly before her, at the back of the sanctuary, was an ancient statue depicting the pain and anguish of Christ on the cross. It brought to mind one word: Atonement. *What an appropriate setting*, she thought. *Tonight Edwina Deveaux will most definitely atone for her sins.* She contemplated a second Christian message, this one from the Sermon on the Mount: Turn the other cheek. She looked at the venerated icon thoughtfully, but without blinking. *Not tonight.*

Yumi glanced at her watch. It was almost time for the concert to start. Jacobus had been certain Deveaux would not pass up the opportunity to confront her, to find out what her cryptic note was all about. She looked at her watch again and found a grand total of thirty seconds had elapsed since the previous time she had checked. St. Mary's version of Elizabeth Twitchell stepped forth to make the pre-concert announcements that no one ever listened to. A smattering of polite applause when she finished—one never knew if applause in that situation was expected. As Faux Twitchell departed the stage along with much of Yumi's confidence that Jacobus's plan would succeed, Edwina Deveaux slipped into the seat next to her. Yumi kept her eyes forward, not taking any notice, as if she was paying attention to the evening's proceedings.

"What do you want?" Deveaux said. No hugs this time. No tears. Not even a preamble. Her face was as stony and rigid as the gargoyles in the eaves, and even less sympathetic. Jacobus had been right.

Yumi turned to Deveaux and smiled. "Edwina, so nice of you to come," she said. That was all. She returned to her focus on the stage and said nothing else for the remainder of the concert. As it had been for the past three hundred years, Vivaldi's *Autumn* was a popular favorite, particularly at this time of year. And since it isn't overwhelmingly difficult, so much the better, Yumi thought, especially for tonight's ensemble, an uneven assortment of well-meaning but technically challenged local amateur instrumentalists. Well, it was for a good cause. Dear old Giant with his erection frozen in time. And, of course, there was Edwina. No better cause than Edwina.

Yumi sat patiently throughout, pretending she was entirely absorbed by the musicians' enthusiastic efforts, but mediocre skills as a million details raced through her mind as to what would soon transpire. During the last movement of *Autumn*, she was brought back down to earth for a moment as she reflected upon Vivaldi's sonnet: *"The hunters emerge at dawn, ready for the chase, with horns and dogs and cries. Their quarry flees while they give chase. Terrified and wounded, the prey struggles on, but, harried, dies."* The story of a hunt. And the hunt was on.

When the performance ended, the sympathetic, if somewhat undiscerning, audience rallied to the musicians' defense with a standing ovation. As Deveaux turned to depart, half-believing and fully relieved she was about to escape unscathed, Yumi said, "Before I forget, greetings from Donald Stroud."

"By mentioning his name," Jacobus had predicted, "that's when it will hit her like a sledgehammer that you know she's Jasper Killingsworth. She will be in shock. Before she has a chance to recover, that's when you say—"

"Please join me for tea, Edwina. We have a lot to talk about."

"Deveaux won't be able to refuse," Jacobus had said. "She'll be desperate to find out what it's all about. How much you know. No one has ever gotten this close to the truth. Ever."

As Deveaux had become immobilized, Yumi took her arm in her own, accompanied by a beaming smile for an old friend. For the first time, Yumi noticed Deveaux was dressed in the same outfit that she wore outside the Royal Albert and also when she emerged from her car in front of her house. The long, gray wool coat. Maybe it was not so much an outfit as her default disguise. *What, no red poppy for me tonight, Edwina?* Dazed, Deveaux allowed herself to be sleep-walked toward Crosby's Fine Teas & Coffees, with Yumi continuing to chat in an amiable tone.

"Dearest Edwina, tell me about your poor daughter who died," Yumi said.

"What daughter? I never had a daughter."

"I didn't think so."

"Then why do you ask an absurd question like that?"

"Because that's what you told me outside Royal Albert Hall. To gain my sympathy. To get me to trust you."

They walked the remaining distance to Crosby's in silence.

Nathaniel, Leonia, and Kate had left the concert immediately after the last note, forgoing their show of appreciation for the musicians' efforts in order to beat the crowd to the coffee shop. By the time Yumi arrived with Deveaux, Nathaniel was already seated at one table, and Kate at another. Leonia sat at a table in between the two, and as soon as Yumi arrived with Deveaux, Leonia rose and moved to sit with Nathaniel. Yumi, taking Leonia's vacated seat, sat opposite Deveaux, with her back to her grandmother, Kate.

"You have to remember," Jacobus had reminded everyone, "that until the moment Deveaux read in the news that it was Archibald Hunter who killed Natasha, she was as in the dark as everyone else. She did not know who had done it. All she wanted to do was to capitalize on the crime and write a book about it ASAP. So she took a guess and fingered Stroud because, at first, he was the easiest one to pin it on. In fact, he was the only one. And, on the opposite side of the coin, remember this: If Stroud was the first person in the world she would have guessed, Archibald Hunter was the last person. But, the second she read in the papers that Mattheson said it was Hunter who had shot Natasha, she would have realized immediately that Hunter's bullet had been intended for no one other than her."

"What can I get you, Edwina?" Yumi asked. Deveaux was unresponsive. Obstinate or in a stupor, it was hard to tell. Her lower jaw, which Yumi now noticed had a few white hairs sprouting from her chin, slid from side to side, pulling the wrinkles in her gray cheeks along with it. Her eyes alternately widened and squinted in apparent confusion, as if she couldn't decide whether to act the innocent or go on the attack.

Yumi, her smile as gentle as ever, gave Deveaux a gentle squeeze on her forearm and asked her again, ever more sweetly. "Coffee or tea? Choose one, Edwina, or the customers might begin to get suspicious. You don't want that, do you?"

"Tea, then," Deveaux said, wiping her chin. "Whatever." Was that drool?

Yumi ordered two Earl Grey teas. With milk, please. No sugar, thank you. The post-concert crowd began to trickle in, the excitement of the performance breezing in with them, bubbling with cordial conversation.

As they waited for their teas, Yumi prepared herself to begin the litany, telling Deveaux everything they knew. Everything. She had spent all afternoon memorizing it. But no drama. That wouldn't do. In a quiet voice. Two friends, a sweet old lady, and a smiling, young Japanese companion. Two tea-loving cultures brought together over their common love.

The teapot arrived. "Ah! Here we are!" Yumi said. She poured for them both.

"Mmm. Don't you just love that bergamot?" she asked. She inhaled deeply. She was the maestro, and it was the moment for the downbeat.

Yumi began her lengthy narrative. By the time she finished, the teapot was empty, and the coffee shop was full.

"And so, Edwina, we know that Archibald Hunter's shot was meant for you. On the symphony's third hammer stroke. But, at the last moment, you moved, and he missed his target."

Deveaux, in a rare candid reflection, recalled, "Yes, the third hammer stroke. I leaned to my right to get a better view. I had to. The bloody poofter in front of me wouldn't stand still."

"To be very honest," Yumi said in disgust, "I'm doubly sorry Hunter missed." The comment seemed to rouse Deveaux into the present.

"What is it you want?" she asked. There was no missing the hostility.

"Me?" Yumi replied. "You mean, like money? You think I'm extorting you?"

"What else, if not that?" Deveaux said.

"Edwina, I don't want anything."

Did she see Deveaux's shoulders relax?

"But," Yumi said, "though I don't want anything personally, the public has the right to know everything. Who you are. The innocent lives you've destroyed: Donald Stroud's and Fritz Wohlfart's and Archibald Hunter's and"—she struggled mightily with the final one—"Natasha Conrad's and her family. I've prepared a list of all the verdicts you got wrong, and I predict that even the ones you've settled with out of court will find a way to circumvent their NDAs and sue the pants off you for libel. You may not have broken any laws, but you've ruined too many lives to get away with what you've done. I hope, Edwina, that exposing you will ruin *your* life."

Deveaux attempted a laugh. There was no humor in it. Perhaps it was merely a release of tension. It was the kind of laugh one hears from someone who had expected a much worse outcome when you receive probation and community service instead of ten years. Relief.

At their morning powwow, Kate had asked, "What if Deveaux shows contrition at this point? Can someone truly be that heartless?"

"You mean a come-to-Jesus moment?"

"Of sorts, yes."

Jacobus got down on his knees (with some difficulty) and clasped his hands together. Imagining the sound of Deveaux's voice, which he had never heard, he wailed, "Oh, please, please, please forgive me! Oh, thank you for letting me see the light! I've been *soooooo* evil, but now and henceforth, I shall be good! Hugs?"

"I take it you don't think that will happen."

"Help me up, and I'll tell you what I think. After what she's done to innocent people in all those books for so many years, I'd bet my worthless soul there's not a jot of remorse in Deveaux's makeup. The only concession you'll get from her is she'll try to make you a deal. That's when she'll be dangerous, because she's a pro at that game."

With that assessment in mind, Yumi was prepared for intransigence, and was not disappointed.

"You won't get away with it, you know," Deveaux said. "No one will believe you. Why should they? Look at me. I'm just a sweet old lady living in the countryside. You're a high-powered, jet-setting, pushy musician who's lashing out, trying to get revenge for your little student's untimely death, which, by the way, you acknowledge I had nothing to do with. I hate to break this to you, dear, but I've been dumped on with a lot worse manure than what you've got, and came out the other end smelling like roses. But, if it will make you feel better, tell me what you want. Maybe we can come to an accommodation."

"If she fights back, Yumi, go to the nuclear option," Jacobus had said. "You've got the right to push the red button, if anyone does."

With no hesitation, Yumi removed an item from her purse. That was the signal for Nathaniel, Leonia, and Kate to be on alert.

"As I said, I don't want anything, Edwina. In fact, I have something for you."

She laid a small, brown paper bag in front of Deveaux.

"What's that?"

Yumi brushed an imaginary, errant hair off her face. That was the sign for action. Go!

Leonia bounced up out of her chair, shamelessly showing off the mink stole wrapped around her shoulders—she had to do something to get everyone's attention—and brandishing a familiar paperback in her hand.

"Look what I've got, everyone!" she chortled. *"Murder at the Royal Albert!"* Customers looked up, their focus, for a moment, pried away from their raisin scones and berry tarts and custard eclairs. Noël Coward could not have directed a more effective freeze frame.

"And wouldn't you know, here's Jasper Killingsworth!" Leonia persisted, pointing at Edwina Deveaux. "Would you be a sweetheart and autograph it for me? Does anyone have a pen I could borrow?"

"I don't know what you're talking about," Deveaux said, trying to hide in full view. Her head spun in every which direction, almost like afflicted Regan in *The Exorcist*, gauging the crowd's level of credulity.

"Of course you do, dear! Listen, everyone! I've a secret to unveil. Jasper Killingsworth *is* our very own Edwina Deveaux from Sydling St. Nicholas! Isn't that a lovely surprise?"

That shocking revelation produced a noticeable if mixed response: disbelief, denials, laughter, some *"really!"*s. But none of the reactions in the crowded café were the one Deveaux was hoping for: lack of interest.

"I'm leaving," she said.

"Don't you want your going-away present?" Yumi asked as Auntie Leonie continued to flail her book and her fur. This was the critical moment. Do or die, Jacobus had said. Do or die. Be convincing. But not anxious.

"What is it?" Deveaux asked for the second time.

"Take a look," Yumi said.

Deveaux put her hand in the bag. She removed a small revolver. A Luger. Would she try to use it? Yumi had asked. Would she shoot me?

"It doesn't really matter," Jacobus had said. "As soon as she takes it out of the bag, her fate is sealed. Anyway, Small will make sure there ain't any bullets in it."

Deveaux looked at the gun in her hand in confusion. What was this all about, she must have been thinking. In that split second, two things happened simultaneously. Kate Padgett stood up with her teacup in her hand, and Nathaniel got ready to press the icon for a special ringtone on his phone.

With Deveaux still holding the gun, trying to make sense of a situation that was beyond her comprehension, Leonia looked at her and screamed a convincing "No!" at the top of her lungs. Yumi dove to her left. Nathaniel discreetly pressed the icon, which reproduced a remarkably authentic-sounding gunshot blast. Kate released her teacup, which shattered on the ground.

"Oh, my God!" Kate cried. "She tried to kill me!"

"Someone call the police!" one of the customers yelled. Others ran to aid Kate, who appeared terribly shaken by the dramatic turn of events.

In the pandemonium, Deveaux dropped the gun on the table and raced out of the coffee shop into the night. With everyone's attention fixed on the fleeing woman, or on Kate feigning a Jane Austen swoon, or on Auntie Leonia, who continued hooting and hollering, "Oh, dear! Oh, dear!" Yumi inconspicuously slid the gun and bag back into her purse with the dexterity of a world-class violinist.

Deveaux bolted toward her teal Ford Anglia as fast as her elderly, brown-stockinged legs could carry her. Jacobus and Small had easily identified her car, parked earlier in the evening three short blocks from the church. There they had maintained a comfortably obscure vigil a few feet away, under a darkening evening sky and beneath the awning of Markham's Fresh Fish Market, from time to time checking the hour. The two had been engaged in a discussion of the stark dissimilarities in violinistic style between Antonio Vivaldi, a Venetian, and his contemporary, Arcangelo Corelli, the Roman, when Small spotted Deveaux careering in their direction.

He gave Jacobus a pat on the rump.

"Showtime, old man," Small whispered. "Are you totally sure you want to do this? It could be dangerous."

"What is it you limeys say? Into the breach?"

"Very well then. What is it that you Yankees say? Break a leg." He gave Jacobus a small shove forward, perhaps a little more forcefully than was absolutely necessary.

Deveaux tore open her car door. As she got in, Jacobus approached the back of the vehicle. When he heard her turn on the ignition, he slammed his arm against the car's boot and fell heavily to the ground.

"*Achhhhh!*" he cried.

Deveaux revved her engine and raced from the scene. Jacobus writhed, moaning in theatrical pain. He had even pre-broken his cane for added dramatic effect.

"Help!" Small cried. "My friend's been hit by that car!"

A young Black woman with a Nigerian accent stopped pushing her two toddlers in a pram and yelled, "I saw it! I saw it! Wasn't that Edwina's car?"

Another pedestrian joined in. "I saw it, too! A hit-and-run."

And another. "And to a poor blind man! Horrific!"

"How could she do such a terrible thing?" the woman said, in profound disbelief, before slipping quietly off into the night.

"That secretary of yours is worth her weight in gold," Jacobus whispered, lying on his back.

"And a return train ticket," Small replied.

Chapter Twenty-Three

"**B**rilliant scheme, old man," Small said. "Absolutely brilliant. Ha-ha! I think it's done the trick!"

Small, with typical erect posture, sat in the window seat of Auntie Leonia's parlor, nattily dressed for a special occasion. Late morning sun shone through the window, illuminating the stack of newspapers by his side as if it was heaven blessing the Gutenberg bible. He held open one of the papers, thus prompting his comment.

"Whatever," Jacobus replied. He lay on his back on the settee, with bare feet hanging over the edge. His buttocks were still sore from his overly enthusiastic pratfall the night before. Pittums lay, purring, on Jacobus's chest in the wrong direction, its tail making a tickling mustache in Jacobus's face.

"Oh, do tell!" Leonia piped up, ushering in a tray of freshly baked raisin scones with clotted cream and a pot of jasmine tea.

"The tabloids are absolutely skewering Deveaux," Small said. "All of them. *The Mirror, The Guardian, The Daily Mail, The Sun, The Daily Express.* Here are a few headlines: *'Verdict: Edwina Deveaux!' 'Killingsworth Exposed! And He's a She!' 'You Be the Judge: Guilty!'*"

"I do like that one," Leonia said.

Nathaniel sat at the coffee table with Yumi, where, appropriately, they were drinking coffee. "Give us the gist?" he asked.

"Gladly," Small said. "The gist, as you say: Deveaux, as expected, protested adamantly to the police that she hadn't fired the gun or run over Jacobus, but, of course, everyone in the coffee shop saw her with the gun in her hand

and heard the shot go off, and everyone saw and heard her knock Jacobus off his feet before speeding off, so all of her denials have fallen on deaf ears."

"Which direction are the tabloids leaning? With her or with the customers?"

"As you would expect. Less interested in her denials than in the sensational story," Small said. "As our Mr. Jacobus predicted."

"The papers say that the police are continuing to search Deveaux's house for the gun. She claims she doesn't know where the bloody thing is since it wasn't hers. She says she left it on the table at Crosby's, but none of the many witnesses corroborated her claim."

"Thanks to Leonia," Kate said.

Leonia did a slow, dignified curtsy in the most proper English manner.

"Deveaux doggedly insists she'd been framed," Small continued. "She showed the police the note Yumi left on her doorstep. She said that will prove it was a setup."

Everyone in the parlor looked at Yumi. She shrugged.

"Prove? Prove what?" Yumi said with wide-eyed innocence and a hint of a smile, which was nice to see after such a long time without one. "I don't know what she's talking about. If the police ask me, this is what I'll tell them: The note I wrote said, 'So looking forward to seeing you at the concert tonight at St. Mary's.' It was my response to her asking me if I was planning on going, from when she bumped into me in Cerne Abbas. Such a small world! No, sir, I don't remember exactly where or when. I'm surprised she doesn't remember, either.

"And I *was* looking forward to seeing her, wasn't I? After she was so kind when she consoled me after the Mahler concert in London. That's why I left her that note on her doorstep. It was the least I could do. And wasn't it kind of her to invite me to Crosby's after the concert? Oh, the paper bag? No, sir, I have no idea why Edwina brought it, until she pulled the gun out, of course. No, I have no idea what happened to it. I wish I did. But don't you think it's striking how similar it all was to Archibald Hunter's murder of Natasha Conrad? The one she wrote about in such detail in *Murder at the Royal Albert?*"

"No doubt that's what must have given her the idea," Kate said, playing along.

"And it just gave me the creeps. Me thinking she was such a sweet old woman."

"Nope!" Jacobus said, without moving from his horizontal position. "Nope, nope, nope! You just screwed up, Yumi. They'll throw us all in jail if you say that. Haven't I taught you how to lie better than that?"

"What do you mean?" Yumi asked.

"It was Donald Stroud who Deveaux incriminated. She didn't know about the paper bag until it was in the news after Mattheson announced that Hunter had killed Natasha. And that was *after* she wrote *Murder at the Royal Albert*."

"Ooh. Right. Sorry about that. How about this: After reading all about it in the papers, then."

"That's better. Use your head."

"And what would you say if the police asked what Madame Deveaux's motive might have been to kill you?" Small asked. "After all, she hardly knew you."

"I would say that if the police can't even always be sure of a murderer's motives, how could I? Didn't DCI Mattheson himself say that 'why' is often an unanswered question?" Yumi replied, having rehearsed all this thoroughly in her head, just in case. "But if I *had* to take a guess, I'd say this: Edwina Deveaux, aka Jasper Killingsworth, and Archibald Hunter were both colleagues at Stone Cottage Press. Hunter murdered Natasha Conrad, my student, for a motive we may never learn. But for some reason, it made Edwina believe she needed to finish Hunter's job and kill Natasha's teacher. Me."

"So you'd say Edwina and Hunter were in cahoots? Co-conspirators. Is that it?"

"Let me be devil's advocate for a moment," Jacobus said. "That sounds like bullshit to me?"

Yumi was unfazed. "But, sir, I can't think of any other possibility. Can you? She must have been planning to kill me for some time. God knows why."

"Good thing you ducked," Nathaniel said.

"Yes," Yumi agreed. "I literally dodged a bullet. Thank God it missed my dear grandmother as well."

"The papers are saying that if there was any doubt about her guilt, the hit-and-run confirms it," Small said.

"Even if she hadn't fired the gun," Kate said, "I would imagine she'll be in serious trouble for the car accident."

"You don't have to imagine," Small said. "The police have not taken kindly to Miss Deveaux's conduct. She is being charged on an impressive list of counts. Her career and her reputation would seem to be—as Mr. Jacobus might say—flushed down the toilet."

"And Jake, it's a miracle you were not badly injured," Kate said, tongue firmly in cheek. "You could have been killed."

"Yeah, that's what the doc said when they took me to the ER," Jacobus said. "Miracle. Goddamn miracle," he chuckled, rousing Pittums from his stupor. The cat slid off Jacobus's chest, flopped with a thud onto the floor, vocalized the standard feline objections to being disturbed, and lumbered into the kitchen.

Yumi's phone rang. It was DCI Mattheson. Like everything else, the call was not unexpected.

"I see you had an eventful visit to our pastoral English countryside," he said.

"Much more eventful than we planned on," Yumi said, her spiel readied.

"I want to let you know, I have a firm idea of what might have transpired," he said, "the speculations of the tabloids notwithstanding."

"Do you?"

"Yes. Anything with the fingerprint of Branwell Small leads me in such directions. In fact, I had considered sending Littlebank down there to investigate. Pranks can be dangerous, you know."

"Pranks?"

"Yes, pranks. Disguised as sting operations. We take a dim view of sting operations. You see, we have laws in this country. Have you ever heard that term?"

"Yes, of course."

"And our laws weren't made to be toyed with, regardless of the perceived justification."

"I'm not sure I understand what this conversation is about."

"I'm sure not," Mattheson said, trying unsuccessfully to hide the sarcasm. Or maybe he wasn't trying at all. "But I just wanted to let you know I eventually decided against pursuing one."

"One what?"

"One investigation."

"I see." Yumi waited for the next shoe to drop. She was not going to take the bait and ask why or say thank you.

"Yes. Quite. Well..." He hesitated. Unlike him. Did she hear him tap his pipe? "Well, I'm glad to hear you're all safe."

That surprised her. There would be no other shoe. "Thank you."

"Have a pleasant journey back home, Ms. Shinagawa. Good-bye."

They finished their coffee, tea, and scones, and it was time for farewells. Yumi's departure was set for late the next day to return to work in New York. Jacobus and Nathaniel would depart the day after, heading for Jacobus's home in the Berkshires—the American Berkshires. Kate would remain one more week with her sister before returning to the mountains of Kyushu, Japan's southern island. It was unclear when they would all see each other again, if ever.

Branwell Small was the first to say his goodbyes.

"We certainly have made a jolly good team," he said. "Sorry that we have to break up the band, in a manner of speaking."

"Don't get too bent out of shape," Jacobus said. "All bad things have to come to an end."

Yumi suggested a future musical collaboration.

"I'm not on your level, though, am I?" Small demurred, his modesty only being a touch false.

Yumi insisted it would be her pleasure, to which Small responded with a polite, respectful bow.

"And we *must* plan a reunion!" Leonia said. There was general agreement, but everyone knew it was a symbolic gesture.

"Well, I'm off then," Small said. He departed into the brilliant sunlight of an autumn day in England.

Chapter Twenty-Four

That evening, Auntie Leonia fluffed the embroidered cushion of the piano bench and began the first strains of "Roses of Picardy" while she sang, not the least bit concerned that her singing was as out of tune as the instrument on which she was accompanying herself. Nathaniel said, "I think I'll take a stroll around the block." Jacobus decided it might be a good idea for him to join Yumi, who was going to her room to pack, though both of them knew he would be useless helping her. Yumi's phone rang just as she placed her foot on the first step of the stairway.

"Jake, it's for you," she said.

"Tell him to call back another time."

"He's a her, and she says it's important. I'm not in a hurry. It's okay."

Yumi handed Jacobus the phone.

"Can you tell Auntie to put a sock in it for a minute?" he whispered to her. "Hello. Who's this?" Jacobus demanded into the phone.

"My name is Claudine McConnell."

"That's nice."

"I am Claudine," she repeated, as if he should know her.

"I am Spartacus," Jacobus said. "What the hell do you want?"

"Branwell Small! I'm Branwell Small's Aunt Claudine!"

Ah! The daft one, Jacobus thought. Small warned us about her.

"I see," Jacobus said. He changed his tone. Sweet as sugar. "And what may I do for you, Aunt Claudine?" *I'll give her ten more seconds, and then I'll hang up.*

"Is Branwell there?"

"No. Why should he be? Don't you have his phone number?"

"That's the point. I don't want him to know. I must meet with you immediately," she said. "It is vitally urgent."

"Vitally urgent? Or urgently vital?"

"Please, you have no idea how important this is."

"If I may ask, how did you get Ms. Shinagawa's number, Aunt Claudine?"

"From Branwell, of course. Who got it from Rosalind Langstone, who got it from Miss Shinagawa herself at the concert last month. Now, sir, will you stop patronizing me for a moment? I have taken the train to Victoria Station, which is my present location. Tell me exactly where you are, and I will be there in fifteen minutes. I must see you!"

She didn't sound totally off her rocker. Jacobus considered what else was on his agenda, which was nothing, plus the prospect of having to listen to more of Auntie Leonia's piano playing, and decided.

He said, "Okay, Mrs. McConnell, I will await your arrival with bated breath," and provided the address. "I'm starting to hold it right...now!"

He hung up and handed the phone back to Yumi.

"Sounds interesting," she said. "Do you want me to stick around?"

"Only if you want. Probably wants a donation to the concert society."

"In that case, I'll go pack."

The doorbell rang in the middle of Leonia's rousing rendition of "Pack Up Your Troubles in Your Old Kit Bag."

"Cease and desist," Jacobus ordered Leonia. Kate went to the door and ushered Claudine McConnell into the parlor. To Jacobus's ear, McConnell was either very aged or very infirm, because she moved with very slow, halting steps, sliding her shoes along the floor. Of course, she was. She was old! Branwell was pushing seventy, and this was his aunt. She was probably in her nineties or even her hundreds. As she shuffled in, Jacobus also heard the rhythmic tapping of a walking stick on the entrance foyer's marble floor. *She's like me,* Jacobus realized. *She's blind.*

Kate sat McConnell on the settee next to Jacobus.

"May I get you a cup of tea, Mrs. McConnell?" Kate asked.

"Yes. That would be lovely. Thank you."

"And you must be Mr. Jacobus," she continued.

"How did you know I was sitting here?"

"Because I heard you shift your bloomin' arse. How else do you think I knew?"

Jacobus guffawed. He had rarely been on the receiving end of underestimating blind people. It gave him an immediate appreciation of his visitor.

"Well, you got me there, Mrs. McConnell. Sorry I gave you a hard time on the phone."

"Oh, no bother. I'm used to it. People think us old, blind folks are a sandwich short of a picnic basket, but I suspect you and I will be able to see eye to eye. Don't you?"

"I don't see why not."

"I wasn't always blind as a bat, either. It came slowly, so I got used to it. By the time it was all gone, and I had to admit I couldn't see the side of a barn, I didn't miss it a whit, really."

"Mine happened overnight." Jacobus almost never talked about his blindness. Though he often sang the praises of the many advantages of being blind, he also knew that others considered it a frailty, and so he had built a tough, protective shell around his condition. "Big deal. That's life."

"I understand," McConnell said.

"Do you?" He had had enough introspection for the day. "You said you had something urgent to tell me."

Jacobus heard footsteps on the stairway. Yumi was back.

"We're in here," Jacobus said.

"Oh," Yumi said. "I'm sorry to interrupt."

"This is Claudine McConnell. Small's aunt."

"Nice to meet you," Yumi said. "Can I get anyone some tea?"

As if on cue, Kate returned from the kitchen with tea and yet another round of scones, and Nathaniel from his walk.

Jacobus cleared his throat. "Everyone, please sit down. Claudine has requested this meeting. I'd really like to get this over with, if you don't mind."

"Thank you," McConnell said. "Well, to begin with, let me say that dear

Branwell has been like a member of our family."

"Like?" Jacobus asked. "What do you mean, 'like'?"

"I'm getting to that. You'll just have to be patient, please. You're quite the impatient young man, aren't you, Mr. Jacobus? I have to tell this in a certain order.

"Yes, it is true that my sister, Louisa, and her husband, Harvey Small, had a son, Branwell. It is also true that he enlisted at age sixteen to enter the infantry and serve in Germany."

McConnell stopped.

"May I have that tea, please?" she asked.

"Thank you," she said after an interval of fortifying, if noisy, sipping.

"I'm sorry. This is very difficult. I've never told this to anyone. Never."

No one said anything. Jacobus waited.

"After four months, Branwell was wounded. A grenade exploded at his feet. It was very serious."

"And that's how he got amnesia," Jacobus prompted, running out of patience.

"No, Mr. Jacobus. That's not what happened. That's how Branwell actually...well, that's how Branwell actually died."

Jacobus recalled Branwell Small's comment about the questionable reliability of his Aunt Claudine's faculties. It now sounded like a point well taken.

"Go on, Mrs. McConnell," Kate said. She squeezed Jacobus's hand, as if to say, "Just be patient. The old lady's harmless."

"So many young boys were getting killed," McConnell said. "So many. The field hospitals were filled to the brim. Overflowing with wounded soldiers. In and out they went. In and out. It was chaos. The surgeries, the amputations, the gangrene. Broken and frozen limbs and damaged organs. Hell on earth, it was that and more. Branwell died almost as soon as he arrived at the infirmary. They removed his body from his sickbed in order to put the next casualty there, but, you see, they neglected to remove his identification from the foot of the bed.

"The next person they put there had a head wound. He had been found on the side of a road, lying face down in freezing mud. He was in a coma."

"You said 'person,'" Jacobus said. "Not soldier?"

"You're a very observant young man. Yes, the person was not a soldier. They could have left him there, in the road to die, and none would have been the wiser, but they didn't. They took him to the infirmary and put him in my nephew's bed."

Jacobus smacked his head.

"I get it! I get it! When this person woke up, he didn't know who he was. He had amnesia from the wound, so he couldn't tell anyone he was *not* Branwell Small."

"That's correct, Mr. Jacobus," McConnell said. "Though you may be impatient, you are observant and astute, if not polite or clever. With the medics and doctors and nurses and patients swirling around, as far as anyone knew, that person was Branwell Small, who had suffered a head wound and lost his memory and, for a time, the ability to speak. He was in a fog. He could answer simple questions with a nod, but that was all."

"But what about Branwell Small's parents?" Kate asked. "Clearly, they must have known this stranger wasn't their son."

Claudine McConnell laughed a sad laugh that turned into a whistle emerging from deep in her throat.

"You know how bureaucracy works, don't you?" she said. "And we English are the worst. All the paperwork. All the confusion. The left hand doesn't know what the right is doing. It was war! It was madness! Paperwork was the last thing on anyone's mind.

"My sister and her husband were notified that their son had died on the battlefield of wounds from a grenade, defending the free world from the Nazis. Before they had even finished mourning, they received another letter saying their son Branwell was being returned to them. That he had suffered a head wound, causing him to lose his memory, but that in his family's tender care, it was hoped he might soon return to normal. That letter didn't mention anything about defending freedom.

"My sister, Louisa, and her husband, Harvey, didn't know which letter to believe, but if they had a choice, they wanted to believe that their son was alive. Wouldn't you? The moment the military vehicle delivered him home, of course, they knew it wasn't Branwell.

"They had to make a decision. Right there, at that moment. They looked at each other and then at this total stranger who had a pleasant smile but no memory and said, 'Welcome home, son.' They signed whatever papers they had to sign. This poor, unknown teenager was now their son. Branwell Small."

"But everyone in the town must have known," Jacobus argued. "*You* must have known. Why didn't anyone say anything?"

"Think for a moment, Mr. Jacobus. Think about what you would have done. Would you have sent the young man back? Return to sender? To where? These two loving parents had lost their only child, and through a miracle, God granted them the chance to have another. Yes, you are absolutely right. People knew. That is so. But people were wise. Branwell Small did not die. Branwell Small came back from the war, wounded but loved."

The ensuing silence affected even Auntie Leonia, who entered the parlor and sat down without saying a word.

"What a remarkable tale," Kate said. "Remarkable and touching."

"Does Branwell know any of this?" Jacobus asked.

"No. Not a hint. His mum and dad went to their graves with the secret, and so would I have…."

"Except?"

"Yes, except. 'Except' is the reason I am here today. Louisa and Harvey promised each other never to try to find out who the lad really was. They didn't want to open Pandora's box. Even if they wanted to know, how could they have without saying to the young man, 'We think you're our son, but maybe you're not'? They didn't want to lose him, don't you see? But the night Branwell met you at his concert, he called me, Mr. Jacobus, and told me he felt something. He felt like he knew you."

"Knew me?" Jacobus asked. "You think he and I knew each other before he was wounded? But how? I had never been to England."

"Well, that's another part of the puzzle. When he was in the military hospital, when he awoke from his coma, and his head started to clear, and he began talking again, he didn't speak in English though he seemed to understand it well enough. He spoke in German."

"German?"

Suddenly, Jacobus became lightheaded. His breath caught in his throat.

"His new parents, Louisa and Harvey, persuaded him that he had been a translator in the war, and the wound must have rewired the part of the brain that controls language. He did speak some English, though, so it was a plausible explanation."

Oh, my God.

"And then, when he showed an interest in music, they got him a gramophone and then a piano. Within a year—it was a miracle—he was off to conservatory."

Jacobus's head fell back. He toppled off the couch, unconscious, onto the floor.

"Oh, dear!" Kate said. "Water, please. Quick."

Kate sat on the floor and placed Jacobus's head on her lap, patting him on the cheek. It seemed the right thing to do. When he shook himself awake, she put the glass of water to his lips. He drank in small sips.

"I'm okay," he said. "I'm okay. He's Eli, isn't he? My brother. Help me up. Please."

Nathaniel and Yumi lifted Jacobus gently and placed him back on the couch, a cushion behind his head. Kate handed him the water. He breathed deeply.

"I am so sorry," McConnell said. "I couldn't think of any other way to tell you."

"No," Jacobus said. "Not your fault. It's just that after all these years... Not knowing... And now..."

"What do we do next, though?" Kate asked. "We *think* this man named Branwell Small might be Jake's long-lost brother, Eli. But how can we be *sure*? And we must be sure, mustn't we, before we tell Branwell. Because one way or another, this will tear his life apart."

Claudine McConnell insisted she could get home on her own via a taxi and then the train—"After all, how do you think I got here?"—but Nathaniel insisted even more strongly that he accompany her. It must have been exhausting for her, not only to have made the trip, but to have divulged such a tightly held and deeply embedded family secret. She acquiesced, but before leaving, she reached out her right hand in order to shake Jacobus's. Kate saw the gesture and, taking Jacobus's hand in hers, directed it to McConnell's, connecting their lives.

After McConnell departed, Jacobus excused himself. He went out to the veranda, where he was left alone to sit and contemplate. What the others chose to do was none of his concern. The roof over the veranda, which until yesterday had provided them shade from the sun, now protected him from rain, falling steadily.

He was having a difficult time processing. So many years had passed. So much futility. Though he had told himself over and over again there was hope his brother was still alive, he had never really believed it. It had been easier to concede that he was dead. The finality of death was comforting in its own way.

But now! Not only alive. Alive, and in their midst! After all his efforts to track him down—the letters, the phone calls, the historical documents, all dead ends—here it was. A coincidence! A mere coincidence. But here's where life pulls its tricks on you. Neither brother, their same flesh and blood, had been aware who each other was. If not for Claudine McConnell—God bless her—they would have passed, two ships in the night. Branwell's amnesia. Not Branwell's amnesia. *Eli's* amnesia. Jacobus's blindness. Would he even have recognized his brother if he could see? Probably not. They had been boys, and after so many years…

So, now what? If Eli had no recollection of his past, what good was it that they were brothers? What was there to share? If Eli thought he was Branwell Small, why shatter that happy life by replacing it with a tragic one? Why tell him of his true parents' fate in the death camps? Why not maintain the illusion? Why not let him continue to be the respected Baroque scholar and musician? The enlightened amateur dabbler in criminal investigation?

CHAPTER TWENTY-FOUR

Would it really matter that Eli didn't know the truth, as long as Jacobus did?

And how could he be sure that it really was Eli? Yes, yes, it was true all the pieces seemed to line up. The two of them looked similar, so his friends said. They were both musicians. The chronology. Their respective ages. He spoke German. His story was plausible, if almost unbelievable, at the same time. After all, couldn't there could be hundreds, maybe thousands of men who shared those same similarities with him? Yes, McConnell *sounded* like she was telling the truth. That she hadn't lost all her marbles. But Kate was right. Somehow, they would have to be sure.

But how to prove it was really him? Really his long-lost, dear brother, Eli? The only other surviving member of the Jacobus family. Was there a way?

A sudden uptick in the breeze sprayed a misty rain on Jacobus, chilling him.

"Shit," he said and went inside.

"Very kind of you to invite Aunt Claudine and me," Small said to Yumi that night. It was a going-away party for Yumi. Last minute. Impromptu. Auntie Leonia could never pass up an occasion. Small introduced his aunt to everyone. She pretended she had never met them. "So generous of you," she said.

There was an additional guest Small had brought, unannounced. He hoped he wasn't being too presumptuous. It was Halima Danjuma, stunning in a new, royal blue dress. She was smiling and clear-eyed and had had her hair cut very close to her scalp, highlighting a pair of dangling silver earrings. "She's become my indispensable assistant. Soaking it all up like a sponge. Don't know how I ever managed without her. Like a daughter."

"Don't be silly," Yumi replied. "We're happy to have Halima. But don't thank me. Thank Auntie Leonia. She did the cooking."

"And Nathaniel got some good cheese," Jacobus said.

"Aha!" Small replied. "You remember my vulnerable spots well."

The conversation meandered. Yumi took Halima by the arm as, one by one, by prior arrangement, they all drifted off to their own quiet conversations, leaving Jacobus and Small alone.

"I've got something I want to talk to you about, Small," Jacobus said.

"Yes? By all means. What would that be?"

"I know you're a Baroque expert and all, but do you do anything else?"

"You mean about the guns? The 'crime fighting'?"

"No, no, not that. I mean, do you play other repertoire?"

"Ah! Sadly, I have to confess not. I'm afraid I've become quite the specialist. What's the saying: If you keep learning more and more about less and less, eventually, you'll know everything about absolutely nothing? That might be said about me, I'm afraid. Anything after the sad day in 1750 when Bach shuffled off his mortal coil is uncharted territory for me."

"So, no nineteenth-, twentieth-century stuff up your sleeve?"

"No, no! But don't get me wrong. It's not that I don't think it's good music. Beethoven, Brahms. They're all marvelous. How could one go wrong? It's just that I've become so at home with the Baroque, and there's such a limitless repertoire there. I'm 'discovering' a new composer every day. I don't think I'm even a third of the way through the Scarlatti sonatas!"

"Well, even so, I was wondering if you might help me with something," Jacobus said.

"Willing to give it the old college try. After all, you've been so kind. How could I refuse?"

"Good. You see, I really admired the way you realized the harpsichord part in the Vivaldi concert last month, and I wanted to hear what it might sound like on the piano if you kind of improvised the piano part to a little piece by Dvořák that I'm fond of."

"Dvořák!"

"Yes, Dvořák. The *Four Romantic Pieces*."

"But that's totally out of my depth, Mr. Jacobus. That's a hundred years beyond me. Why, Stravinsky's much closer to Dvořák than Bach is. I couldn't imagine—"

"Yeah, yeah, I understand. It's a crazy idea. But it's our last night here. How about you give it a shot? Then, if we go down in flames, we can go off to the pub for a pint. On me."

"Ooh, I'd love to hear it, Branwell," Halima chimed in, having returned with Yumi.

"Would you? I can't imagine why."

"Please?"

"Oh, very well. Wouldn't want to disappoint the young lady. Wraps me around her little finger, that one."

"I have to caution you that Auntie Leonia's piano needs tuning," Jacobus said.

"That will be the least of my difficulties, I'm sure."

Jacobus had borrowed Yumi's violin for the experiment. She, Kate, Nathaniel, Leonia, Halima, and Claudine McConnell sat around the room. Waiting.

Jacobus had learned the *Four Romantic Pieces*, Op. 75, in childhood. It was an obscure little suite, though typical of Dvořák, with each of its short movements rich in melody and distinctive in character. Well within the technical capability of young musicians, the pieces provided an ideal introduction to that composer and to the esthetic of nineteenth-century Romanticism.

But the reason he had challenged Small to improvise the piano part had nothing to do with pedagogy or music history. Jacobus and his brother, Eli, had played the pieces together for hours on end as youngsters, so enamored were they of the music's richness and of their fraternal collaboration. It became their default repertoire on the many occasions when their parents requested performances for friends or family visiting for dinners, parties, or holidays, representing the happiest of times in their lives together. Daniel and Eli had reprised the Dvořák pieces so often that after the first dozen performances, they never bothered using the music. They had even forgotten where they put it.

"Could you give me the part to look at?" Small asked. "I've never even heard of this piece."

"I don't have the music on me at the moment. It's somewhere on the other side of the pond."

"But how do you expect me—"

"Give it a whirl. Just see what happens."

213

"But—"

Jacobus didn't wait for any further objections and began to play the first piece, *Allegretto moderato* in B-flat Major, a touching, heartwarming little tune supported by a gentle rocking chair of a piano accompaniment. It conjured up the image of sitting by a warm fireplace on a cold winter night. It was the kind of tune better played by an old man, like Jacobus, than a budding young virtuoso, out to show the world there was a new Heifetz on the scene. Better played by someone whose vibrato had slowed and widened a little too much for public performance, and whose exaggerated intonation might have led someone less informed, someone who only listened to CDs, to believe it was out of tune. Someone who was not out to prove anything, but only to share something beautiful. So when Jacobus played, he only played the way he thought the music was supposed to go, not realizing the effect it had on his small audience. He didn't see the tears he was bringing to everyone's eyes, because of the music and because of the moment.

For twenty, thirty seconds, there was no sound from Small, seated at the piano, his hands on the keyboard, flexing his fingers, searching for direction, seemingly bewildered. Then, a few tentative chords. Then, the outline of a counter melody. Then, the exact piano part, note for note, that Dvořák had composed.

Both musicians stopped at the end of the three-minute miniature.

"I don't understand," Small said. "I am totally befuddled, Jacobus. I swear to you, I have never even heard of this piece in my life. I'm mystified. How do you explain it?"

Now with tears in his eyes joining the others, Jacobus said, "It's a long story. Sit down, and I'll explain, Eli."

"Eli?"

"I think we should leave these two gentlemen alone," Kate whispered to the others. "They have a lot to catch up on."

They all left except for Aunt Claudine, who bore silent witness to the miracle.

When they returned from a long walk—Yumi, Kate, Leonia, Nathaniel, and

Halima—it had gotten quite dark, but the rain, at least, had stopped, and the chill of autumn, which would inevitably be upon them soon, was still being held at bay. Standing outside the door, they heard music coming from the parlor. Music for violin and piano. Lovely music. Schubert duos, Yumi informed them. They didn't want to interrupt and so continued to wait outside in silence, appreciating a moment all would remember.

After a while, Nathaniel asked, "Do you think it would be all right if we snuck in? I really do have to go to the bathroom."

They tried to be quiet as church mice, but Jacobus and Eli heard them immediately.

"We're so sorry!" Yumi said.

"No problem," Jacobus said. "We were running out of repertoire anyway. And my arm's about to fall off. I haven't played this much in years."

Of course, Jacobus had been playing without music. Yumi glanced at the piano. There was no music in front of Small, either.

"It was just lovely," Kate said. "Simply sublime. Have the two of you had a chance to...?"

"That we have," Eli said. "And I have to say, I'm still in something of a fog. To have reconnected with my brother, a brother who I didn't even know I had. And a past that's such a jumble."

"But you seem to have remembered the music quite well!" Kate said.

"Yes, that is indeed a bit of a miracle. It's music I didn't even know I knew, if that makes any sense. And what's more, the playing of it seems to have jogged my memory a bit. Just little flashes. Images. Nothing coherent. It comes and goes. But maybe the more we keep playing, the more I'll remember. In the meantime, I'll just trust Mr. Jacobus—"

"Daniel," Jacobus said.

"Yes, I'll just trust Daniel to tell me the truth."

"Good luck with that," Nathaniel said.

"And I'll have to start getting used to 'Eli' now! No more Branwell Small. Eli Jacobus! Think of it! Though, how am I ever going to tell everyone?"

"I think that's the least of your problems, Eli," Jacobus said. "Now you've got me for a brother."

Auntie Leonia, who had disappeared during the conversation, returned with a bottle of sparkling Rosé and seven glasses on a silver platter.

"Talk, talk, talk! All this talk," she said. "I think a celebration is in order," she proclaimed and popped the cork.

They all toasted the Jacobus family. And they toasted the memory of Natasha Conrad, without whose tragedy the two brothers would never have reunited.

"And may Mahler's ghost be put to rest," Yumi said, her glass held high.

"Hear! Hear!" echoed through the brightly lit parlor.

Postlude

Dear Reader,

Autumn's last leaf has fallen. Last night, only days after returning to his home after his poignant reunion with Eli, his long-lost brother, Daniel Jacobus, relaxing in his comfortable, if somewhat tattered, living room rocking chair, listened to the String Quartet, Op. 130 by his hero, Ludwig van Beethoven. We know that to be the case because that was the recording still spinning on his turntable this morning. The final movement on that side of the LP is the joyful *alla danza tedesca*. That was particularly appropriate, as Jacobus often said that was the music he wished to have played at his funeral; not the following heartrending *Cavatina*, which he said was "too damn morbid to go with pastrami sandwiches."

It is thus with great sadness we must inform you that sometime during the night Daniel Jacobus passed away peacefully in his sleep, a half-empty glass of Scotch by his side and a cold cigarette butt in his fingers. His bulldog, Trotsky, lay at his feet, faithful to the end.

Jacobus is survived by his older brother, Eli Jacobus. He, along with his friends Yumi Shinagawa, Nathaniel Williams, and Kate Padgett have requested that in lieu of flowers, you, his admirers, donate generously to your local community and youth orchestras, to carry into future generations the music that he loved. As Jacobus was wont to reply to people who claimed to love classical music, "Prove it."

These are links to partial listings to find American community and youth orchestras near you:

The Community-Music Contact List: https://www.community-music.in fo/list.php

Musical Chairs, United States Youth Orchestras: https://www.musicalch airs.info/united-states/youthorchestras

Acknowledgements

Writing a book is an individual labor of love, but the journey from the author'sdesk to the bookstore shelf requires a team of passionately committed professionals. I wouldlike to extend my heartfeltgratitude to Josh Getzler, my agent at HG Literary,Meredith Phillips, who patiently proofreadmy early draft, and Shawn Simmons, my courageous editor at Level Best Books, for taking *Murder at the Royal Albert* out of the concert hall and into your living room.

I also need to give a special shout out to the Boston Symphony and to my fellow musicians who comprise one of the world's greatest orchestras, because if I hadn't had the opportunity to perform Mahler's 6th Symphony with them at Royal Albert Hall, the idea for this book would never have occurred to me. Talk about the hammer of Fate!

About the Author

Gerald Elias leads a double life as a critically acclaimed author and world-class musician.

His award-winning Daniel Jacobus mystery series, beginning with *Devil's Trill,* takes place in the dark corners of the classical music world. He has also penned two standalone novels, *The Beethoven Sequence*, a chilling political thriller, and *Roundtree Days*, a Jefferson Dance Western mystery. Elias's prize-winning essay, "War & Peace. And Music," excerpted from his insightful musical memoir, *Symphonies & Scorpions*, was the subject of his 2019 TEDx presentation. His essays and short stories have appeared in prestigious journals ranging from *The Strad* to *Coolest American Stories 2023*.

A former violinist with the Boston Symphony and associate concertmaster of the Utah Symphony, Elias has performed on five continents and since 2004 he has been the conductor of Salt Lake City's popular Vivaldi by Candlelight chamber orchestra series. In 2022, he released the first complete recording of the Opus 1 sonatas of the Baroque virtuoso-composer, Pietro Castrucci, on Centaur Records.

Elias divides his time between the shores of Puget Sound in Seattle and his cottage in the Berkshire hills of Massachusetts, spending much time outdoors and maintaining a vibrant concert career while continuing to expand his literary horizons. He particularly enjoys coffee, cooking, watching sports, and winter weather.

https://geraldeliasmanofmystery.wordpress.com/

SOCIAL MEDIA HANDLES:
https://www.facebook.com/gerald.elias
https://www.facebook.com/EliasBooks/
https://www.instagram.com/geraldelias504/

AUTHOR WEBSITE:
geraldeliasmanofmystery.wordpress.com

Also by Gerald Elias

The Daniel Jacobus series:
  Devil's Trill (also an audiobook)
  Danse Macabre (also an audiobook)
  Death and the Maiden
  Death and Transfiguration
  Playing With Fire
  Spring Break
  Cloudy With a Chance of Murder

Stand-alone novels:
  The Beethoven Sequence, a political thriller
  Roundtree Days, a Jefferson Dance Western mystery

Self-published:
  Symphonies & Scorpions, a musical memoir, *"...an eclectic anthology of 28 short mysteries to chill the warmest heart"*
  Maestro the Potbellied Pig, a children's book, also an audiobook in English and Spanish versions.